Shades Of Love

HENRY PITT

Shades Of Love

iUniverse, Inc.
Bloomington

Shades Of Love

iUniverse books may be ordered through booksellers or by contacting:

iUniverse
1663 Liberty Drive
Bloomington, IN 47403
www.iuniverse.com
1-800-Authors (1-800-288-4677)

ISBN: 978-1-4759-8909-0 (sc)
ISBN: 978-1-4759-8935-9 (ebk)

Library of Congress Control Number: 2013907970

Printed in the United States of America

iUniverse rev. date: 04/29/2013

CONTENTS

Dedicated with love

This book of short stories is dedicated to my late mother who passed away September 6, 1999. She was a very special loving parent and my best friend. She was a strong woman who gave me life. Without her I would not have made it as far as I have. I know that she is still looking down on me, and watching each and every step that I take. She is still right here in my heart.

I will always love her.

Our Love

It was a cool fall day, and I was just getting off of work. I had been thinking about going out for some fun after work. Believe me it was about time that I did something to relax. Well it's like this I work in a big company where every day I wear a suit and tie. It's hard to be relaxed when you have to deal with other big businesses, and the you can only wear black, navy or gray suits. I have not been out in months; there are several nightclubs and bars in the area. While sitting in my car I was trying to make up my mind on what place I would hit first. After taking about 45 min. for me to get home I was ready to get out of these clothes, and take a shower. Once I was out of the shower and had dried off I started trying to find something to wear. When I looked at the clock I knew that it was time for me to hit the road if I wanted to go to more than one place tonight. My first stop is going to be a nightclub where a lot of the people I know hang out.

When I got to the nightclub there was a lot of people all ready there. I made my way inside this place was rocking. There was a woman standing near the door, somehow we started to talk. From that point on I started to enjoy myself, but I had no idea what this night would bring. After spending a few hours in the nightclub I decided to go to a bar. I asked the woman I had met if she would like to join me. She informed that she could not, because she was there with some friends. I asked her if I could call her sometime? She said that she was not ready to start any type of relationships with any one at this time. I did not ask any more questions. Being 35 years old I learned when a person did not want me around. So, I left and started my drive to find the nearest bar. I did find a new one that I had not seen before. The name of this bar was Jody's place. As I got inside I noticed that the lights was lowered and the waiters were wearing very little. I thought nothing of it at that time. I walked over to the bar and ordered a drink. While I was sitting there a man came over and sat down he ordered his drink. Then he spoke to me, responded by saying hi or something like that. He did not say anything else to me the whole time we were at the bar. My time there went by a little slow, and then I went to leave, as I was going to another nightclub. I was on my way, when noticed someone on the side of the road, which was having car trouble. I stop to see if there was anything that I could do to help. After pulling over and getting out of my car. I walked up to the car to see what was wrong. The driver was a man that looked to be just a little older than I am.

I asked him if he needed some help? He replied by saying that his car would not start, and went on to say that it just cut off on him and he could not understand why. He popped the hood then he got out of the car, we both walked around to the front of the car so we could look under the hood. We could see nothing wrong. I asked him to try and start it again. He went back and turns the key nothing happened. At point I asked if he needed a ride. He said he was on his way to meet some friends at a motel just down the road. I told him that I could drop him off there. When we got to the motel, he asked if he owed me anything for be so helpful. I replied no. Then he went on to ask me to join him and his friends in the bar for a drink. I did agree to that. Once on the inside of the motel we walked into the bar where there were 4 other men waiting for him. They all looked like the same type of businessmen I had to work with all week. After two drinks one of the men said why don't we go up to the suite that I have, it has it's own bar. Another of the men replied that sounds like a real good idea. The man that I had helped out asked if I would join them. One man said the more the merrier. Without thinking I went up to the room with them. It did not take long for us to start drinking again. I lose count of how many drinks I had that night. One thing I knew was that I could not drive anywhere. The man who rented to the suite said that we all could stay there for the night. Each of them started taking off their clothes, so I did the same. There would enough places for each of us to sleep.

Some time dueling the night I was awaken when I felt someone grab my arms. I had no idea what was going. I tried to talk, but couldn't because something was in my mouth. I could not move because someone was holding me. At that point I realized that I was being raped, they were having forced sex with me. It was very painful, but that did not matter to them at all. I could hear them talking, about how their plan works every time. I knew then that I was not the first person they had done this to. They had sex with me for so long that I just stop even thinking about it. The next thing I knew there was no more voices, and I was not being held any more. I opened my eyes to find that no one was there. After removing what was in my mouth, I found that they had put my own underwear in my mouth. As I was trying to get myself together the door opened, it was a guy who looked to be about my age. He asked if I needed any help?

I did not know what to say to him, because I was laying there naked, I did not know how to explain to him what had happened to me. He walked over and helped me to my feet. I told him at that point that I needed to take a shower. The young man told me that I should go to the hospital first to be check out, after I made it clear that I just wanted to take a shower, because I felt dirty. That's when he walked me into the bathroom. It was hard for me to stand up on my own. He had to help me. He sat me down on the stool and I watched as he undressed, so that he could stand with me in the shower. For some reason I started to fear that he too was going to rape me or something like that. Before I could say anything he walked over to me and stood me up again. He helped me to step into the running shower, where he helped me to wash. Then he dried me off. I was worrying that he was going to hurt me just as the other men had done. As he helped me to get dressed, he looked into my eyes, and told me please do not worry I am here to help you. I know that you have been hurt. I asked how did you know that, he said I work for the motel, and I over heard the men talking about what they had done as they walked though the hallway. From what I heard they had done the same thing to other young men. They talked about how they had burst his tight sweet ass, and how they had filled him up with their cum. One man even talked about how he had fisted fucked the young fucker's ass.

I knew that who ever they were talking about needed help, so I came up here to see if any one was still in the room, and if they were okay. I did not know who you were. I still feel that you need to go to a hospital to get checked out. They may have hurt you on the inside. You also need to call the police. I did how ever agree to call the police, but I did not know how I was going to tell them what had happened, when I knew that a man telling the police that he had been raped. Was going to be very hard for them to believe. Once I was dressed, he picked up the phone next to the bed where I was sitting. I listened as it rung. A man's voice came over the line. It was hard for me to find the words, but the young man standing there in front of me took the phone out of my hand and talked to the police officer. The officer told him that I needed to go to the hospital for testing. He told the officer that he would make sure that I got there.

Once he had put the phone down he asked me if I had a car. I told him that my car should be down in the parking lot. I reached into my pocket to find my keys. I handed them over to him. As he reached out his hand he said by the way my name is Thomas. What is your name, I replied my name is Tony. We slowly walked down the hall to elevator. It was good to see my car sitting where I had parked it. He helped into the car, and then he drove to the nearest hospital. I was taken into a small room where a Doctor came in and asked me to remove all of my clothes and put on a hospital grown. Thomas was there to help me. After getting on the table the doctor started to exam me. The only thing I did not like about what he had to do was when he told me to get up on all fours so he could exam my asshole. He put some thing inside of me. I did not know what he was doing but it hurt. It seemed like the exam took forever. When it was over I got dressed and waited for the police officer to come in a questioned me about what had happened. I answered each of his questions the best I could. He told me that I should go home and get some rest. The doctor gave me an order that stated that I should stay off of work for at lease 10 days. I did not want to do that but the Doctor told me that I needed to, because the rape had injured my body. When it was time for me to leave the Doctor gave me something to take to help me sleep. Thomas asked if he could drive me home. I agreed, and then I asked him how he was getting him from my place. He said that could call a taxi. I still needed some help walking, he was right there for me to lean on. Once at my place, I knew that I needed to get undress and lay down. So Thomas did everything he could to help me. He asked me if I wanted to take what the Doctor had gave me so I could get some much-needed sleep. I did just as the Doctor had said. Thomas sat in a chair beside my bed, and we talked for a while.

Before I started to get sleepy I found myself asking Thomas if could stay here with tonight. I was scared to be alone. He agreed to stay. I fell asleep with him sitting in a chair beside my bed. When I woke some time that night he was right there in the chair. I called his name and he almost fell out of the chair. The first thing out his mouth was what's wrong? I replied nothings wrong, I saw you sleeping in that chair. Why don't you get in bed there is enough room for us both. He said I did not know how you would feel about me doing that. I know that some guys do not like to be in bed with another man. I have a brother like that. Once he turned 12 he did not want us to sleep in the same bed. We could not even wash up in the bathroom at the same time. I never understood that kind of thinking, because we were brothers. I on the other hand did not think that way. In college I had to share a room with two other guys. One night we had to let two other guys stay in other room, because their room was being worked on. So that might that I had to sleep in the bed with one of the guys. Plus we dressed in front of each other all of the time.

I told him to stop talking and get into bed, so he could get some rest. With what little light that came though the window. I watched him undressed. Then he got under the covers and laid there on one side of the bed while I was on the other. The next morning I awoke to find him still sleeping. I eased out bed to go to the bathroom. I had to walk slowly, because it still hurt me to walk. While in the bathroom I heard him call out my name. I answered him. Then he opened the door to see if I was ok. I told him that I had to use the bathroom. He asked why didn't you call me to help you. I told him that he was sleeping so good that I didn't want to wake you up. Plus I felt that I could do it myself. By the way I will have to do things for myself once you leave. He walked over to me and sat down on the side of the bathtub. Looking right into my face he said I will stay right here as long as you need me.

My reply to that was I could not ask you to do something like that for me, when you don't know me. Plus you have a job and a life of your own. Thomas said I have a few days that I can take off. Well I live alone so I can be here for you. I just had to ask what would make you want to help me? He said I feel in side my heart that you need my help. I had to agree, because I did need somebody to help me. After everything those men had put me though. Plus the fact that I did not want my family to find out about the rape. He stayed right by my side for a week. I know that I could never repay him for everything he did for me. He told me that he had to go back to work on the next Monday, but he would still stay with me every day before work and night after work. One night Thomas asked me if I felt like talking about what happened that night in the motel room. I started out by telling him about the broken down car and the man that I tried to help. Then I told him about taking that man to the motel to meet his friends. After a few drinks they asked me to join them in the suite one them had rented. Somehow they talked me into spending the night there with them. Everyone started taking off their clothes, so I did the same. It didn't take me long to fall asleep, then some time dueling that night I woke up with someone raping me. I forced myself to tell him everything that I could remember. Then I said the rest of the story you already know. I broke down and started to cry, which was not like me. He seemed to understand he put his arm around me and told me to let it all out. I could not stop crying He just held me. Once I had stop I asked him to forgive me for doing that. His reply was, you did not do anything wrong. I had always been told that a man should do a lot of crying.

That was the first time I had ever let another man touch me in that way. It was a different feeling. We were going to spend two more days together. On the last night, while we were watching TV. While laying on the bed together we start talking about him. Since this thing started this was the first time He was able to talk freely about his life. He told me that he was the youngest of three children. Thomas was 29 years old, working for a hotel as an assistant manager. Went to college for four years, for business law. He has a girl friend, which he has been with for three years. His father passed away about eight years ago. After hearing about his life I ask him again why he was doing this for me? He told me that in his heart he knew that I needed him. At that point I felt that I needed to tell him some things about the person he is helping. I started out by telling that I was 35 years old. I am the 5th child out of 6 children. The oldest is a set of twin boys. I also have two older sisters, plus one sister that is two years younger than I am. She lives with our parents. For the pass few years I have been playing the field. There was a woman in my life until she found a job a 1000-mile away. We tried to keep things going but things went bad, and we broke up.

The days and nights went by fast enough, the next thing I knew it was Saturday night and Thomas will be going back to work on Monday morning. He told me that he needed to run out for a short time, and he will be back. So what could I say? He left for about an hour or so. Then he came walking though the door. I was in the bedroom laying on the bed watching TV. It took him a while before he came into the room where I was. When he did Thomas informed me that he had some thing to show me. I slowly got off bed, and started to walk towards the living room. As I got into the room I could hear music playing and I saw that the room was darkened, the only lights were candles. I also smell food. He helped me over to the sofa, and then he came and sat down beside me. I hope you like what I have here. He had gone to the hotel where he works and got some food. While we were sitting there eating, he told me that he had some thing to tell me. It seemed to take him a long time to get his words out. I asked him to just come out with what ever he had to say. I had my mind made up that he was going to tell me that once he goes back to work that he would not be seeing me any more. I had hoped that we had become friends, and I did not know what I was going to do if he was not here for me. When he finally got his words out I almost fell on the floor, because he told me that for some reason he has found him self wanting to be around me more and more every day. Then he asked if he could move in here with me until I was back on my feet and ready to go back to work. The only thing I could say was that would be all right with me. He went on to say that it has been so nice being here with me for the pass few days.

At that point I found myself asking myself the question why would I want to be so close to another man. My father has always told us that we are to find a woman and fall in love just as him and our mother had done. Well my two brothers had done just that. I thought that I was on my way, when I had met a girl about 5 years ago. We had a 4-year relationship. Then one-day things just fell apart. I had dated other women, but I just had not found the right one yet. Now I do not know if the right woman will ever come along. The woman I was dating before rape. I do not know how she will take what I have to tell her. About that time the phone rang. When I answered it the voice was that of my girl friend. It like she knew that I was just thinking about her. She wanted to know why I had not call for about a week. I told her that I had been busy with work. She knew that I had a job that could keep me very busy. Then she wanted to know when we were going to get together. I told her that I would have to wait until things are wrapped up. Her reply was I understand. Then we talked for a while longer. I told her that I needed to get back to work on a few things.

I know that I should have told Neisha the real reason for me not calling her, but how would explain what had happened that night. Then a thought hit me I still had not told my parents anything, they didn't even know that I had been hurt. What was I going to do? At that time Thomas called out my name. That's what brought me back to reality. You went away from me for a while. What's wrong? Well that was my girl friend she wanted to know why I had not called her for a while. A knock cut what I was saying short. I went to the door, and opened it. To my surprise my parents were standing there. I do not know how Thomas will handle the fact that my parents are a mixed couple.

Well my mother is a beautiful black woman and my father is a handsome white man. I asked them to come in. when they came though the door, there was Thomas sitting on the sofa. I said mother and father this Thomas he is a friend of mines. Then I went on to say Thomas these are my parents Mr. and Mrs. J.A. Brookerson. My parents said their helloes, and then Thomas replied by saying hi. My father said we were out for the night so we decided to stop by to see how you were doing. Well I am doing ok. Just sitting here talking with Thomas. My said that they had to run because they are going to dinner and then to a play. It wasn't long before my parents left.

Once again it back to the business at hand. I was waiting for Thomas to say some thing about my parents, but he never said a word. As I looked over at him I started to notice a few things that I had never though about before that moment. Why was my mind playing tricks on me like that? There I was thinking how his body was build and what his face really look like. Maybe I was just going crazy, or could been because of all the help he had given me. Thomas was a very handsome young man. I had never thought like this before. The two of us talked for along time, before he asked me if I wanted to ride with to his place to get a few things that he would need at my apartment. I wanted to say no but my fear got in the way and I said no, but you going a head I will be all right until you get back. Went he left it seem to me that he was gone for a very long time, but in reality he was only gone for a few moments. He had just taken enough time to pack a bag, which he brought back with him. It wasn't long before we got in to bed, because Thomas had to work the next day. That night I had a dream, in which the rape was happening all over again. Thomas woke me up, because I had been yelling in my sleep. I found myself crying, will this nightmare ever end? He put his arms around me as I tried to stop crying. I must have cried myself to sleep, because when I awoke there I was laying in his arms. What was going on with me? Why was I doing these things? There were so many questions that I could not answer.

When the clock went off to wake him up, his first words were good-morning. I replied by saying good-morning. He removed his arms so that he could get up to get out of bed. I watched as he got up and walked towards the bathroom. After the door had close I heard the water in the shower running? I laid there in bed with so many thoughts going though my mind. My eyes were closed, when I heard the bathroom door open. When I opened my eyes there he was standing in the doorway with only a towel around his waist. He walked across the room, to get to his bag of clothes. He picked it up and brought it over to the bed and laid it down. I watched as he went though his things. Only to see him pull out a pair of briefs, then He turned his back to me and without removing the towel he pulled on his underwear. The towel dropped to the floor then he walked over to the closet door to get his pants and shirt. I watched as he dressed, and then he went back into the bathroom. It was a few moments before he came out. He asked me if I needed anything before he leaves for work. I told him that I can handle things myself I think. Then he said I have left my office number on the nightstand, if anything comes up and you need me just call. After I heard the front close I eased out of bed and walked to the door to check it. Then I went back to bed. When I awoke it was about 11:00am. I got again this time I went into the bathroom to take a shower; it took me a little more time. I was getting better, so I have to start doing things for myself. It has been nice having Thomas here taking care of me, but I am hoping that I will be able to go back to work in a few days. Once I had dried off I walked back into the bedroom to find something to put on. I just dressed in a pair shorts and a T-shirt, because all I was going to do is lay around mostly. I went into the kitchen to find something to eat before I took my pills. When I got into the kitchen there was a cover plate of food with a note, that said I know that you would need to eat before you take those pills, I fixed this for you, Make sure you eat. There is also something in the refrigerator for later, I will be back as soon as I get off of work.

After eating I with back into the living room where I got onto the sofa and watched TV. At some point I fell asleep. When some one ringing my doorbell awaked me. I got up to answer the door as I opened the door there was a salesman standing there. He started trying to tell me about his company's product. I told him that I did have the time to talk to him about this right. So he said thank you and walked away. As I sat back down on the sofa the news was on. The news reporter was talking about a rape that had happened in the area. That's what made me pay attention to the story. She said that another young man had been raped last night. Then she went on to say that he could be another one in a group of young who had been raped by the same group of men. These men trap the young men by one of them posing as if his car had broken down on the side of the road, while the others wait at a motel. Where they have rented a room, once at the motel they talk the young men in to drinking, and spending the night at the motel. Once the young man had fallen a sleep, they undress and rape them. These men are between the ages of 40 and 50 years old. They come off as businessmen, they are also well dressed. If any knows anything about these rapes please call 1-888-284-3791. The police need help in taking these men off the streets. As I sat there my mind was racing and my heart felt like it was going to jump right out of my chest. What was I going to do? I was one of men who those crazy men had raped. About that time the phone rang. I reach over and picked it up. When I said hello, a voice came though and said my name is detective William Delocke I am calling because I need you to come down to the police station. We would like you to take a look at some pictures to help ID the men would rape you. I asked when he wanted me to come in. he asked what would be a good time for you. I said that I could be there in about an hour. When I got off the phone, all of my fears hit me full force. I knew that I would not be able to go down there alone, but I did not want to call Thomas. Then I realized that calling him was the only thing I could do. So I did make the call. When he came to the phone I told him about detective William Delocke calling, and asking me to come down to the station. Thomas asks when do you have to be there? In about an hour I replied. He said ok I will be there in a few minutes. After hanging up the phone I started to get myself together. When Thomas got there we felt for the police station. Once there detective Delocke got us into a small room where he started to asking me questions about that night. I did the best I could to tell him everything I could remember, which was almost everything. There was a few things that Thomas also. When asked if he had seen the men he said yes very well. At that point the detective laid out a group pictures, and asked us does any one look like the men. In this group both of us picked out the same two men. Then he laid out another set of pictures for us to look at. As I looked over them no one stood out, Thomas said the same. Then once another group was put before us, we again pick put the same person. Now this is the last group please take your time and see if there is any one in these. It did not take us long before we picked out the two men. That's when I asked what is going to happen next. The detective said once they are found we will make arrest, and then we will give you a call.

Thomas and I left and went back to the apartment. When we got inside he asked me if I was ok? I said I will make it. Just then some knocked on the door. Thomas went answer it, the person on the other side of the door asked for me. I did not know who it was. The next thing I knew a man's voice asked if I was one of those young men who had been raped? I did not say a word, but at that time the man tried to push his way passed Thomas. Before I could get off of the sofa Thomas was able to back the man into the hallway, and close the door. After he made sure that the door was locked, then he walked back over to the sofa where I was sitting doing my best to hold back the tears, because of what had just happened. Thomas put his arm around me, and said don't let it get to you. As we sit there I could not say a word. We both just sat on the sofa with nothing being said. My mind was spinning, I did not know what was going to happen next.

I had no idea what was going on around me. It seemed that I could someone talking, but I just sat there. Thomas called out my name; it took me a few moments before I could answer him. When

I did he told me that someone had call, and asked for me. I asked with they left a message. He told me that it was a man who said that his name was Frank. I said that he was a co-worker. Thomas informed the man that I would call him back at a later time. I slowly tried to pull myself together, was still upset and Thomas knew it. He tried to talk to me so that I would relax. I reached for the remote so that I could turn on the TV. Just as we started watching the some show that was on, the station broke in to give a news bulletin about the rapes that had been happened within the pass few months. The reporter said that police information said that there were at lease 12 young men had been raped by the same group of men. These men are wanted by the police. And anyone with any information are asked to call the following number 1-888-284-3791. Just as the report went off the phone ranged again, this time I answered it. There was Neisha's voice you said that you were going to call me back, what's going? I had to find the words to tell so that she would just leave the matter alone. So I said I'm sorry baby, but I have had so many things on my mind today that I forgot. She was like you always do this to me. You let everything come before me. What am I to you, just someone you come to for sex? I said girl you know that you are more than that. We have something special, and you are my boo. It won't be much longer before things cool down more. I knew in my heart that things were about to hit the fans, because once the police make an arrest it will be all over the news, plus I will have to go to court. Neisha asked me if I heard what she were saying, I said I'm sorry I was reading something. Then she said never mind, I will talk to you later and hung up the phone. I knew she was mad with me, but what was I going to do, I couldn't tell her the truth right now.

Once I had put the phone down, I start trying to watch TV again. That's when Thomas walked into the living room from the kitchen with something for me to eat. He said you know that you have to eat something; I almost wanted to say that I was not hungry, but I knew he was not going for that. So I tried to eat what I could. Thomas picked up the phone and made a call to his girl friend. I could tell by what he was saying that she was upset with him for not being home when she went there. He told her that he was at the home of a sick friend. She did not want to believe him, but he said I am telling you the truth. He did not say on the phone long. It looked like we both were having bad luck with our girl friends. All because of those men raping me. Hopefully it will be over soon and maybe our lives will get back on track. Tomorrow is the day that I will have to go back to the doctor's office for a check up. I really did not want to go anywhere; I knew that it was something that could get around. The appointment was for 9:00 in the morning with my family doctor, who has known me since I was little. Now I will have talk to about the rape. What is he going to think about me?

After taking those nasty pills I went in the bedroom and got myself ready for bed, because those things make me sleepy. Once I got into bed it did not take me long to fall asleep. The next morning when I awoke, I looked for Thomas, but he was not in the room with me. I wonder where he could be. It was to early for him get up for work. I got up and walked into the living room to find him asleep on the sofa. He was sleeping so good I did not wake him, I allowed him to sleep until I knew that he had to get ready for work. When I called his name he looked up at me and asked if anything was wrong, said no I am just waking you so you can get ready for work. He said oh I forgot to tell you that I am not going to work this morning, so that I can take you to the doctor's office. Tony I am glad that you woke me, that gives me time to cook us breakfast, and get dress for your appointment. Do you want to take your show first, and then I can go in a shower before I start breakfast. I told him to go ahead and take his shower, I would take mine's while you are cooking. So he went in to the bathroom and took a shower, while he was in the bathroom I decided to turn on the TV. The first thing I saw was a news report about the rapes. I did not need to be hearing about it all over again today. It was enough to be going to the doctor, and having to tell him what had happened. I will be so happy when everything is over. That's when he came out of the bathroom wearing only a towel. It did not take him long to get dress, and then it was my turn to shower.

Once in the shower it gave me time to think, one thing that crossed my mine was how good of a friend Thomas had become. He has been there for me though everything that has happened. Now if my girl friend will be here for me once she finds out what happened. As I came out of the bathroom I could smell food. So I got dressed as fast as I could get something to eat. When I got in to the kitchen he had cooked a wonderful meal. We took our time eating, after we had finished there was just enough time for him to clean up the kitchen, I asked if I could help, but he said that's all right I can handle it. I looked at my watch; it was time to head for the doctor's office. When we walked into the office I let them know that I was there for my appointment.

The lady said that the doctor will be with you in a few moments. I did not have to wait long; Thomas sat in the waiting room while I was being examined. My doctor explained to me that I could go back to work, but I will have to still take it easy. I told him that I have a fairly easy job any way. When I walked out in to the waiting room Thomas asked me about what the doctor had to say. I told him that I had been released to go back to work.

When we got back to his car I turned my cell phone back on, to find that I had gotten a call from the police it most have been detective Delocke with some news about the case. I pulled out his card and called him. Sure enough he did have something to tell me. He said that all six of the men who were doing the rapes. Each of them are sitting in jail with chance of bond. That was good news in a way, but now I know that things are going to hit the fans. After ending the call I told Thomas what the detective had said. He said that things will be coming to an end soon. Then you will not need me hanging around. That's when I made the statement that I hope we will all ways be friends. Yes we can be friends if you want us to be he said. As we got into the apartment he turned on the TV, and the first things we saw was news report about the arrest of those men. I watched as they show their faces. The report told how they were arrested and where it took place. Each one of them would have to stay in jail until we go to court. From the day they were arrested until the day we went into court. I had to find away to tell my parents and my girl friend what had been going on. It was very hard for me, but I had told them before they heard it from the news. Because once the trial starts there will be no way that everyone would know. I remember the night I went to my parents and talked to them about the rape for the first time. They both were understandably upset. They never blamed me for any of it. When I told my girl friend (Neisha) she almost walked out of my life. I did everything I could to make her understand that those men used me in ways that no one should use another person. With the court date coming up in about a week, Neisha didn't want to talk to me or even see me. The way she acted had really hurt me, but I had to be strong. On the first day of trial the courtroom was full of people and news reporters. There were 12 of us who had to relive what those men had done to us. It was very painful to have everyone listening to the details of how 6 men pared and used each one of us until they were arrested.

I wished that it were over. I had to thank the Lord for my parents' support. Both of them were right there each day. I had to be thankful for having a true friend in Thomas, he were sitting in the courtroom listening to every word even though he all ready knew what had happened to me. He had been there for me from the night of the rape and though the trial there are times when I missed him. Since he had moved back into his own apartment, but I know that he is still a real friend. He calls and come by to check on me. If I was to ask him to come over he would. There is one bright spot in all of this madness. Thomas and his girl friend are planning their wedding, which he asked me to be one of his bestmen. They are about a month and a half away from their big day. Hopefully this trial will be over soon. Each day could be the last, but it seem to be going on and one. It has been almost two months to long. On the last day of the month things came to an end. Each of the six men went to prison for 15-20 years. When I walked out of the courtroom for the last time with my family and friends, I felt that a weight had been removed from my shoulders. The 12 of us had to make our way though a sea of reporters and people to get out of the courthouse.

That night I called Neisha and tried everything I could to get her to understand that I still love her. We were able to talk this time. She said that the last two months had given her time to think. So we got together and enjoyed a night of pleasure. Three days later I asked her to become my soul mate, and share everything part of our lives together, her reply was yes. She wanted to get married on Christmas day next year. I was going to tell Thomas about our plans, and ask him to be in the wedding.

When I got home I called Thomas to let him know the news. He was very happy for me. Then that's when I ask him to be apart of the wedding. He said I would be honored. We started talking about his wedding. I asked him when I would have to be fitted for my tux for his wedding. He said that we have another two weeks before I will get every body together to go to the store. Jessie was having all the ladies dresses made so the woman has all ready started on them. While we were talking I had the TV on, when a report came on about the trial. I hope that this will be the last one I would ever have to watch. I tried my best not to pay any attention to what was being said. Thomas and I talked for about an hour; I think he might have known that I needed to talk. The next few weeks were a little crazy, but I was getting back on track. Tomorrow was Thomas's big day. The men of the wedding party spent a night of parting. That next morning we got up and started to pull ourselves together. The wedding was going to be at 2:00 that afternoon and we had to be there at 12 noon. When we got to the church, we were shown to a large room were we would be changing clothes. There were 14 men and 5 young boys in the room. The best men tuxes were ivy with rose color vest, while the groom and the bride's escort's tux were all ivy. Then the groom's men tuxes were ivy with light pink and rose vest. The 5 young boys were also dressed in all ivy. Our shoes and canes were also ivy. As we finished dressing a knock came at the door. When the door opened it was the wedding consultant, she wanted us to come into the church to take pictures. It was not long after was had stop taking pictures that's when people started to arrive, Thomas, his brother and myself along with the bride's escort had to return to the back of the church. The groom's men escorted people to their seats. The church was filling up, and it was getting close to the start of the wedding. When the ladies and young girls came around to the front of the church. The guys saw them for the first time. Each one of them had on tea length dresses. The maid and matron of honor had on dresses and shoes that were in the color rose, while the bride's maids dresses and shoes were lt. Pink, each woman's bouquets were mad up of rose, lt. Pink and ivy flowers to match their dresses, with ribbons that flowed down wards. The flower girls carried lace and satin covered ivy baskets, which match their ivy dresses and shoes. They had flowers in their hair.

The Jr. bride had on a dress ivy that looks as if it was two dresses one over the another. The under dress was made of satin; the second part of the dress was made of lace which flowed into a train. She also had a headdress that was made of flowers, peals and a Vail. Her bouquet was made mostly of ivy with some rose and pink mixed in.

No one had been allowed to see the bride, not even the ladies of the bridal party. So we did not know what she was going to look like. I know that Thomas was ready to see her, because they had not seen each other for three days. Well it is now show time. The pastor, Thomas and his brother, and myself came out from the back of the church. As we stood in our places, the doors to the church opened for the wedding party to start entering. Then the first groom's man to come in with the bride's sister on my arm. As the music played they slowly made their way down the aisle. Once he had escorted her to her place, he made my to where he was going to stand. I stood watching the rest of the wedding party making their way in to the church. The two ring bearers came down the aisle carrying pillows made of ivy satin trim in lace. Then the Bible boy take his walk down the aisle with an Ivy lace covered Bible in his little hands. After that the Jr. bride and groom made their entrance in to the church once they had taken their places, the doors were closed. It seems to have taken a long time before the door were reopened for the bride (Lanetta) to make her show stopping entrance. She was a very beautiful bride. Her dress had a form fitting under dress that was made of ivy satin with an over lay of lace and peals which flowed into a long train, that followed her as she slowly made her way down the aisle to the man she loved, escorted by her father. The two of them were about to start a new life together.

I was standing there thinking to myself that I will be stand in Thomas's place in just a few months. Neisha was sitting there watching everything that was going on and I know that she was making note for our wedding. I watch as my friend took his vows to make her his wife, and life partner. When they took their first kiss as husband and wife the church went wild. The pastor had to tell them to break it up. I was so happy for the two them. After the wedding was over, we had to take more pictures before we could think about going to the reception. Once at the reception every one had a good time. The newly weds found a way to get a way from without any one knowing it. They will be gone for a week on their honeymoon.

When Thomas and Lanetta came back from their honeymoon. Thomas called me and asked that Neisha and myself could come over. I told him that I would give Neisha a call then we would be there. So we got to their apartment in about a half an hour. The four of us sat around and had a nice long talk. Thomas and I had a special bond; our ladies seem to be getting closer. None of us spoke about the rape. That was a thing of the past. That night Neisha asked Lantetta to be one of her bride's maids, she said yes. Thomas was going to be one of my groom's men. I had asked my twin brothers to be my bestmen. He told me that it was going to be a real honor just to be apart of our special day. On my way to take Neisha home we talked about how the four of us are so close.

As the days passed, and our wedding got closer. Things were going the way we had planned them. Neisha wanted to do what Thomas and Lanetta had done, which was not to see each other for three days before the wedding. The weather was cold, but I was feeling so happy. I was going to make the woman I love the center of my world. The days turned into hours, it was the night before our wedding and there we were 14 men spending the night together.

Everybody cut up and showed just how crazy we could be. The next morning we got up and got breakfast in the motel's dinning room. The women were in another motel to keep us from seeing them before the wedding. The wedding was going to be at 6 o'clock that evening. So we had to get to the church about 5 o'clock, we were going to dress there. Neisha brother and I were dressed in winter white from head to toe. My twin brothers had winter white tux with sliver vest. My groom's men would be in winter white tux and gold vest. The 6 boys in the wedding would be dressed in winter white from head to toe also. We had no idea what the women were going to look like. Neisha would not tell me anything about that.

We loaded up and left the motel about 4:30 to go to the church. When we got there, we were shown to a room to dress. Things went about the same as Thomas's wedding. We waited for someone to come and get us for pictures. When the wedding consultant did knock on the door, she told us to come into the church. It did not take long for the pictures to be taken. There I was standing in the back of the church waiting for things to start. Ok guys its show time. That's when the pastor, myself and my twin brothers walked back in to a full church. Our parents were seated on the front row. The music started and the doors opened, Thomas and Lanetta were first two people of the wedding party to come in, she was wearing a long gold dress. Her bouquet was gold, sliver with a touch of red. I watched as each bride's maid came down the aisle. Then Neisha two sisters followed they were her maids of honor their dresses were sliver. The 5 flower girls were the next to come in; they were dresses in winter white with matching baskets. Then the Bible boy followed them, then the ring bearers, with the bellboy behind them. My nephew was the candle carrier. He came in right before the Jr. bride and groom. Then the doors closed, and I waited for my bride to make her way down to me. The lights were lowered then the doors reopened again, this time there she was looking like an angel from heaven. Her brother was at her side. He escorted her down the aisle. I wanted to run up and take her right there, but I knew that I couldn't. My time was coming. When it got to the point when the pastor said you may now kiss your bride. I took her in my arms and gave her a kiss that she would never forget. I paid no attention to the pastor when he asked me to stop. When I did stop Neisha almost got weak in her knees.

When we got to our reception, we enjoyed our family and friends. Once we had cut the cake and had our first dance. I took my new wife by the hand and we ran out of the building to my car. Then we were off to Fla. for our honeymoon.

That night I made love to Neisha I ways that I had never had before. The six days and nights we spent in Fla. was filled with passion and hard core sex. On our last night there we did not get any sleep. When we got back home Neisha wanted to call Lanetta and Thomas, so we could get together to talk and have fun. They were our closeness friends. That evening Neisha and Lanetta cooked dinner, while Thomas and, I sat watching a game and talking. The next day I went back to work, where my co-workers had fun joking me about how they thought our honeymoon went. They were enjoying themselves. I have to say that I was also having a good time. By the end of the day I wanted to get home and see my wife. While in my car I started thinking about the things we did on our honeymoon, my dick got very hard. I just wanted to throw her down on our bed, and rip her panties off and fuck the hell out of her. I also wanted to taste her sweet juice. She was filling my every need. I hope that our honeymoon never ends. If we could only stay this happy for the rest of our lives.

When I got to our apartment Neisha was in the living room sitting on the sofa. I walked in and without saying a word I sat down beside her. I pulled her to me and started to kiss her. At the same time I was trying to undo her pants. She tried to push me away, but I was holding her tightly. Once I got her pants undone. I was doing everything I could to get them down. Once we stopped kissing, Neisha allowed me to pull her pants down. She pulled her clothes off while I undressed. I made love to her right there on the sofa. Then I eased her body to floor and enjoyed her more. As we laid there on the floor wrapped in each other's arms. Someone knocked on the door. We worked hard to get some clothes on.

I answered the door wearing just my pants, while Neisha picked up the rest of our clothes and ran into the bedroom. When I opened the door, I got a real surprise. Standing in front of me was the woman I had loved for 5 years, until she moved away for a better job that's was the reason for our break up. Now she was here, but she is going to get a surprise. I asked her why was she were here, her reply was I came into town to see my sister in the hospital, so I also wanted to see how you were doing. About that time Neisha walked back into the living room, and stood next to me. I told the woman standing on the other side of the door that I wanted her to meet my wife Neisha. The look on her face was worth a million dollars. I do not know what her real reason for being there was, but I had stopped her in her tracks. There was nothing else that she could say, but congratulations. Then she turned and walked away. I closed the door and turn to my wife kissing her. When our kiss was over, she asked who was that woman? I said that she was an old girl friend. It's been over for years. Now that you are here it will stay over.

As the month passed the four of us built a very strong relationship. Thomas and Lanetta' 1st anniversary was coming up and they had invited so to dinner to help them celebrate. We went out to a very nice restaurant where we had dinner and soft dinner wine. Then we went out to a club to do some dancing. After a night out with our friends, we returned home where I took my wife in to our bedroom and made love to her. I did everything I could sexually and more to give her the pleasure she wanted and needed. I did things to her that night that she may have only wished that I would do. By the time we finished it was early the next morning. As she laid in my arms I kissed her sweet lips. Then I closed my eyes to rest with her head on my chest, and our warm bodies wrapped together as one. I laid there thinking about how much I loved my wife, and how much I would do for her. I woke up when the phone rung to find Neisha still in my arms. I reached over and picked up the receiver, saying hello. Then I heard boy I know that you are not still in bed, have you forgotten what we were going to do this morning? I replied no I have not forgotten I just had along night. It was my brother Alton, one of the twins. I told him that I would be there in a few min.

Once I hung up the phone, I woke Neisha up and told her that I had to meet my brothers to make plans for our dad's birthday. She said ok. I went in to the bathroom to shower. When I came back in to our bedroom, she was fast a sleep. I dressed, and then I kissed her and left her in bed while I went to meet my brothers. They were waiting for me at Allen's house. We wanted to a party that he would remember for along time. His birthday was a month away. So we did not have much time to put the finishing touches on our plans. The last thing we had to do was to address the invitations, and put them in the mail. We are hoping to have over a 150 people to be there. Our mother and three sisters did not have any idea about the party, and dear old dad maybe thinking that we have forgotten his birthday all together.

We were sitting talking when Alton ask what happened your woman kept you up late last night, that's why you couldn't get up this morning? Since you must know I was the one that kept her up all night. I gave it to her hard and strong. You should have heard all the noise. Man the bed was really rocking, and we were rolling. It was late when she gave out on me, so I let her get some sleep. Allen had to get his two cents in, he asked are you sure she gave out, or did she wear your bony ass out. I loved my brothers even though they love to pick on me all the time, but we do have fun together. One thing they had never joked with me about the rape.

My brothers had all ways been there for me no matter what. You know boys will be boys. We are just three little boys at heart.

While we were playing around Allen asked me how my buddy little T was doing these days. I said yesterday was his 1st anniversary, and the four of us went out to celebrate it. Both Allen and Alton told me to tell him happy anniversary. You know that Neisha and I will be married one year in just a few months. Then Alton said that's right she got her hooks deep in your little ass real good. Man you are crazy I love my wife, I replied. Those two was having fun teasing me. It took us about three hours to finish up. I had to leave these two nuts to go home and check on my wife. Do you have to check on her, or check in with her Allen asked.

When I got home Neisha was still in bed. I undressed and joined her; I got up close to her nake body. Without really waking up she covered me with her arm and leg. We laid there for along time, then the next thing I knew my wife was giving me a blow job, she was working hard on me, once I was hard she got on top of me and road my hard dick until both of our juices flowed. When it was over she just laid on top of me. I wrapped my arms around her, and held her warm wet body. Both of our hearts were racing, and our breathing was deep. My wife whispered in my ear I love you, I replied I love too.

Then she laid one hell of a lip lock on me. Then she led me into the shower where she washed my body, and I washed her. I went down to my knees just to taste her sweet juice, and then I got her again right there in the shower. The warm water was running over our bodies as we stood there making love, for a while we became one. Once our lovemaking was over we finished cleaning up, then dried each other off. When we stepped out of the shower I watched my woman walk away from nake, what a sight to see. I followed her in to the bedroom, where we dressed. We spent the rest of the day sitting around watching TV.

On Thursday we started to get replies to the invitations we had sent out for dad's birthday party. One reply came from Thomas and Lanetta they were looking forward to being apart of this celebration. The four just sat around for a while and talked. We decided to make it a short night, because all of us had to go to work the next day. Our wives were making plans to get together for lunch. Thomas and I both knew that was their code for shopping. After they had left. My wife and I started to get ready for bed. Before we could get in bed the phone rung.

When Neisha picked it up, she said hello, then she gave it to me. I said hello, the voice on the other end was a voice from my past, and it was my ex-girlfriend. She asked have I called at a bad time? I replied by asking why are you calling? You know that I am married. Plus we have nothing to talk about. I didn't know what kind of games she was trying to play, but I knew that I wanted no part of it. I hung up the phone, and then I turned to my wife. The look on her face told me that I have to explain, who it was on the phone, and why she was calling. I told her who it was on the phone, but I couldn't really tell why she was going. When we got in to bed Neisha would not get close to me as she had done each night. I could tell that she was upset, so I moved closer to her and put my arm around her, and said baby you do not have to worry about that woman. She means nothing to me at all.

I knew what I had to do, so I started to kiss her neck, and then I moved down to her nipples. Once there I kiss, lick and suck them. I made my way down her body. When I got to her legs I opened them and took my place between them. I performed oral sex on her until she begged me to make love to her. Once we had made love, we got cleaned up, and got by in to bed. The next morning we started our day off with a kiss. When I got to work I started thinking about that phone call. I called Thomas and told him about it. He told me that I need to put a stop to that crazy woman before she causes trouble. I said that I told her last night that we have nothing to talk about, and then I hung up on her. We did not talk for long, because it seemed that we both had meetings that morning. After getting off the phone I started getting my reports and other papers together for my meet. It was in about 10 min. I headed down to the boardroom. I was not the first one there, and it did not take long for the room to fill up. The company's CEO came in and started the meeting. It lasted for about two hours, and I for one was ready for it to be over. When she did close the meeting, every one went back to their offices to go to work. I took one look at my desk and the mound of paper work that had to get done. So I reached for the top file. As I sat there reviewing it the phone rung. When I answer it, and heard the voice on the other end I got mad. Because it was my ex-girlfriend, told that if she does not stop calling I would call the police. That's when I hung up on her. I went back to work, because I had to get all this work done before I could go home. By the time I finished my work it was almost 6:15. I called my wife and told her that I was on my way home. When I walked into the apartment I could smell the food. She had dinner ready, and I was hungry. We sat down and eat, then we talked about our day went along with what new things she do gotten while shopping. We also talked about my dad's birthday party; it was only two weeks away. I had the job of getting my parents to the party. One of the lodge members would make sure that my sisters and their families were there. While we were talking the phone rung. I went over to answer it. My brother Alton was calling to tell me about the head count for the party. He said that all the replies were back and it seems that there was going to about 250 people at the party. We had to let the caterer know by Wednesday, so they will have everything ready. The lodge where dad was a member had worked with us. They had planned a dummy black tie affair, in which they had invited to come and bring his family. He was going to call the caterer the next day.

Those two weeks pasted very fast, it was the day of the party and everything was in place. Once we had dressed Neisha and I went over to my parents' house to get them. My sisters were going to meet us there. Alton and Allen told my dad that they would also meet us there. The starting time was 7:00pm. Once we had left the house Neisha called Lanetta let them know that we were on our way. They also had someone watching for us. When drove up one of the members were out side showing people where to park. Once we got out of the cars, we walked up to the door. When we opened the door the room was filled with family and close friends, along with the lodge members. Everyone was dressed in suites and ties, and dresses. There was a banner that said happy birthday Jay A. Brookerson. My dad was very surprised, along with my mother and sisters. Dad was given many gifts that night. Everyone there enjoyed themselves; the party was a big hit. The lode member did a little play to honor my dad. The band that played for the party was one that dad was a member of years ago. They got my dad on stage to play a song with them. He had fun doing it. The party lasted until 12 mid night. All the work that my brothers and me had done was worth it. When Neisha and I got home we went right to bed. The next morning the phone woke me up. When I picked it up, that crazy ex-girlfriend was the one on the phone. Before she could ready say anything I hung up on her. When I got up that morning I call to the police station to report what was going on. The officer told me that they would check in to the matter. About a week later the police officer called me back about the matter with my ex-girlfriend. He told that had been serviced with paper, and if she calls my wife or mc again, that she would arrested.

In a few weeks Neisha and I would be married for one year. I was working a surprise for my wife. Thomas had helped to setup dinner and a suite at the motel. The four of us were going to have dinner there and then spend the night there. The only thing I had to do now was to buy her a gift that would knock her socks off. I went to a jewelry store where I found a diamond and emerald ring. On the day of our anniversary I acted as if I had forgotten it. I went to work without saying a word. I did not send any flowers on her job, or to the apartment. When I got home she was mad with me for forgetting. Thomas and Lanetta were going to get her to go with out. So when Lanetta called Neisha agreed to go. The three of them left. Neisha had no idea that I was going to meet them at the motel. When I got there they were sitting at the table. I walked over to them and dropped down on one knee and ask for to forgive. There I was with a doz of long stem red roses and a big wrapped box. She would have to go though 10 other boxes before she would get to the ring. My wife could stay mad with me after that. Plus when she found out that our friends were in on the whole things from the start. We got her that time. Thomas and I had also planned a strip show for our wives. Once we got up to the rooms. We left the girls in one room while we went into the other one to get ready. We undressed and put on thongs and tear away pants and shirts that we had brought. When we got back into the room with the girls, we put on the CD that we had with the music on it that we were going to dance to. It did not take us long to end up wearing on our thongs. Our wives had a good time watching us dance and strip for them. I had to say that be the time we were finish we all were turned on. So Thomas took Lanetta by the hand and led her into the room, while I led Neisha over the bed. I made love to every inch of her body from her head to her toes. We seem to fall asleep as soon as our heads hit the pillows. The next morning the four of us got up and went down to the dinning room for breakfast. Check out was at 1:00; we had just enough time to make love one time. So I got my wife back up to the room did everything I could to rock her world. On our way the four of had smiles on our faces. Thomas and myself were two very happy men.

The next day Thomas called me and said that he needed to talk to me about something that was going. I agree to meet at the motel; we sat in his office while he told me about what was happening with his brother. He said that Edward's wife had left him. I asked what happened they seem to be so happy. Thomas looked and me with a look on his face that told me it was bad. He said I will try to explain it to you the best I can. My sister-in-law had been having an affair. Last week while Edward was at work she called him and told him that she was leaving him. He had no idea why until he talked to her brother, who informed him that she was moving in with this woman from her job. I asked do he know who she was having the affair with? He said he found out that the woman she was moving in with was the person she was cheating with. Man they had been married for over 8 years. They have two kids, and he loves those kids. I don't know what he is going to do now. This has upset him very much. I talked to him last night and he was in tears then. Over the weekend she called him so that he could talk to the kids, when they got off the phone. He asked if he could talk to her? What she said to him at that point hurt him. That woman told him that he was not man enough to please, so she had to get someone who could, and the woman she has knows how to make her happy. Before she hung up the phone she said we do not anything else to talk about from this on. As I sat there listening to him I started to wonder how I would feel if I was in Edward's place and Neisha had done that to me. Thomas asked me not to say a word to any one about what had happened, because Edward did not want any one to know. I did agree to take, when I got home to my wife I wanted to talk to her about it, but I could not. Later that evening Neisha got a call from her baby sister. She had some news for her, that news was that she was getting married in about three months. She had called to ask her to be in the wedding. Of course she agree to. They talked on the phone for a while. Once they had gotten off the phone Neisha told me about what was going on. She its about time for them two be thinking about getting married they had been together for a long time.

After a few days Thomas and I talked about what was going on with Edward. He said that he was not doing to good. The only things he do is go to work and come back home, I have been going over there to help him with things like paying his bills, and buying his food. Some time I wonder if he is even eating. I just hope he does not get really sick because of this. At that point his phone rung, when he picked it the person on the other end told him that he needed to come to the hospital, because his brother had been brought in, and he was in bad shape. Once he had gotten off the phone he looked at with tears in his eyes, I asked what was wrong he said Edward had been taken to the hospital. The first words out of my mouth was do you want me to take there. His reply was please I don't think I can drive. So we went to the hospital, when we got there the nurse at the desk told that the doctors was in the room with, and they will be out to talk to him in a few moments. As we sat in the waiting area I could tell that Thomas was almost at his break point. He sat there with his head down not saying a word. The door open to his brother's room, and one of the doctors came out and asked if any of Mr. Peliford's family here, the nurse point him to where we were sitting. He walked over to us, and said are you Mr. Peliford's family. Thomas said I am his brother, what's wrong with him doctor. The doctor said we are not sure at this point, but we do know that he is very weak. He told him that he could go in to see. Thomas turned and looked at me, and asked me to go in with him. When we opened the door Edward was laying in the bed with tubs and wires everywhere. At that point Thomas could not hold back any longer he started to cry, I reached out to him, I am glad that I did, because he fell into my arms. I had to help him to a chair that was next to the bed. He sat there crying. I stood beside him with my hand on his shoulder. I did not know what to say or do. He said I have to call mom and Sheneil to let them know about what is going on. I told him that I would make the calls. I walked over to the phone and made the calls for him. I also called Lanetta and told her that Edward was in the hospital, and Thomas needs her here. It was not long before every one was at the hospital, Neisha was there too.

We all stayed there for hours waiting to see how things were going to turn out. Every thing hit the fans when Edward's so call wife showed up at the hospital. When Thomas saw her he went off on her about what she had done to his brother. She stood there in front all of and said remember I am still his even if none of you like it or not. Then she came out her mouth with a statement that made their sister tell her off too. She said I know that he wasn't a real man, he couldn't take care of his business in bed and now he can be man enough to handle losing me. That's when one of the doctors came out of the room and told us that it was going to be a long night. We are doing everything that we can for him. As we all sat in the waiting area a man walked and handed Edward's wife an envelope, when she opened it and started to read the paper enclosed in side she got really mad. Come to find out Edward had filed for divorce, the man had serviced her with the papers. She left and did not come back. That we all stayed right there, the next morning the doctor had some good news for us, he was going to make it. The next few were going to be spent in the hospital, but he was getting better. Each day we each went to the hospital to visit him. When he was ready to come Thomas and I went to pick him and take him to their mothers house, every one was there waiting for him to get there. He got out of the hospital a few days before he had to go to court. When we came into the house every one hiding, but once we got in to the den they came out to welcome him home.

On the day that Edward had to go to court, we were all there to support him. It did not take long the judge to grant the divorce, plus Edward would be able to spend time with his children. When it was over he was a very happy man. We walked out of the courtroom feeling good about a lot of things. The next day Neisha and Lanetta would be leaving to go to her sister's to help her with the finishing touches for her wedding. Thomas and I would drive down there Friday night after we got off of work. That night my wife and I got into bed early, but we did not go to sleep until late. I wanted to give as much sex as she could handle. That night we fell asleep on the bed nake, the next I was woken up with my wife sitting on top of me riding my hard dick. I laid back and enjoyed the ride; I tried to hold back as long as I could, when I did unload inside of her. I almost past out. We got up and went in to the bathroom where we took a shower together, then we dressed I had to go to work, and she was getting read for their trip. I knew that she would not be home when I got off of work, but she was going to call me when they got there, and Lanetta was going to call Thomas. I kissed her and said I will see you in a few days, I love you.

That day at work I could not keep my mind on my work, because I was worrying about my wife driving that few, but I knew that they would be all right. About lunch Thomas called me. We talked for a while, and then he asked me to come over to his place after, so we both could be there when the girls called. So after work I did go over to his apartment. Lanetta called him, and I also talked to Neisha. They were a little tiered, but ok. After talking to them we went out and got us something to eat, then we went back to his place and watched some TV and talked. For the next few days we spent time together. Thursday night we were sitting in Thomas's apartment on the sofa, when some thing happened that I would never be able to explain. We were sitting there when some how we shared a kiss. From that point on things got very heated, we ended up in their bedroom. Thomas and I laid there on the bed together. We begin to touch each other in ways that we never had before.

With out saying a word we started to make love to each other. I remember placing myself between his legs, and I allowed myself to taste his dick for the first time. It was not long before he had moved me around so he could also taste my dick. We laid there for a while, what he was doing to me felt good. The next I did to him was, I enter his tight opening slowly. I knew that he was in pain, but he did not ask me to stop. I made love to him that night. Then I in turned laid there on my back and let him make love to me. After it was over we went in to the bathroom and cleaned up. Then we spent the night together. The next day we were going to go to meet our wives. I knew that I could never tell Neisha what had happened. The next morning when we woke up the two of us talked about our love making, and how we could talk our wives any thing about it. We left my place about 4:00 that afternoon; the trip took about three hours. When we got there the two of them was waiting for us. The four of us had dinner together. That night I made love to my wife, she wanted me so much and I wanted her. It had been almost a week since we had seen each other.

The next morning every body got up and started to get their selves together for the wedding. At the church Thomas and I took seated beside each other. When the wedding party started to come in to the church we saw our wives as they came down the aisle. It took me back to the of our wedding, and how Neisha looked that day. What was happening to me I was in love with my wife, but I was also having strong feeling for my best friend? How was I going to handle this? As I sat there and watched the wedding, I felt as if I was in a dream. When it was time for us to leave out. Thomas touched my hand that's what made me realized that I was not dreaming. While we were standing out the church waiting for them to finish taken pictures, we talked, but we did not say any thing about what we had done. As we road to the reception we dance with our wives on a slow song, I held her close to me and smelled her sweet scent. Later that night we drove back home. Thomas and Lanetta drove one car while Neisha and I drove the other one. When we got back home we all got in one car so that we could take Thomas and Lanetta home.

Over the next few months Thomas and I made love to each other, whenever we could. The two of us loved our wives, but we seemed to need each other in ways that we could not explain. Our wives did not know what was going on. We did not have to hide what we were doing, because every one knew that we were friends, and if any one saw us together they did not think anything about it. Out wives never mined us spending time together, because they spent a lot of time together also. Maybe they were enjoying each other in the same way that we were. They would have girl's night out, just as we would have boy's night out. From time to time we would take trips together the four of us, or it could be just the girls or just us boys.

Here we are now ten years later, and we are all still together. Both Thomas and I are happily married to our wives, and enjoying the pleasures of being with each other. Our family and friends never knew that the two of us was bisexuals. One-day Thomas came to my office; he said that we need to talk about something. He pulled out picture and laid it face on my desk. Thomas told me that I needed to see what was on the picture, I turned it over and there were our wives kissing each other. He said that someone had sent the picture to him. Then he asked what are we going to do about this? I told him that we won't do any thing, because if we don't say any thing to them we will not have to tell them how we feel about each other. Let them do their thing and we can do ours. One night the four of us were having fun at our apartment. When some thing happened that changed every thing. We were playing spin the bottle, the rules were when you spin who ever it lands on is the person you had to kiss, no matter who it was. On the first spin I had to Lanetta, when Neisha took her spin she had to kiss Thomas. The next spin was Lanetta, and she had to kiss Neisha, man what a kiss. Thomas was the last one to spin and guess who he had to kiss, me. We gave each other a real kiss. Every one was having a lot of fun; by the time it was over we all knew what was going on. That we talked about it openly, and made an agreement that we would all stay married. We also agreed to not hide our love affair from each other any more. From that point on whenever Thomas and I got together, we knew that our wives were together. This made things easier for us all. A year later the four of us went out of town for a weekend. That weekend we decided to share our pleasure together all four of us. I truly believe that we were turned on by watching each other making love.

I am going to end by telling you that we are all still very happy with each other. The four of us now live in one house, and share our bodies with each other. The sex is great, and we love each other. It's been 12 years and I am happy with my life. This could the dream of many people, but we are living it, and it is not a dream. Bye now its time for me to get in to bed.

Shades of Love

On Saturday June 27, I turned 21 year old. Like so many other young people I wanted to share my new freedom with someone. After thinking it over for a while. I then decided to go to a bar that a co-worker told me about. Well my story really started about 8:00 that night, after I got had dressed, and went out to my car. As I headed to the bar I was on top of the world.

Maybe I need to explain why I used the word freedom. If any one remembers being under 21 years old knows how it feels to live at home with your parents. Well my parents were totally against me having a place of my own. Because I was the youngest child out of three children. Plus given the fact that my mother couldn't have any more children. She kept us all close to home.

Two days before my birthday I was able to move into an apartment of my own. This made me feel that I should go out and have some fun. Well I got to the bar's parking lot. I found a park and got out of my car and locked the doors. As I looked around I noticed that a lot of men both young and old were around the front of the bar. Some were going in to the bar as I stepped on to the sidewalk. Once inside I went up to the bar and order a beer while drinking my beer a man came over to where I was standing and spoke. He also orders a beer. For one time in my life I had more than one beer. Plus I talked to a number of people who I did not know. After a while I lost track of time. I do remember some of the things that happened that night. A guy asked me to play a game of pool, So I did that's when things took a turn. Anyone who has ever had beer to drink knows that it will make you have to use the restroom, which I did. As I walked out of the restroom, two people took a hold of my arms. The next thing I knew I was being forced into a back room. Once inside of the room, the door was closed hard behind us.

The two men held me so tight that I couldn't move. As I stood there I looked around. I couldn't believe my eyes, there were nake men everywhere. That's when I started to do my best to get away from the men that were holding me, but I couldn't do anything. I tried to speak, but I was told to keep my mouth close. Until I was told to speak, one man got up and walked over to me and ripped my T-shirt off of my body. Then he undid my belt and jeans. I watched as my clothes were being taken off. As I stood there nake and scared. Men came over to me and rubbed my body all over. Not knowing what they were going to do, I knew that I was in deep trouble. I could hear everything that was being said about me. They were saying that I had a good-looking body and it was soft.

As I was held there a big man walked around me and ran his fingers between the cheeks of my butt. I felt it when he touched my asshole. That's when he made the statement that they had a cherry. I didn't think that any one knew the feelings that were running though me. Someone said that he wanted to see what my cherry looked like. That's when the two men holding me, turned me around, and made me bend over. Someone behind me pulled my cheeks apart. I felt something rubbing against my hole. I heard a voice say get him ready! There was noting I could do to stop anything that they were going to do to me. I felt something pushing into me. What ever it was hurt like hell. It moved in and out of my ass for a while. Then it was pulled out, but not for long. The next thing that was pushed into me was bigger. A voice said open him up good. I could feel my hole getting loose. Believe me I didn't want any of these things to be happening to me, but no matter how many times I said stop or no. It didn't do any good.

A voice from the room asked is he ready for us to ride him good and deep? I want get my load of hot cum off deep inside of his hole. Soon after that was when the first man of many started to rape me. this went on for hours. I must have blacked out from the pain, because most of the rape was a blank to me. Some time doing the rape a low voice asked if I was ready for a good hard fucking? Someone said yes we've got him loosen up just for you. Then I could feel something big being pushed into me. I must have blacked out again because I didn't feel the pain from the fucking. I do remember being pushed to the floor by a big pair of hands. I heard the low man's voice say; he was a good little damn fuck.

As I laid there on the floor crying. I felt something hit across my butt. Not only did it hit me one time, but again and again until my butt burned with a hot pain. I couldn't move at all. After a while I heard people leaving the room. When there was no more noise. Someone touched me. I tried to fight but it didn't do any good. Who ever it was, put his arms around me and held me. When he spoke his voice was soft and filled with care. He said I'm not going to hurt you. Let me help you get your clothes on. So I slowly got dressed, but that was about all I could do. He asked if I had a way to get home. I tried to answer him, but my voice just didn't sound right when I said my car is in the parking lot. He replied let me help you to your car. As he helped me to my feet, I could hardly walk. He walked out to my car where he asked if I could make it home all right. The only thing I could say as I held the keys in my hand was I don't know. He told me to let him drive me home. I gave him my keys and told him my address. It only took a short time to get back to my new apartment.

This young man that I didn't know was being so caring to me. After he helped me out of the car he locked the doors, then he helped me into my apartment, I asked him to help me into the bedroom. All I wanted to do was lay down, so he laid me down on the bed. That's when he told me his name. He said my name is Quinton, I know what they did to you tonight, because one night they did the same thing to me. That's why I had to help you. Because when it happened to me no one helped me. It took me over three hours to make it home. Not before I was raped again by other men in the bar. Some how I was able to make it to my car, but still to this day, I don't know how I got home. When I woke up the next morning I was in my bed with what was left of my clothes still on. Quinton told me his story as he was helping me get of my clothes. There wasn't much to take off, because we never found my underwear in that damn room.

I laid there nake with my life in this man's hands. He told me that I needed to get cleaned up, before I went to sleep. He asked if I wanted to take a shower. I replied that I don't know if I can stand up long enough to do that. So he said well maybe I should run you a bath. Once the water was running Quinton came back to the bed and picked me up and carried me in to the bathroom. Where he placed me down on the side of the tub. The water felt good to my body as I lower myself into it. While I laid in the tub, trying my best to relax and forget what I had been though at the bar. There was one thing on my mind, and I had to know the answer to my question. So I asked Quinton why he was there at the bar tonight? He replied I can't really explain why I was there, when I have tried my best not to go there. But for some reason I felt that I needed to go there. Tonight. Now I'm glad I was there, you needed my help. Are you feeling better Quinton asked me? Yes I am, was my reply. But in my mind I didn't want to be alone. For some reason I wanted to ask him to stay with me. But I didn't know what would happened if I did. After helping me out of the tub he dried me off then he carried me back to my bed where he laid me. He asked if I wanted him to do anything else for me, before he left that's when my mind took over and I asked him if he could stay with me that night. Quinton did stay. He decided to sleep on the sofa. Sometime that night I had a nightmare about what had happened. I must have cried out in my sleep. Because I heard Quinton calling my name.

That's what woke me up. Once I opened my eyes he asked if I was all right? My reply was I think so. Sitting on the side of my bed was a well built young man, who looked to be about 185 pounds and stood 6'0" tall. With shoulder length hair, and the skin of a child. He told me that he would stay right by my side. Without taking off his clothes, he got into bed with me. This man held me all of that night, until the next morning when I woke to find him watching me as I slept.

The first word out of his mouth was good morning, my reply was good morning. Then he said you know I don't know your name. His smile was cheerful and warm. Well my name is Dennis I said as I laid there next to him. Well I think it's time that I tell you more about myself. You just found out my name, and you know what I went though last night, but you did not know that I just turned 21 years old yesterday. I'm about 5'8" and 150 pounds. With short to mid length hair. I work and I'm also a full time student.

I was hoping that everything that had happened to me was a dream. But you know that it's not a dream when you wake up in your bed with another man. I never have thought about being with a man sexually. Being raped doesn't make it any better. Quinton seem to understand what I was going though. He had done so much for me with out asking for sex nor had he tried to hurt me in any way. When he got up from the bed he was still fully dressed. I got up right behind him I was nake as the day I was born. Once I had taken a shower and gotten dressed I asked my new found friend if he wanted something to eat. He replied that would be nice to have a home cooked meal for once. I told him that I can cook all right. So I fixed us a meal. While we were eating, we had a long talk. I found out that he was living from place to place, because his grand mother put him out after he told her about the rape. So that's why I was out that time at night. Quinton told me that there was something else he had to tell me, but he didn't know how I was going to react. I told him to tell me, what ever it is because that's the only way we could get to know each other. About that time he said that he gives his body away for a place to stay. The men that I stay with, I have to sleep with them sexually. As Quinton talked to me the only thing I could do was to look at him. I asked him how old he was, he replied that he was 20 years old. No job, and doesn't go to school. For some reason we ended up spending the day together. Later that evening I asked if he wanted to stay the night? For the first time Quinton called me Dennis. He asked if I really wanted him to stay after what he had told me. I watched his face. There was a look of suddenness. I took a hold of his hand and said you don't have to worry. I want ask you to do anything that you don't to do. Quinton started to cry, he looked up at me and said you are a real friend. Everyone else always want me to do something for them. As we talked Quinton told me that he needed to go and pick up some clothes. So we got in to my car and drove to an apartment building. Where he went into, when he returned with two bags. He put them into the back seat, and then he got into the car. After closing the car door. He told me that the guy who lived in the apartment had told him to leave. Because his girl friend was coming back to town. So now he had all the clothes he owned in two paper bags.

At that point my heart went out to this young man. I wanted to return the help that he had given me the night before. There was something about Quinton that made me feel at ease around him. I felt that I could understand some of the things that had happened to him. He was only 20 years old and very much in need of someone to help him get his life back together. Once we got back to apartment, Quinton and I sat down in the livingroom area. And talked some more. We talked for hours. I found out that Quinton had wanted to go to college. I had found away to help my new friend to get a job. The next step I wanted to take was to help him to get in college as a student. That night Quinton and I went to bed in the same bed, but this was the one time he didn't have to perform any sex acts, the next morning we both got up and went to work. It was the longest eight hours of my life, because I wanted to see what had happened. I waited for him in the parking lot. A few moments later Quinton walked out to my car, with a big smile on his face. What's up, was the first words out of his mouth when he got into the car. My reply was all I want to do is to go home and relax, this has been along day. So we went to the apartment. Where we decided to take turns getting cleaned up. I didn't have much time before I had to be in class. I asked Quinton to come with me to my class; I told him that we could bring visitors to classes. He agreed to come and sit in.

After we both had cleaned up and gotten dressed Quinton and I headed for the collage, as we road we talked about a lot of things. He told me that he has been looking for someone that he could love and share his life with. Someone who would want him just as he was and not for what he could do for them. Well believe it or not I have been looking for the same type of person. The more we talked the more it seemed that Quinton and I were a like in many ways. When we got to my class, the teacher was already in the room. I informed him that I had brought a visitor to sit in on the class. His reply was it's good to have you here tonight. Please take a seat. As our class started Quinton seem to really get into what was going on He surprised me with how much he knew.

Once the class was over the teacher came over and talked to Quinton for a while, when we got into the car, he told me that teacher wants him to come to the class each night. That's good, I replied. I could tell that Quinton was very happy about what happened. We didn't talk very much as we drove back to the apartment. When we got into the apartment Quinton headed for the kitchen. His words were sit down and relax, I've got something in store for you.

About 45 min. later he came out of the kitchen carrying two plates, he placed them on the table. Come on and eat. I got up from the sofa and walked to the table where I took a seat. The food looked good, I didn't know that he could cook. When he returned to the table. Our eyes met and we didn't say a word for a few moments.

The he was the first to speak. Well how's the food my friend? Once I got my mouth to working again I said it was very good. Getting back to the eye contact. I don't know why, but when I looked into Quinton's eyes there was something. I didn't know what or why. Well the night went by to fast. It seemed that by the time we fell a sleep, the clock was going off for us to get up for work. Once I had taken my shower and came back into the bedroom. Quinton had laid out some under clothes for me to put on. I hope you don't mind me doing that, he asked.

As I walked over to the bed. As he walked across the room towards the bathroom's door. My eyes followed him until he stepped though the door. For some crazy reason I was doing something that I had never done before. After getting dressed I found myself looking though his clothes to find him a pair of underwear. Well when I started looking there were underwear of many colors. I have grown up thinking that men only wore white underwear.

I was one of those people who's mother always brought their underwear. I found a pair of red underwear. So I laid them on the bed. The next thing I to do was to find a T-shirt. Because he only wore T-shirts. I picked out one that said, "I Love the Beach Life". About that time Quinton came back into the bedroom, wearing only a towel. I watched his every move as he removed the towel and then what seem to be in slow motion, he put on his underwear and T-shirt, then his jeans slowly moved up his manly legs.

I don't know what came over me. I have never been entrusted in other men, but now I find myself drawn to Quinton. Maybe its do to the way we met or how caringly he treated me that night.

After he finished getting dressed we headed to work for another eight hours. Once we got into a parking space at work. We wished each other a nice day. Then we headed for our jobs, not to see each other again until we got off. I had to try my best to keep my mind on my work. But it was real hard, because I was thinking about the things that were going on in my personal life. Why should a young man like me who has always wanted to find a girl to marry and have children. Here I am now having thoughts about another young man. Plus I seem to be drawn to him in ways that no man should be to another man. Maybe what ever it is will just go away. How can I say that when I don't even know what going on?

I wonder what Quinton is thinking; maybe he knows what I should do about this matter. Should I say anything to him about what has been going though my mind, or could the right thing be for me to keep it to myself? My thoughts was cut short when a buzzer went off to let us know that it was break time. I went on break and I sat and watched the people around me carrying on with their lives like they were all as free as the birds in the sky.

As I went back to work I thought to myself that I needed to talk to someone, but who. I didn't know any one that would understand what's going on in my mind. When I can't understand it myself. My whole day was long and crazy. I'm glad that I don't have a class tonight.

My last two breaks went fast, the next thing I know it was time to go home. When I got half way to the car I noticed that Quinton was already waiting. As I walked towards him, he began to smile and his face started to light up. Once inside of the car. He asked do we have a class tonight? I answered him by saying no; we'll have a whole night alone. I just happened to turn and look as Quinton, he was looking at me with a childish look on his face. After making one stop at the store to pick up a few things, we headed home.

Once we got inside the apartment. Quinton and I raced to the bathroom to get cleaned up. He got into the bathroom just before me. I stopped at the door. I stood and watched as he pulled his T-shirt off and kicked off his shoes, the next thing to go was the jeans that covered his body so neatly. I couldn't take my eyes away from what I was seeing.

Dennis why didn't you come on in with me, when I heard Quinton's voice calling out to me. It seemed that I was watching a movie. I watched as the actor undressed and walked into the bathroom. My mind was racing with thoughts. I couldn't stop myself. I don't even know if I wanted to. Once inside the shower Quinton started to rub soap over my body. He took his time, and all I could do was stand there and let him do what ever he had on his mind. His hands moved over me very gently.

After he finished with, my hands seem to have a mind of their own; they took the soap and started to rub it over his body. With out saying a word I worked on him the same gentle way he had done me. When we finished we stepped out of the shower and dried each other of. Then Quinton took me by the hand and lead me into the bedroom. Where he laid me down on the bed and slowly gave me a massage. By the time he finished my body was so relaxed. I moved aside to allow him to take my place on the bed; I let my hands move over his body, touching every part of him. Before I knew it I found myself kissing him around the neck. Which seem to be turning him on,

What I was doing was also turning me on. My dick was hard as a rock. I wanted to make love to Quinton so bad; well I didn't have to wait for long. The two of us seem to know what the other person wanted. There was touching, kissing and making the heat rise. When we got into making love everything seems to fit just right. When I enter him I tried to take things slow and easy. But for some reason things speeded up and I was giving it everything that I had. Quinton was voicing his feelings, and he was using his hands to keep me hot as I could be. After I had finished making love to him I felt that I was still on fire, I rolled over beside of him. I put my arms around him and pulled his on top of me. From that point on he seem to know what I was feeling so he started to work on me. I was willing to let this Man do what he wanted to my body. I never knew that another man could make me feel so wonderful. When Quinton raised my legs I knew what was about to happened. Part of me wanted to say no. But my mouth wasn't working. When Quinton's hard dick entering my ass hole, he seem to push a button that I didn't know was there. Believe me he took pleasure to the highest point. Man let me tell you when I reached that point my body felt like it had never felt before.

My friend how could I explain how I could allow myself to make love to Quinton. When I've never seemed to be turned on by any man before. But you know I wanted everything that he had done for me, as we laid in bed together I held him in my arms. With his head on my chest. Our bodies pressed together. His skin was soft and warm against mine's. All I knew was that people wouldn't understand how a man make me feel so much better than a woman that I've ever knew.

As the hours went by we both fell a sleep. The next morning when I awoke Quinton was still in my arms, and sleeping like a baby. His face seemed so peaceful. I laid there and watched him. His body was almost uncovered. There was something about being here next to him that sent a feeling though my heart. My mind raced with many questions none of which I had any answers for. Luckily I awoke about an hour before we were to get up, and get ready for work.

As I watched this beautiful young man, and trying to keep my thoughts together. The clock went off, and woke him up. When he opened his eyes, his first words were good-morning. I replied by saying good-morning to you too. He started to jump out of bed; I stopped him and gave him a kiss. He kissed me back so sweetly and tenderly. After our kiss we got out bed, and both of us headed for the shower we washed each other's bodies. Once our shower was over we dried off and went back into the bedroom to get dressed. As we dressed, we talked. I tried to explain what had happened last night. Quinton told me that there was no need to explain anything, because he wanted it to happen.

Just then the phone rang, it was my girlfriend. She wanted to know why I hadn't called her. The only thing I could say was that I had been busy trying to get my apartment right. I told her that I couldn't talk, because I had to get ready for work. And that I will call her later. I didn't waste any time getting off the phone. One thing I knew was that I couldn't explain to this woman about the things that I am feeling about another man. When I put the phone down I turned around to see Quinton standing there in front of me wearing a pair of jeans that made me want him all over again. My eyes were locked on him; he walked over to me and gave me a kiss. That kiss brought me back to the real world.

Look we've better get moving or we wont have time to eat. Do you have a class tonight? Quinton talked to me as I dressed. Then he went into the kitchen and fixed us something that we could eat on the run. Once out of the apartment we walked to the car. Once inside the car, we started on our way to work. Quinton reached over and touched my leg. Then he asked me if I had enjoyed the things that happened last night. My reply was yes. How could I have done that to when I knew that you had been hurt before? He replied don't worry about making love to me. Because like I said earlier, I wanted you to do everything that you did.

After he finished speaking I told him that I didn't know how to explain it, but I also wanted him to make love to me too. By that time I drove into the company's parking lot. That meant that we would have to finish talking later. I hope that I could get some work done.

Well believe me those eight hours wee the longest hours of my life. As I walked out of the door. On way to the parking lot.

There was Quinton standing there waiting for me. As soon as he saw me his face lit up with a smile. He seemed to be happy about something. And when I got over to where he was standing. Quinton started talking a word a second. I had to tell him to slow down because I couldn't understand what he was saying. His words were "Dennis" I was put on a new job today. Which means more money for us. My supervisor came to me and asked if I wanted to move up to a better job. Well you know what I said to that. Now I can help you with all of our bills and plus I will be able to save some money for when we really need it.

There's one thing I need to talk to you about when we get home. Once we had gotten into the car Quinton seem to slow down a little, but I could tell that he was still wired up. My mind started racing, what could he want to talk to me about? Is it about the job or about what happened last night? What ever it is I hope I can take it. Once we had gotten home, Quinton and I walked into the apartment door. I felt like two big men were standing on my shoulders. It seemed like everything was moving in slow motion. When I had made it to bedroom door, my eyes fell upon Quinton standing in the middle of the floor nake.

As I stood there watching him, he turned and walked into the bathroom. Just then everything seem to speed up into fast-forward. It didn't take me long to stripe out of my clothes and made my way into the bathroom. I took matters into my own hands. I ran a tub of water. Then I stepped into it and asked Quinton to join me. He did and we laid there together and let the water relax us.

My mind went into a state of crazies, and all I could do was ask the one question that was in bedded into my mind. So the words came out of my mouth, what was it that you wanted to talk to about? Quinton's reply was don't worry it nothing bad. I just wanted to talk to you about our relation ship. He said I don't know how to explain what's going on in my head. I broke in with the following words why don't you just come on out with what ever you want to say. At the same time I took a hold of his hand. That's when he started telling me that he was wondering what type of relationship I wanted out of life. And have I ever thought about maybe having a relationship with someone like him. Before I reply. He asked what kind relationship do we have? Believe me I didn't know what to say. By that time my mind had went into over drive, and I some how my mouth took over. The words I spoke was a surprise to me as well Quinton. When I told Quinton that I wanted us to be ore that just friends. Then I asked him what he was looking for in this rclationship?

Quinton looked into my eyes and told me that he had no idea what he wanted, but he would be willing to take the chance to see how things will work out. I told him that I would also be willing to take things one-step at a time. He also told me that we needed to talk about what bills I would like him to pay. My reply was that I haven't thought about it, well I guess that we could go half on everything. He said that it sound good to him. Now we need to think about what we were going to have for dinner? After we had eaten dinner, I noticed the time; I knew that we only had enough time to make it to class. So I told Quinton to get his stuff so we could leave for school.

After driving to the school, we got there just in time for class. We went though a three-hour class on the act of report writing. For some reason that night we had a good time. The time went by fast. After the class Quinton and I started on our way back home. When we walked up to the door of the apartment, I heard the phone ringing. So I hurried to open the door, and ran to answer the phone. When I picked it up I found that it was my girlfriend. Who I have not talked to within the past few weeks.

She had called this morning, but I didn't talk to her then. She was wanting to talk to me about something. I knew that I was going to be faced with something that I had wasted to prolong for as long as I could. Now I will have to tell her what happened. She may not be able to understand that I never wanted any of this to happen, but now I have to go on with my life.

I told her that I would be there with in a little while. After we had hung up the phone. I needed to talk to Quinton. He understood what I was going to do, and that there was no way of knowing how it will turn out. I let him know that no matter what happed we would still have each other. With no other words spoken, I left to go and talk to Pauline. When I pulled up in front of her apartment building. My mind was racing right a long with my heart. I almost did a U turn, but then I was hit in the face by reality. Which was making me do what I knew had to be done.

When I got out of my car and walked up to her front door, she was waiting for me to get there. Once inside we took a seat on the sofa. Where we started to talk, we didn't try to sometime to the points that were needed to be made. Then I told her that I had to tell her what happened on my birthday. "Pauline" do you remember the night I went out to a bar alone. She didn't say anything, so I went on to say that there was something about that night I hadn't told anyone, but I was about to tell her everything. And that I don't know how you will handle it. The only words she said was go on and tell me.

So I tried to find the words to say, but I knew that the only thing I could do was to tell her the truth. The facts were that I had been raped in a back room of the bar. Where I had to go though a nightmare. After she heard story. About that time her whole mood changed. Pauline was mad as hell, and she didn't care what words came out of her mouth. And before I knew what had happened she told me that she never wanted to see me again.

Then she said you freak I want you to get the hell out of my house. Because I couldn't talk her down, went off on me again. This time she made a statement that sent my head in to a spin. She said I'm going to have a baby. Before I could react, Pauline told me to get out and that she never wants to see my face again as long as you are alive.

I walked out and left her crying. Once in the car I sat there unable to move. With my head in my hands. It took me a while to get myself together. The drive back to my apartment seem to take forever. I was feeling so hurt and alone. With Pauline's words still ringing in my ears my car must to have been on auto ploit, because I don't remember how I got from one place to the other. After I packed my car I walked up to my door. It seemed that Quinton knew I was standing there unable to move. He opened the door and took me by the hand and lead me into his arms and held me. That's when I lost, I started to cry.

Quinton didn't say a word. He seemed to now that I needed someone to lean on. When he opened his arms, I once again felt alone. He looked into my eyes with such warmth. Baby what's wrong? Was the words that he spoke so tenderly. It was so hard for me to speak. I took a deep breath and said that she never wants to see me again.

Then I said she is going to have a baby. My words seemed to hit him; just as hard as they had they had hit me when Pauline first spoke them. Quinton's eyes dropped from mine's and his face sadden. I reached out and lifted his face, that's when I saw the tears steaming down his face. Which was the most handsome tanned face that I've ever seen. At that time I didn't know what to say. Before I could say anything because Quinton spoke, he said that he would leave. Then he turned and started to walk away from me. I knew that I couldn't let him leave. So I reached out for his arm, and told him that I wanted him to stay.

When he turned to face me. He was still crying, Quinton asked why should I stay when you have a girlfriend and a baby on the way? That's when I took him by the hand and leads him over to the sofa where we sat down. I explained that Pauline couldn't handle the facts about the rape, so she broke up with me. As I was walking out of her door, she loudly stated that she was going to have a baby. I don't know if the baby is mine's or not. One thing I can believe is that Pauline will not have anything to do with me, because she thinks that I am no longer a man. I don't know what got into me. We both knew that people can not deal with the facts when it comes down to a man being raped by other men.

I just let all the words come out that were running around in my head. At that point Quinton and I took our next step together. We both knew we could let our feelings run free. After my mouth stop running. Quinton took over; he had a few things to say.

He said that Pauline didn't know what she was giving up. And that he would happily stand by my side. We seemed to know what each other was thinking and it ended in a long kiss of passion.

After our kiss I stood up and took off all of my clothes, then I walked over to Quinton and sat on his lap. It didn't take him long to get the idea, and take off his clothes too.

There we where nake, playing around like children. Running and jumping around, wrestling. This went on for a long time. Before we headed for the shower. Once in bed we held each other all night. The next morning when we awoke, Quinton and I knew that another day was waiting to be faced. I told him that we were going to take our showers together all the time. So we got up and went into the bathroom, where we washed each other's bodies down. After getting dressed, we went in to kitchen to eat breakfast.

Just as we were getting ready to leave the phone ranged. The voice on the other end was my mother's. She said that Pauline had called her last night, telling her that she never wanted to see you again. Mom asked me what was going on? I tried to explain to her that I couldn't talk right then, because I had to leave for work.

Once in the car I told Quinton about the phone call. He asked how I was going to handle my parents? My only reply was I don't know. For some reason that day seemed to be a day in which nothing went right. First we were late for work because someone had lost a full load of bricks. That closed the road for about an hour and a half.

Luckily we were not the only ones who were late. Then when I did get to work, things just seemed to go crazy, the next thing I knew I was being told that our line had to work over for two hours. Plus we had a class to go to. Well I think that you know how I felt by the time Quinton and I finally got home.

I just wanted to get into bed and hide. But as soon as we walked though the door, the phone ranged. It was my mom and this time she was going to talk to me one way or the other. So I had to agree to come over to my parent's house, after hanging up the phone, I told Quinton that I was going to have to face my parents tonight. We went to our class, when we finished at school I drove Quinton back to our apartment. That's when he asked me if I wanted him to come with me. My heart wanted to say yes, but my mind knew better.

I had to talk to my parents alone. I wonder how would they handle what I was about to tell them? After giving Quinton a kiss, I walked out the door. Not knowing what was about happened. As I got into my car, I took a deep breath and started on my way, the trip was only six blocks. Then there I was sitting in front of my parent's house. Man you know this was something that I never thought I would have to do, but none of us can know what changes our lives will take from day to day. It was only a short time ago I was living at home with my parents, with a girlfriend. Now look at me. This has been so hard for me to go though, because there are no people who can understand what I have been though, nor can they understand my feelings.

When I got to my parent's house I used my key to get in. They were sitting in the living room waiting on me to walk in. After taking a sit across from them, I could only look at them. My father was the first to speak. His words were to the point. What's going on with you and Pauline? My reply was did it's a long story. That's when my mom said go a head we got the time. I tried to explain to them that it was hard for me to talk about. I could see that they just want some answers. So I slowly started to tell them about the rape that I went though on the night of my birthday.

It seemed to take forever for me to get my words out. I didn't have to see my father's eyes to know that he was looking at me, I could feel his eyes. When Quinton's name came up in my explanation. My father stopped me and asked who is Quinton? I went on to tell them that after the rape was over he was the only one who did anything to help me. Or should I say that we helped each other. That's when my mother asked with force, what do you mean that you helped each other? I told her that he had come to my aid after I was rape. Then I helped him get a job, plus he is staying with me.

There was a long pause, and as I looked into the faces of my mother and father, I wondered what they were thinking. Then with out any warning my father spoke, his words hit me like a brick. I didn't bring a faggot into this world. So until your get yourself together, I want you to leave my house and don't come back. My mother just sat there with tears running down her face.

The only thing I could do was get up from the chair in which I was sitting and walk out of the house. When I got to my car, I could hardly open the door. Once inside I asked myself over and over again, what did I do wrong? My father's words still in my head. It was a long drive from their house to my apartment building. After parking I sat in my car for a while. When I looked up there was Quinton standing on the steps, waiting for me. So I got out of the car and locked the doors. Then I walked over to the one person who still wanted me around. When I stepped up to where he was standing, Quinton put his arms around my shoulders and walked me into the door. Once in the apartment, he told me not to say a word. Then while we stood on the middle of the floor he slowly undressed me. Next he picked me up and carried my nake body into the bathroom. Where he sat me down on the side of the tub. That's when he undressed, and then we both got into the warm water that filled the tub.

The bathroom was lit with scented candles. That Quinton had placed around the room. I want to you to lay back in my arms and relax, those were the words hi whispered in my ear. Believe me I did what he asked, and tried to relax. It was hard when I couldn't forget the words I had heard from my parents and Pauline. The words still cut into my heart. Some how the scent of the candles and the warmth of the water along with his arms. Made me fall asleep. When I work again Quinton was still holding me in his arms. When I opened my eyes, he was looking over me. Are you feeling better now, he spoke in a soft tone of voice. My reply was I'm feeling a little better. How can I explain the way I felt that night. I was hurt by the two people whom I loved, and the woman I thought that I was in love with. Also I was feeling a pleasure like no other that I have ever known. These things that were going on in my life were so different from what I had been told about all of my life.

Here I am now twenty-one years old and trying to make something out of my life. The person standing by my side is not the woman that I was told should be my better half, But a young man. Maybe I need to let you in on a few things. First of all I'm a black man from a middle class family. Everyone always told me that relationships were to be man and woman. There couldn't be anything in between. Picture a man 5'8" at 150 pounds, with short black hair and brown eyes. If I should say so myself I do have a nice body. Pauline seem to enjoy it before I was raped. Now on the other hand Quinton stands 6'0" at 175 pounds with shoulder length brow hair and light brown eyes. Oh I forgot to tell you that's he is a white male. Who is twenty years old? He was living from place to place.

Now can you see why I said that things are different, because the thought of having a gay relationship had never crossed my mind? After a few moments Quinton and I got out of the tub and dried off. We got into bed, that night we didn't have to say a word. We just laid in each other's arms. I could feel his heart beating. And his breaths were long and slow. It took me along time to fall asleep again. So I just laid there enjoying the feeling of his body next to mine's. I don't know when I fell a sleep, but the next morning when I awoke, I was holding Quinton in my arms. My body felt as if I had not gotten ay sleep at all. The sound of the clock going off woke him up. The first thing he did was to give me a kiss. We held each other for a while, and then we released the hold that we had. At that time both of us jumped up from the bed and raced for the bathroom.

I don't know why we did that because we always ended up in the shower together. Our showers together were both fun and relaxing. We knew every part of each other's bodies. My hand seems to always find just what I was looking for Quinton's nice round butt for white boy. Believe me every chance I got I would touch those buns. I don't know how to explain what was going on, you see I was a man who had never wanted to have a relationship with another man, but this one really turns me on in every way. We took our time to shower and dry off and to dress.

Once dressed we fixed breakfast together, then we ate. On our way to work Quinton and I talked and played around. It seemed as if it fast and before we knew it the day was over and we were on our way home. We had a little time before it was time to head to school.

Once at school things took a crazy turn, and everyone in class seemed to be off the wall even Mr. Peterson, our teacher was acting crazy. It was a fun class. About three and a half hours later we were on our way home again this time to try and come back down to earth. Wouldn't/t you know it we were a little crazy ourselves, so for some reason we decided to stop at the park, where we took along walk together.

While in the park we sat on a bench and watched the stars dance around in the darken sky. As we looked out over the park we could see the lake, plus there were other people walking and spending time with each other. We stayed in the park for about two hours. Then we made our way home. Once at home Quinton and I acted like two kids, playing around. The two of us ended up on the living room floor making love to each. Man by the time we finished there was nothing left, but to sleep, and that's what we did. The next morning we woke up the floor nake, and the sound of the clock. I jumped up so that I could see what time it was. The clock had been ringing for 30 min. We were running late and we only had time to take a quick shower and get dress. I was hoping that we would make it to work on time. After parking the car we had just enough time to get to our jobs and start to work. Once we had pulled our eight hours, we just wanted to go home and spend a restful night alone. First we took a long shower, and then we went into the kitchen to cook dinner. After that we sat down in front of the TV, and ate.

I found away to talk about what I feeling. It was hard for me to explain the thoughts I had running around in my head. There was a pain in side of me that hurt so bad. Also there was a pleasure that Quinton had brought to my life. My words came out of my mouth in such a way that it didn't even sound like I was doing the talking. After I had finished what I had to say. Quinton then took his turn; he told me that he was glad that we had met. Not because of what had happened, but because he was in need of a friend. There was one thing that we had never thought would happened, and that was we had fallen in love with each other. By the time we got into bed both of us had opened our heart and minds. Now that we had laid our feelings out on the table. What would happened next. No one could say.

Anniversary Gift

On my way home from work, I stopped at the mall to buy my wife a gift for our 1st anniversary. I went into one of the jewelry stores located inside the mall. I looked around for a while before picking out a diamond heart pendant, which hung from a gold chain. After getting it wrapped, I went to another store to buy a bottle of Champaign. While driving home I started to think back to the day that I married her. I remembered seeing her for the first time that day. As she appeared in the doorway of the church. Looking like an angle from heaven dressed in white. She slowly glided towards me. We stood there together vowing to be one for the rest of our lives. Each day that we have been together my love for her has grown stronger.

When I drove into our driveway I thought about the surprise I had planned for her when she walks though the door. I went into the bedroom and undressed, I was going to be wearing only a red thong and a black bow tie. Just as I pulled on my bath robe, the doorbell rung. I went to the door, when I opened it to found the deliveryman standing there with the 3 dozen roses I had order. He placed them inside the doorway. I tipped him, and he left. I started to work, I took one dozen of them and pulled the petals apart ad drop them on the floor making a path from the front door to the bedroom. Then I took another dozen and made a rose petal spread for our bed. The last dozen roses were going to be sitting on the table by the front door. When I looked at the clock I knew that she would home in a few moments, so I took off my robe and laid on the bed and drop some petals on my body. The scented candles were already lit and ready. While the music was playing soft and low.

I heard the front door open and close. I knew she was on her way to the bedroom. When she stepped into the doorway, I show the look on her face. She was very surprised. I guess she thought that I hear forgotten, because I had not said anything to her about our anniversary. As she stood there looking at me, I said happy anniversary baby. She walked over to the bed, and picked up the gift that was sitting on my chest. When she unwrapped it I watched her face light up. It did not take her long to undress and join me in the rose peltols. I held her close to me as I kissed her sweet lips. Then we made love, that night was wonderful. My wife and I shared our love and pleasure with each other. I was the started of another year of happiness. That year was so wonderful; we shared so many things together.

Now here I am getting ready for another anniversary. This time I left work early to cook dinner and to pick up her gift. When I got home I went to work. I had everything ready a few moments before she walked though the door. I was hoping to surprise my wife again. Well she was surprised, but the real surprise was going to be on me. She had an unbelievable surprise in store for me. We eat dinner, then danced right there in our living room with the lights down low. I was ready to take her into the bedroom and make love to her. I slowly moved her towards the bedroom. As we laid on the bed she told me that she had a special gift for me. I asked where it was; she said you will have to wait a little longer. I didn't know what she had on her mind.

I only had to wait for a few moments. When the doorbell rung, she got up to answer it. I could hear her talking to Norrell, which was her best friend. The two them walked into the bedroom. While I was laying on the bed half nake. I wondered why he was there. I didn't ask, because they were so close that they were like sisters. Maybe I need to explain. You see Norrell is gay. I watched as my wife (Miona) started to undress with him standing in the room. Then she said baby your gift is here. I didn't know what she was talking about, but I was about to find out. As I laid on the bed my wife joined me on the bed, then something happened that really took me by surprise. There in front of us stood Norrell nake as the day he was born. Miona told him to join us, so he came over to the bed and sat down. Before I could ask what was going, Miona kissed, then she said I wanted to give you something extra special, and Norrell is it. What are you talking about? I asked. She said I know that you do not understand any of this, but you will, just lay back and enjoy.

The two of them started to massage my nake body. I closed my eyes and relaxed. They touched every part of my body. With my eyes closed I could not tell who was doing what. Norrell's hands were just as soft as Miona. One of them started to give me a blowjob, while the other one was licking my balls. They were making me very hot and horny. My dick was so hard that it hurt. I wanted to make love to my wife. I opened my eyes to find Norrell sucking my hard dick, while she was licking my balls. What was a man to so when he is getting good sex. The next thing I knew Miona was on top of me, riding my hard dick. That's when she tells to get ready and lay down on the bed beside me. He did just as she had asked him to do. She road me just long enough to grease my dick with her juice. Then she got off of me. That's when things took a turn. My wife told me to have sex with her best friend. She wanted to fuck him in his ass. I had never thought about doing anything like this before. My wife kept telling me to do it. So I looked over at him laying there face down on the bed. I moved around so that I could get between his opened legs. He took my hard dick into his hand and put it in to place. I then slowly pushed forward, I could feel myself going deeper in to his warm hole. I could not believe that I was fucking another man.

I did not understand why my wife did this, but I had to say that she did surprise me this time. I found myself fucking him until I short my load inside of his body. While I was doing this I felt that he was enjoying what was happening, because of the sounds he was making. Once it was over I pulled out and rolled over on my back. My wife came over and sat down on the bed beside me. I asked her why did she do this? What was on her mind? She told me that she wanted me know how it would feel to have the best of both worlds. Then she went on to say a lot of men thinking about doing what you just did, but worry about what people would say if they were to find out. How you think about this not only did you do it, but you had sex with both of use at the same time. It's not over with yet baby. That's when she took my hand and said lets all get cleaned up. So the three of us went into the bathroom, where we got into the shower together. There I was being washed by both of them, they touched every part of my body. Some body's hand went between the cheeks of my ass that was a spot where I had never thought about another person touching me.

My Doctor had never touched there before. I did not know whose hand it was, but it made me feel something I had never felt before. Once every body had been washed we dried off. Then we returned to the bedroom where we got back on to the bedroom.

This time Miona did every thing she could to get me hard again, she did not have to work to hard on that. I had in my mind that I was going to make love to her this time out. That's what I did, but some thing happened that I did not plan on. While I was fucking her Norrell had an idea of his own. He started to lick the cheeks of my ass. Then I felt his spread them. I did not know what he was going to do next. I did know that no man was going to go up in me. I kept fucking my wife while he went on to lick my asshole. It was some thing about what he was doing that made me hot as hell, what was going on here? He stop doing that, but he got down to where he could lick my balls, and my dick as it move in and out of her wet hole. I was about ready to pop my load inside of my wife when he took both of my balls in to his mouth and started to suck and lick. Man I thought that I would never stop cuming. What were these two people doing to me? This was a pleasure that I had never felt before. I know that I may sound a man who has not seen the light of day, but that was some thing a lot different than we had ever done. I found out the hard way that the night was a long way from being over. There I was weak as hell, when they pulled me from the bed and led me into the bathroom, were we got back into the shower.

Once we were washed and dried, the two of them led me back into the bedroom. It all starts all over again. The two of them worked my body all over from head to toe. I didn't know who I was going to make love to this go round. Norrell got on top of me and road my hard dick; he slowly roused and lowed himself the length of my dick. My worked on my nipples, then she moved down to my balls and started to work on them. Man I got lost in the whole thing. I know that I was in another world all together. My mind was reeling and my heart was racing. That night after every thing was over Norrell got cleaned up and went home. Moina got in bed and I took her in my arms as we laid there, slowly falling a sleep. The next morning when we awoke I try and find out her reasons for doing what she did. When I asked her, she said that she wanted me to get the best of both worlds, and that she wanted to give me full pleasure. During that day we talked about the things that went on the night before.

A few days passed, and I found out that my wife had another surprise in store for me. On Friday when I got home from work. She asked me if she could talk to me about some thing. Once she sat me down she started to talk to me about the night of our anniversary. She asked me how I felt about what went on that night. I told her that she had surprise, and I did enjoy what she had done. I went on to say that what we had done would be some men's dream comes true. She went on to ask me if I would want to do that again? I answered her by saying only if that's what you want. Well that's what I want to talk to you about. How would feel if Norrell came to live with us, and we were able to do this whenever you want it. At that time my mind went in to over drive. I had so many thoughts running around in my head that I didn't know what to think. She said that way you could have your cake and eat it too. You would have two lovers' right here with you at all times. My first words were why do you want to do this. Well I just want you to be happy she replied. I wanted to make my wife happy and if this is what it would take then I'll do it. I told her that we could try this to see how it would turn out. We agreed that Norrell would come and spend the weekend with us, and see how things go. That's when she got on the phone and called him to tell him that I had agreed, and for him to come over.

When he got there we sat around and talk almost like nothing had happened. That night when it was time to go to bed. The three of us got into the same bed. There I was with my wife on one side and Norrell on the other. As I laid there the two of them started to take off my t-shirt and underwear. Then they slowly started to kiss my nude body. Was I ready for what they were going to do to me? I did not know, but I was going to find out. That night was a repeat of about a week of ago. Man they did their best to drain me of my cum. After we had cleaned up, the two of them laid there in my arms. The next morning I awoke to find myself laying in bed with my wife and her best friend. This must be a dream, how am I going to handle this. I was the first to wake up so I laid there waiting for them to awake to see what was going to happened. I did not have to wait long, because my wife was to next person to open her eyes. She noticed that I was awake she said good-morning, she smiled at me saying I hope you enjoyed yourself last night. I did not know how to answer her, because I did not know how she would handle my answer. How do a man tell his wife that he was beginning to enjoy having a three way with her and another man. I did how ever tell her the truth, by saying yes. That's when she kissed me on the lips. Before I could say any thing, she woke Norrell up, by touching him. Once he had awaked he also kissed me. Man this was all new to me, but I was beginning to like this. By Sunday night I was thinking so many things that I did not really understand my own thoughts. My wife told me that Norrell was going to spend the night with us and the next morning he was going to work from the house. It would be up to me how things will turn out. Will I be able to allow Norrell to move into our home. I asked her how long I had before I had to give an answer? She said that I could take the rest of the day, why don't the three of us come back here after work and sit down and talk. I agree with that, and then she went into the kitchen to talk to Norrell.

When I got to work I could not wait to talk to my best friend. I did not know how he would handle what I wanted to tell him. But I did need to talk to some one. So when we had our break, I ask him if I could talk to him about that was going on. We sat down and talked, when I told him about what was going on with Miona, Norrell and myself. The only thing he said was man you got it made. A lot of men would love to be in your shoes. What are you going to do? I told him that on one hand I want to let him move in, and then I feel a fear, because what if someone found out what we were doing. He asked why are you worrying about other people, when every one is grown. On top of that your wife is apart of this. He had helped me to make up my mind. I told him that I was going to tell my wife that Norrell can move in. so when I got a change I called Miona at work and told her the answer. After work the three of us went to Norrell's apartment to get his things. We used all three cars so that we would only make one trip. It did not take us long to load up and drive by to the house.

Once at the house we unloaded the cars and put everything a way. I had a funny feeling that things were just getting started. I asked myself how was I going to explain this once people found out what was going on. Then I remembered what my buddy had told me. Then I just started to think about how the two of them had made me feel. I was in another world; I did not realize that my dick had gotten hard as a rock while I was sitting there. I did not hear Miona and Norrell come into the room. I was brought out of it when I felt someone touch me. When I looked up there they were standing there in front of me, with big smiles on their faces. Miona said I see that you must been thinking about us, then she leaned over and put her hand on my hard dick. I couldn't hide it, so I replied yes I was thinking about what has been happening the pass few days. That's when she said now you can have it whenever you want it. Before I could respond they both kissed me. There I was being kissed by my wife and her best friend who was a man. The night was just beginning. After dinner we sat in the living room and watched TV, and talked. It was kind of funny to have the two of them all over me. It did not take me long to get into swim of things. I started to play around with them. Doing things like touching and kissing.

My buddy called to see how things were going. I told him that we were sitting around watching TV. He asked that's all? I said for now. Before getting off the phone he said I can't wait for you to tell me all about at work tomorrow. When I looked at the old clock on the wall it was about 9:30pm, and getting close to our bedtime. I asked myself what do those two have on their minds? That's when I asked them if they were ready for bed? With smiles on their faces they both said yes. The three of us got up and walked to the bedroom.

Once we were there the two of them started to undress. I watched their clothes come off. I was getting turned on by seeing their bodies. As I stood there, their underwear came off and I was hot as hell. My dick was hard as a rock. Before I could start taking off my own clothes, Norrell and Miona walked over to me and went to work on undressing me. Once I was nake the two of them started to lick and kiss my bare skin. They started by kissing me in the mouth, and then they worked their way downward. Man when they got below the belt line. It was on, Norrell moved behind me, he parted my ass cheeks and licked my asshole. At the same time Miona was sucking my hard dick. I was about to loose control; I did everything I could to keep from screaming. As they worked I started to moan.

When they stopped I was lead to the bed, where they laid me down. As I laid there Norrell lifted my legs, then he started to licked my asshole. Then he slowly played with my tight hole with his finger, and Miona had lowed her body down over my face. I licked her wet pussy. This was the first time I had ever being finger fucked. It hurt but at the same time I was enjoying the feeling. There I was a 26 years old married man enjoying another man's touch. I loved my wife with all of my heart. At the same time she wanted me to be with her best friend. After Norrell had finished fingering my hole, I made love to Miona while Norrell started to licked my back and ass. I tried to hold back on shorting my load of cum so fast. Man the two of them was doing me in. I could get use to this type of pleasure. It did not take long before I reached the point of no return, I cam inside of my wife. I had known idea what could happen next. As I moved backward to get off of my wife, Norrell's hard dick touched my asshole. When I felt it I was a little worry because I never had been fucked in the ass before, and I did not know if I even wanted to. He just allowed me to do what I felt at that time. I just allowed my body to stay right were it was. He rubbed his hard dick between the cheeks of my ass. With out saying a word he seemed to know that I was nerves about it. He pulled a way and laid down on the bed beside me. I moved over and kissed his lips. Then I slow moved over him so that I could lay down on top of him. As I lowed my body down onto his, we kissed and he wrapped his arms around me. I kissed his neck then his shoulder, I worked my way down his body until I got to his legs, I lift them in to the air. Then I placed my face between the cheeks of his ass were I licked his wet hole. He moaned in pleasure, I eased my finger into his wet hole. When my wife came back into the room I had just started to move around so that he could suck my dick. He did just that; I kept working his ass hole. I did not have to tell him that I wanted to fuck him. As my wife watched I made love to her best friend.

Once we had finished making love, the two of us went in the bathroom to take a shower. While we were alone in the shower, we washed each slowly. Then we dried each other off. When we walked back into the room Miona was laying on the bed almost a sleep. We got on the bed with and the three of us went to sleep. The next morning I woke up to see our three-nake bodies woven together by legs and arms. When the clock went off my two lovers awoke. That morning the three of us got into the shower together, they washed my body. I also help to wash each of them. We went back into the bedroom and got dress, then had breakfast before heading off to work. I kiss each of their sweet lips before we walked out of the front door. As I drove to work I could not keep thinking about the night before. When I got to work my buddy Kayrone was waiting for me. I knew what he wanted to know. I told him that we were going to talk. When we got on the floor, our supervisor told us that we were going to be working in the sample room. That was good news to us because then we could talk alone.

He told me to start at the beginning, he wanted to know everything. I started by telling after we had moved Norrell stuff into the house, I sitting alone in the living room where I started thinking about what had happened the night before. Then I just started to think about how the two of them had made me feel. I was in another world; I did not realize that my dick had gotten hard as a rock while I was sitting there. I did not hear Miona and Norrell come into the room. I was brought out of it when I felt someone touch me. When I looked up there they were standing there in front of me, with big smiles on their faces. Miona said I see that you must been thinking about us, then she leaned over and put her hand on my hard dick. I couldn't hide it, so I replied yes I was thinking about what you had done to me. That's when she said now you can have it whenever you want it. Before I could respond they both kissed me. There I was being kissed by my wife and Norrell. That's about the time you called, after that when things got wild . . . Once we were there the two of them started to undress. I watched their clothes come off. I was getting turned on by seeing their bodies. As I stood there, their underwear came off and I was hot as hell. My dick was hard as a rock. Before I could start taking off my own clothes, Norrell and Miona walked over to me and went to work on undressing me. Once I was nake the two of them started to lick and kiss my bare skin. They started by kissing me in the mouth, and then they worked their way downward. Man when they got below the belt line. It was on, Norrell moved behind me, he parted my ass cheeks and licked my asshole. At the same time Miona was sucking my hard dick. I was about to loose control; I did everything I could to keep from screaming. As they worked I started to moan.

When they stopped I was lead to the bed, where they laid me down. As I laid there Norrell lifted my legs, then he started to lick my asshole. Then he slowly played with my tight hole with his finger, and Miona had lowed her body down over my face. I licked her wet pussy. This was the first time I had ever being finger fucked. It hurt but at the same time I was enjoying the feeling. There I was a 26 years old married man enjoying another man's touch. I loved my wife with all of my heart. At the same time she wanted me to be with her best friend. After Norrell had finished fingering my hole, I made love to Miona while Norrell started to licked my back and ass. I tried to hold back on shorting my load of cum so fast. Man the two of them was doing me in. I could get use to this type of pleasure. It did not take long before I reached the point of no return, I cam inside of my wife. I had known idea what could happen next. As I moved backward to get off of my wife, Norrell's hard dick touched my asshole. When I felt it I was a little worry because I never had been fucked in the ass before, and I did not know if I even wanted to. He just allowed me to do what I felt at that time. I just allowed my body to stay right were it was. He rubbed his hard dick between the cheeks of my ass. With out saying a word he seemed to know that I was nerves about it. He pulled a way and laid down on the bed beside me. I moved over and kissed his lips. Then I slow moved over him so that I could lay down on top of him. As I lowed my body down onto his, we kissed and he wrapped his arms around me. I kissed his neck then his shoulder, I worked my way down his body until I got to his legs, I lift them in to the air. Then I placed my face between the cheeks of his ass were I licked his wet hole. He moaned in pleasure, I eased my finger into his wet hole. When my wife came back into the room I had just started to move around so that he could suck my dick. He did just that; I kept working his ass hole. I did not have to tell him that I wanted to fuck him. As my wife watched I made love to her best friend.

Once we had finished making love, the two of us went in the bathroom to take a shower. While we were alone in the shower, we washed each slowly. Then we dried each other off. When we walked back into the room Miona was laying on the bed almost a sleep. We got on the bed with and the three of us went to sleep. The next morning I woke up to see our three-nake bodies woven together by legs and arms. When the clock went off my two lovers awoke. That morning the three of us got into the shower together, they washed my body. I also help to wash each of them. Then we dried each other off, and got dress for work. Kayrone asked me, how did I feel about having a man touching my body. I told him that it's a first for me, but it does make me feel kind of good. As

I looked at my buddy's face he had this smile on his face. I knew that he was thinking something. I ask him what are you thinking. He said man you got it made two live in lovers that you can get anytime you want. Right now I can only hope to find someone to love me the way I would like to be loved. I asked him what type are you looking for. He replied well who will try to understand me for the person I am, and someone who will try to be the best lover they can be.

As I listened to him I couldn't help from thinking that there was something he was not telling. So I just looked into his eyes and said you are telling me something what is it. He had this look on his face like a child who knows they had done something wrong. Then he said I didn't know how to tell you about this, or if you would be able to understand it. I said you know that you could all ways talk to me about anything just as I can you. That's when he said I am gay. It only took me a second to say man that's all. I thought that you were going to really tell me something. Now I know why you really got into this thing with me, Miona and Norrell. Who knows your Mr. Right will come along soon. We had talked all day. It was now time to go home, and I was looking forward to doing just that. I asked Kayrone to come with me home for dinner. He almost said no, but I was not going to take no for an answer. So he followed me home. We got there about a half an hour before Norrell would be home, so I went into the bathroom to get cleaned up. When Norrell got there I Introduced my best friend to my lover. Norrel came over to me and kissed me on the lips. Before he could walk a way I pulled him back and gave him a real kiss. I told him that Kayrone was going to stay for dinner.

Then about an hour later Miona came home. She already knew Kayrone. She came in and said hi, and then she also came over to me and gave me a kiss. Both Miona and Norrell went into the bedroom to change clothes before they were going to cooking dinner. While they were busy doing that Kayrone and I stayed in the living room talking. I told him that they always greet me that way. He said I would love to be greeted that some times. It took about 45 min for everyone to be ready to eat dinner.

The five of us sat down and had dinner together. We had fun while Kayrone was there with us. He left around 8:00pm. Then that's when my two babies started to work on me. Before I could get out of the living room they had striped me nake. Miona started taking off Norrell's clothes so I joined in and helped her. Once he was nake we started in on Miona. It was not long before we were all totally nake. We touched and kissed on each other. That night we did not have all of the wild sex. However we did enjoy each other, we fell a sleep in each other's arms. It seemed that we had just fallen a sleep when the clock went off it was time to get up for work. No one wanted to get up, but we knew that we had to. I kissed both of them before we headed off to work. I felt so good as I drove to work.

When I got there Kayrone was waiting for me. I knew that he needed to talk to me. Once we started to work we were able to talk. He wanted to tell me about what happened after he left my house last night. He was felling a little down when he left last night, so he went to a club that he had been to a few times. When he walked in the place was about half full. It seemed to be the same old faces. He said while he was sitting at the bar drinking a soda, a guy came over and sat down next him. This man ordered a drink. For some crazy reason the two of us some how started talking. We spent about two hours just talking about nothing really. We have a date tonight at my house. I asked him what is man's name? He told me that his name is Marzelle. He is 30 years old, and fine. I can't wait to see him again. There is something about the man that really makes me feel good. Last night as we sat there talking I felt that he really was interested in being around me. Unlike some of the other men who just wanted to find someone to have secret sex with or one nighters. I need some one who could want me for the person I am.

It was time for us to get off of work, and Kayrone was in a hurry to get home so he could get ready for his date with this new guy. I too was ready to get home so I could get cleaned up and fix dinner for my two special people. When I got home the first thing I did was to go in to the bedroom and undress, then I took a shower. I knew that both of them had to work a little late that night. So I had time to get everything ready. By the time they came home I had dinner on the table. I had something planned for them. When they walked though the door, I was standing wearing only an apron and until else. The apron said quick kiss the cook. Believe me both of them are fast readers. And they also follow instructions very well. After being kissed, I told them that dinner is ready. The two them went in to clean up, and then they came back in to the kitchen so that we could eat. I sat at the table with only my apron on. The two of them had fun picking on about it. After eating we clean up the kitchen, then we went into the living room to watch TV. I told them about what happened to Kayrone after he left our house last night. He was felling a little down when he left last night, so he went to a club that he had been to a few times. He told me that when he walked in the place was about half full. It seemed to be the same old faces. He went on to tell me that while he was sitting at the bar drinking a soda, a guy came over and sat down next him. This man ordered a drink. For some crazy reason the two of them some how started talking. They spent about two hours just talking about nothing really, so he. they have a date tonight at Kayrone's house. He told me that his name is Marzelle. He is 30 years old, and fine. He couldn't wait to see him again. I hope they have a good time, and it would be great if they got something started together. I will have to wait until tomorrow to find out how things went between them.

Miona had something to tell Norrell and me about, something had happened at work that was funny. One thing was that some guy had gotten into trouble with the boss by talking too much. He was running his mouth about how the boss was fat and also a dummy. Not only was he go around telling people that he had a picture that he was showing around to every body. The other thing that happened was a woman came to work dressed like a streetwalker. Being a big woman you know that she really looked bad. Every roll she had was hanging out. Them it was Norrell's turn to talk about had happened on his job. He told about an older man who had came in and was talking crazy. It took the police to get him out of there. Now it was time for us to sit back and enjoy relaxing with each. So the two of them got up close to me and laid their heads on my shoulders. I put my arms around them, their bodies felt good next to my almost nake body. Remember I was only wearing an apron. Their hands found their way to special places on my body.

Norrell got down on his knees and lifted my legs into the air, while pulling me to the edge of the sofa. Then he put his between the cheeks of my ass and started to lick and kiss my asshole, and then he started to lick my asshole. Then he slowly played with my tight hole with his finger. I allowed him to finger fuck my tight hole. There was something about what he was doing that turned me on. I knew that I had started to moan from the pleasure I was feeling. I closed my eyes and allowed myself to enjoy what was going on. What happened next was really unexpected. I felt something happening to my body, he had removed his finger and now I was feeling something trying to enter my ass. The head of his hard dick popped into my tight hole, the only thing I could was to let a sound. I felt each inch as it went deeper and deeper in to my body. His movement was slow and gentle, the pain went away, and was replaced by a special pleasure. While he was making love to me for the first time he lends forward and kissed me. He shot is hot load of cum deep inside of me. After he had pulled his dick out of me, I looked over at my wife find out her reaction. The only thing she did was lend over and kissed me. My mind was racing I did not know how to feel at that moment first I felt like Miona was going to be hurt by what had happened, at the same time I was still feeling the pleasure. I stood up and turned to look at my wife, with tears in my eyes and reached out for her. She in turned reached her hand out to me, and stood up. I pulled her body close to me. She looked into my eyes and said don't worry, I understand and I love you. It seemed as if the two of us were alone.

At that time I had a flash back to our wedding day, I picture seeing her for the first time standing in the doorway of the Church. Her white body forming dress flowing into a train behind her as she walked slowly toward me. The next I knew the three of us started to walk toward the bedroom. They laid me down on the bed, where my wife kissed my body. It did not take long for my dick to get hard. I wanted to make love to my wife so bad. I took my time making love to her this was also a pleasure to me. After it was over I laid between the two of them, and wonder to myself how could be happening to me. I have two lovers and both of them have found ways to please me. how was I going to explain this to Kayrone, he is going to enjoy hearing this.

Before I fell a sleep I started think about how things were going with Kayrone and his date. I knew that I was going to hear about it Monday at work. When I awoke the next morning there I was wrapped up in their arms and legs. By that being Saturday we did not have to get up until later. So I just laid there and watch the two of them sleep. About 8:30am they started to awake. Once they had kiss me and told me good-morning, we all went into the bathroom to take a shower. There I was being washed by both of them, they touched every part of my body. Once every body had been washed we dried off. Then we returned to the bedroom where we got back on to the bedroom. Where we got on the bed and played around like children, we had a lot of fun. The phone rang, and it was Kayrone he wanted to tell me about his date. He said that the two of them did a lot of talking, mostly about music, TV, food and movies, we found out that we liked a lot of the same things. The night was fun, because we were able joke around and plays with each other. We even had a pillow fight that was something. I really like this man he make me happy. We will see each other again tonight. While I was on the phone Miona and Norrell were trying to play with me. They were acting like two small children who want their parent to play games with them. We did not stay on the phone very long. When I hung up, I started a pillow fight with the two of them. We were having a lot of fun that morning. We laid around nake for about 3 hours. We even had breakfast in bed nake.

That after noon I told them that I wanted to run out for a while. I went to Kayrone's appointment I want to talk to him about last night. When I got there he was cleaning up. We started talking

I filled him on the facts. Norrell got down on his knees and lifted my legs into the air, while pulling me to the edge of the sofa. Then he put his between the cheeks of my ass and started to lick and kiss my asshole, then he started to lick my asshole. Then he slowly played with my tight hole with his finger. I allowed him to finger fuck my tight hole. There was something about what he was doing that turned me on. I knew that I had started to moan from the pleasure I was feeling. I closed my eyes and allowed myself to enjoy what was going on. What happened next was really unexpected. I felt something happening to my body, he had removed his finger and now I was feeling something trying to enter my ass. The head of his hard dick popped into my tight hole, the only thing I could was to let a sound. I felt each inch as it went deeper and deeper in to my body. His movement was slow and gentle, the pain went away, and was replaced by a special pleasure. While he was making love to me for the first time he lends forward and kissed me. He shot is hot load of cum deep inside of me. After he had pulled his dick out of me, I looked over at my wife find out her reaction. The only thing she did was lend over and kissed me. My mind was racing I did not know how to feel at that moment first I felt like Miona was going to be hurt by what had happened, at the same time I was still feeling the pleasure. I stood up and turned to look at my wife, with tears in my eyes and reached out for her. She in turned reached her hand out to me, and stood up. I pulled her body close to me. She looked into my eyes and said don't worry, I understand and I love you. It seemed as if the two of us were alone.

At that time I had a flash back to our wedding day, I picture seeing her for the first time standing in the doorway of the Church. Her white body forming dress flowing into a train behind her as she walked slowly toward me. The next I knew the three of us started to walk toward the bedroom. They laid me down on the bed, where my wife kissed my body. It did not take long for my dick to get hard. I wanted to make love to my wife so bad. I took my time making love to her this was also a pleasure to me. After it was over I laid between the two of them, and wonder to myself how could this be happening to me. I have two lovers and both of them have found ways to please me. Then we all went into the bathroom and got into the shower together. We washed each other's nake bodies, then we dried each other off. We fell a sleep in each other's arms. That's the same way we woke up this morning. Its funny I have fallen in love with Norrell, how could I be in love with another man? As I talked to Kayrone I was thinking to myself what am I going to tell Miona? I still love her, but for some reason I also love him. My buddy asked me if it would be so bad to love both of them the same. Even when you know they are different. The only thing I could say was that is that I do not want lose them.

I stayed there talking to him for about 2 hours. I knew that it was time for me to go home to the two people I love. Plus I felt that I needed tell my wife how I was feeling about her best friend. It did not take me long to get home. When I got there they were waiting on me. The two of them want the three of us to go shopping. I agreed to that because it would give me time to talk to Miona. While we were in one of the stores that we went into. I told her that I was falling in love with Norrell. The only thing she did was to take my hand and said I love him too, I love both you equally, and I want the two of you to share the rest of my life with me. About that time he came over to where we were standing, and asked what's going on? We turned to him and said we love you. Then we finished our shopping. When we got home we sat down and talked about how we all were feeling. It had only been a few weeks, but we had each fallen in love.

Now I feel that I should jump ahead for about three months. You will never believe what happened. One day a week Kayrone came to me with this big smile on his face. He stated I need to talk to you about something very important. So I said ok, what's up buddy? He replied you have better sat down for this one. I can take what ever you have to throw my way. He looked in to my eyes and said I am going to get married. I know that my mouth must had hit the floor. I could not say a word. Then I managed to ask who is the fool who is going to marry you? He laughed and said Marzelle asked me to marry him on Saturday night. We are getting married on July 27, which was about three months away. I would like for you, Miona and Norrell to share our special with us, by being in our wedding. I am asking you to be my best man. I replied I would be happy to be there for you, and I know that Miona and Norrell will also be happy for the two of you. Why don't you talk to him about coming over to the house tonight so you can talk to them about being in your wedding? Have the two of you started planning the wedding? Well right now we are still in the talking stage. We have agreed on the colors we would like to use. Marzelle and I talked about using burgundy, gold and ivory. I will talk to him after we get off of work, and I will let you know if we will be able to come tonight. When we left work I went home and waited for my lovers to get home. Once they got home we cleaned up and fixed dinner. We had finished dinner, we were sitting listening to some music. The phone hung Norrell answered it. It was Kayrone. He wanted to know if it was a good time to come over, I told him yes it is. I had told them anything about his news, because I wanted him to tell them his self. Once hanging up the phone, it took about fifteen min. for them to get there. When they got there Kayrone and Marzelle sat down and told my boos about their news. They asked them to be in their wedding. Both of them said yes to their request.

The four of them started planning the wedding, they talked about the colors, and the flowers Kayrone said that he wanted to have roses and bird of paradise with baby's breath. Marzelle said that we have to find the right place to have our wedding. I hope that we can get things together in time to have it on July the 27th, because that's his birthday. That a day I have been waiting for all my life. When I met my baby something came over me, and I knew that we had to get to know each other. I enjoy being around him very much we have so much fun. Sometimes we are like two big kids. One day I started thinking about asking my baby to marry me. I made up my mind that I was going to do it no matter what. So Saturday night I went over to his apartment, while we were sitting around listening to music. I stood up in front of him and reached out for him. Once he was in my arms I pulled him as close as I could to me, and said Kayrone will you honor me by spending the rest your life with me. The first words out of his mouth were what did you just say. So I repeated for him. Only that time I got down on my knees. Kayrone said that's when I replied yes, and then I started crying.

I just had to ask him what did Tayrone have to say when he found out about this. He had the same reaction that you had, you know I was joking trying to keep him from telling any one what I had said earlier. Well he told them any way, what was your words" who is the fool who is going to marry you." Marzelle said well I must be a fool, because I will do what ever I have to do to marry him. We all started laughing; they knew I was only joking. Then Kayrone said he wants to be in our wedding, you know how he is. Him and Marzelle enjoy picking on me when we all get together. They both are crazy, but I love them both. I am glad that they get along so good together. Now I hope that my dad will be able to deal with it. He has been out of town on business for the last week. He should be back by Friday even If so we are going over there and talk to him, my mother knows and she is still talking to me. So I guest she is ok with the idea. This will only give us a few days before will have to face. No matter what he has to say we are still going top get married, I am not going to allow any one to come between us.

The five of us sat around and throwing around ideas for the wedding, by the end of the night Kayrone and Marzelle did have some ideas on what they wanted their wedding day would be like. There was one thing that they both really wanted and that was to get married out doors. Marzelle was going to check with his cousin who worked for the parks and recreation for our local town. Maybe they will allow us to have our wedding in the park. That may be the only way that we would have enough room for both of our families. They left about 10:00pm. The three of us needed to get some sleep, because tomorrow was another work for every body. The night was a very short one. It did not take long for the clock to go off, which meant that we had to get up and get ready for work. When I got to work Kayrone and I got a chance to talk mostly about their wedding.

After work I went home to wait for my babies to get home. Norrell got home first. For some reason I was horny as hell. When he kissed me, I could not hold by what I was feeling. The two of us ended up in the bedroom on the bed making love. Before while his dick was deep inside my asshole Miona walked into the bedroom, she did not say a word about what was going on. After everything was over I looked in the face of the woman that I have loved and married? Once we had cleaned up. I went to her to tell her that I was sorry for what I had done. Her only words were you don't have to feel bad about making love with the person who is apart of our life. Before we have dinner Norrell got a phone call from his grandmother. She was upset about something and she wanted to talk to him right away. So without eating anything he left to go over to her house. Miona and I eat and then sat around waiting to hear from him. When he did get back home he was upset, Miona asked him what was wrong? He said that someone had told his grandmother that he could be going with a married man. That was apart of what was making her mad, the other part was when she found out that the man was me, his best friend's husband. We tried to tell him not worry about that because the three of us in agreement to what we are doing and no one has anything to do with this.

We spent the rest of the night trying to come up with a way to handle this. Miona decided to call his grandmother herself. Well she did just that; his grandmother really did not want to hear that we were all in this together. By the time she had finished talking to her things were a little better. We knew that it was not going to be over, because there are other people in this town will had their own ideas about how we should live our lives. Well they can talk all they want to because this is what we want to do. The next few weeks were busy ones because we were helping with the wedding. It had gotten down to three days and counting. Everything was falling into place. The wedding was going to place on July 27th at 6:00pm in the park. That was just what they wanted. Each guy that was taking part in the wedding had to get an ivory suit, shirt and tie. Marzelle's aunt made each of us a gold vest. The dresses that Miona and the other women were going be wearing burgundy and gold. Kayrone's twin brother gave them and their wedding party a dinner the night before the wedding. Every body had a lot of fun joking around and getting crazy with each other. We all left Tayrone's house about 1:00am. When we got home the three of us did not take long to get in to bed. The next morning was going to be busy, because first we had things to do at home before we had to get ready for the wedding. We had to be at the park about 4:30pm to get dressed and to make sure that everything was setup.

Well when we got up the next morning we cleaned up and wrapped the gifts for our friends. Then we had to shower and dress in our underclothes and sweats. We left the house around 4:15pm so that we could get there on time. I drove Norrell's car that day. When we got to the park, we took our clothes out of the car and took them to the area where we were going to dress. First I had to find Tayrone to see if they needed my help in setup things. Well I did find him putting the finish touches on things. He had started things about 2:30. He wanted to make sure that everything was going to just right for his brother's special day. Other people started to show up, all of the wedding party had gotten there and we got dress. I asked about my buddy Kayrone, Tayrone told me that he would be arriving by car just before we walk down the aisle together. Then someone asked about Marzelle, he was told that he was also going to be arriving by car. One of the guys said I hope it's not the same car. At 5:59 we were asked to get ready to make our way down the aisle. So everyone did what we had to do, then a white car drove up and Kayrone got out wearing an all ivory suit, Tayrone stepped beside him and they started down the aisle. Once he was in place another white car came up, this time it was Marzelle when he got out his parents was by his side. He was carrying flowers which laid across his left arm. His mother was on his left side and his father on his right. He was also wearing all ivory.

I stood there and watched as my best friend commit his self to this man. Miona was standing across from me while Norrell stood next to me. Man I had a feeling to come over me I did not know what this feeling was about, but I was happy. I reached out and touched Norrell's hand. Once the wedding was over everyone who was in the wedding took pictures, then we headed for reception. I shared a table with both of my lovers and the other members of the wedding party. Everything was great and the food was really good. Some how Kayrone and Marzelle was able to get a way from every body. They were going to be gone for a whole week just the two of them. They were going to Brazil. We left the reception about 12 midnights, because we stayed to help clean up. When we got home it was bedtime and that's what we did. The next morning was a late one. We did not rush to get out of bed. Once we did the three of us worked on getting our house cleaned up. We are going to have company later and we want the house to look just right. Both Miona's and my parents were coming over, along with Norrell's grandmother. We asked them over for a family dinner, maybe that way we will be able to answer questions they may have. It was getting close to 2:00pm, and they should be here about 5:00pm. So that means that we really need to start cooking. We are hoping that every one will enjoy them self.

The closer it got to 5:00pm the more we worried. The first ones to get there were my parents, and then Norrell's grandmother arrived. Miona's parent got there last but not late. We had dinner about 5:30 once we had eaten all of us went into the living room where we sat down and talked. By the way it did come up, and we tried to explain things to them. By the time they left we could only hope that they could try to deal with what we were doing. The next few days seem to go by slowly, I was missing my best friend. I had to keep telling myself that they would be back in a matter of days. At work thing just wasn't right, because I he was not there to pick on me the only way he could. I was also wondering what the two of them were up to. The only things that made me feel better at the end of each day. It was that my two lovers would be coming home to me. Kayrone and Marzelle called us on Thursday night to let us know that they would be coming home on Friday night. They wanted to know if they could come by to see us. We told that we have been missing them and really want to see them.

When Friday came around something happened at work that made me mad. There are two guys that work there who do not like me or Kayrone. Well they came up to me and asked if it was turn that Kayrone had gotten married? When I said yes, one of them asked what did he marry a man a woman or one of them? That's when I lost it. I told them both to go to hell and to leave me the hell a lone. Then I turned my back on them and walked away. I did how ever tell a co-worker about what had happened, so that someone would know about it. There was no way that they were going to get me upset with them. After work I stopped by the store on my way home to pick up a few things to have when Kayrone and Marzelle came over to the house. When I got home I was met at the door by two half-nake people, both of them wearing red underwear. I knew then that I was in trouble. We had about three hours before our friends would be arriving. So here we go I thought to myself.

Once they had gotten me into the bedroom it was on. My clothes were gone before I could say a word. Their next step was to cover me in honey, and slowly lick it off. The sex between us was great. When we finished there was enough time to get things ready before they got there. About 7:30pm someone knocked on the door. Norrell went to answer it, when he opened the door the two of them were standing there. All of us spent that evening sitting around talking most of the night away. We mostly talked about their honeymoon. I didn't tell Kayrone about what had happened at work. I could tell him later. I would tell him before we went back to work on Monday. That's just how I handled it, Sunday night I called him and told him about it. He said that he was not going to worry him self over craziness like that. Kayrone and Marzelle seemed to be so very happy. It did not seem like it had been almost six month since the two of them met. Which meant that Miona and I was were six months away from another anniversary. We would be together for two years. And at the same time Norrell would us for one year. How could I top the gift my wife gave me last year? One thing I knew was that I did not want to bring anyone else into our relationship. The three of us were enjoying what we had together.

Before that we had another big event coming up, which was Christmas. I had to come up gifts for the two special people in my life along with my family and friends. I want to give Miona and Norrell both something very special. I had five months to come up with the perfect gifts. I was brought back to the real world by Miona's kiss. The two of us were home alone for a while, because Norrell had gone to do some shopping. We started make out right there on the living room sofa. There we were undressing each other. Man there I was fucking the hell out of my wife, when the front door opened. It was Norrell, he came into house and closed the door back, and he called out our names. We could not answer, because of what we were doing at the time. When he found us I was between my wife's legs fucking her. We did not stop; he just took a seat and watched the show.

That time he did not join in with us. After everything was over I asked him why he did not join in, he said that we needed to enjoy each other alone, with out a third party. Miona told him that he is not a third party, that he is apart of the whold relationship. He did bring up a good point, even though the three of us have a relationship sometime the two of you may need to be together only has a couple. I said well that goes for any two of us. You and Miona should be able to have sometime alone with me, just as you and I should be able to have sometime without Miona. We all agreed to that we knew that we could not get upset when one of us walked in and sees our other partners having sex. Which meant that I could have sex with Norrell even when Miona is not around, or the other way around. There are times when the three of us would be having sex together.

The months pasted by at a normal rate. It was a few days before Christmas and had some shopping to do for my parents and both Miona and Norrell. There was something I had been thinking about doing on Christmas day; I want to ask Norrell to marry Miona and me. I know that sound crazy but the three of us have been together for months and things are great between us. I went in to a jewelry store to find something that I could give to both of them, and also find a bridal set. I was able to find a charm that was made up of three figures all joined together, so I got both of them one along with a necklace. I had them wrapped. When I got home

I put them away so that they could not find them. The next three nights were going to busy for us because we had three different Christmas parties to go to. Miona's job had their party first. The three of us walked in there together, and we did not care what any one was thinking. The next night was Norrell's Christmas party we also went to his together. The last one was mine's now that's when things was really a little wild, because that night Miona, Norrell and myself plus Kayrone and Marzelle all walked into the party about the same time. You know that the two guys who did not like just had to have something to say. They were just talking to the walls. No one there allowed them to course any trouble. The five of us enjoyed the night together, along with some of our co-workers. We made plans to get together at Kayrone and Marzelle's house on Christmas Eve to open some of our gifts. That gave me an idea, I could ask Norrell to marry us then. I needed to talk to Miona about it, but I would have to do it when Norrell was not around. The next morning He had to go over to his grandmother's house to do something for her, while he was gone I sat Miona down and told her that I needed to talk to her about something. So I started out by saying that a year ago you gave me a gift that I could never forget. I fell in love with that special gift. Now I want to ask him to marry us. Her reaction was to hug me and say I love you, and that is a great idea. When are you going to ask him? I told her that I want to do Christmas Eve at Kayrone's. She agreed that it would be the right time.

When Norrell came we did not say a word to him about what I was going to do. We had to keep it from him one more day. It was going to be hard but we both knew it was the best thing to do. The 24th came and we could not wait to go over to Kayrone's. well we got there about 8:00pm the five of us was able to relax and have fun together. When we got ready to open our gifts. I knew that it was going to be a crazy night. I watched Norrell's face as he opened his gift from me. The look on his face when he saw the ring was priceless. I got down on my knees and ask him to please do Miona and myself the honor of marring us on January 18th. He replied yes I will marry you, the three of us hugged and kissed. Kayrone and

Marzelle both were very happy for us. I asked to two of them to be apart of our wedding.

Tomorrow is Christmas day and we were going to be spending it with our families, so I guest we will tell them our plans then. When Marzelle opened his gift from Kayrone there was a jacket. Then Kayrone opened his gift he found a pair of gold earrings, necklacc and ring each them had sets of blue and white diamond clusters. Now it was Miona's turn to open her gift from Norrell he gave her a ring that had an emerald set with diamonds all around it. That made me wonder what had he gotten me? He headed me a big box, I hurried to unwrap it. In the box was a gold suit with a green shirt and printed tie. Miona then gave me her gift. It was two pair of shoes, one pair green and the other pair was gold they matched to outfit that Norrell had given me. I had given Marzelle and Kayrone gold bracelets with their names on them. Moina gift to them was matching pants and shirts; Norrell gave them matching sweaters to go with the pants and shirts. It was after mid-night when we left to go home. We needed some sleep, because we had to get early to get ready for our families. When we got home we gave each other the greatest gift of all our love.

The next morning we got up around 8:00am to get things ready before our families get there. Lucky we had already cooked, so all we had to do was to set everything up and warm up the food. All of the gifts were under the tree. The two of them went into the dinning room to get things setup in there while I started working in the kitchen. We had about 4 hours before every one was to get here. About 12:30 the first of our quest arrived it was Miona's parents they came over to see if we needed any help only to find that we had everything under control. Then Norrell's grandmother was the next person to get there.

My parents arrived there about 1 o'clock, the last person to get there was Miona's sister Shandale. After every one was there we went into the dinning room to sit down to eat. Later that afternoon we all sat down in the living room and opened our gifts. Well after every gift was opened it was time to tell our families the news. Norrell had been wearing his rings, but no one asked any questions.

So it was now up to us to let the cat out of the bag. I got up and asked for every ones attention, and then I said we have some news that we would like to share with you. All of their eyes were on me. Miona, Norrell and I are going to get married on January 18th. That's when they came alive; man they had a lot of questions. The three of us did our very best to answer all of their questions. By the time our were ready to leave they knew that we were happy with what we wanted to do. There was only one thing that would make Norrell happy; he wanted to have his mother here. He talked to his grand mother about it. She told him that she would try to talk to his mother about it. There was something going on between him and his mother. He had never talked to me about what ever it is. I don't know if Miona knows anything about it? Once they had all left the three of us started to get things cleaned up for the night. When we got in to bed Norrell needed to talk, he wanted to try to help us to understand why him and his mother do not have a real relationship.

Norrell went on to tell us; well it started when I was younger. You see my father had died that year. Then when I was younger my mother met this man it wasn't long before he was at our house all the time. One night while my mother was at work he came into my room and started touching me. When I told my mother what had happened she got mad with me. Plus she believed him over her own child, we have not had much to do with each other for about 6 years. She has two younger children, but she does not want me around them. At that point I felt his pain. The only thing I thought to do was to take him in my arms and hold him close to me. Miona also put her arms around him the three of us just sat there holding each other. Now the story did not end there he went to tell us that his mother brought him to his grand mother where he has been since I was younger. At the age of 18 he met a 19-year-old guy who seem to want to spent time with, helping him with his schoolwork and being there for him to talk to. One while they were at this guy's house things took a turn. The guy talked him into having sex with him. That was the day he lost his boyhood. He felt the pain of being fucked for the first time. The sex went on between the two of them for about nine months. Then one day I show him and tried to talk to him he did not want me to be around him. I was truly hurt by that, because I found myself wanting to be with him more and more. From that point on things went crazy in my life.

I was in high trying to make it though. Well Miona and I met, and we become close friends. I needed someone to talk to. She was also in need of a friend. A few years ago I met a man who I thought was going to make me happy. We had a 5-year relationship, then one day he up and moved away. All I have looked for in my life was a man who would love me for the person that I am. It seems to me that no matter who I meet it never works out. Now that I have someone who I feel really cares about me, and at this high point in my life I would like to have my mother to share it with me. In my heart I felt for him, I wanted him to get his wish on the day that we marry him. We did not have much time to work with, because our wedding day was close at hand. We only have a few weeks before our wedding day. As we talked we decided to each wear white on that day. That night the three of us made love to each other for hours before we finally fell asleep. The next morning was a new and wonderful day. We were looking forward to starting our wedding plans. So after getting our self-ready for the day ahead, we shared out thoughts on what we wanted to do for our wedding. We knew that we wanted a small wedding with only our close family and friends. The colors that we wanted were white and Navy, with flowers and candles. 2 weeks passed and there was no word from Norrell's grandmother, about his mother. We were on the last week before our wedding. He really wanted to know if his mother was coming. One day I called his grand mother from work to talk to her about what her grand son was going though. She informed me that she had indeed talked to her daughter, and she had told her that she would think about it. I asked her if she could talk to her again, because this is so important to Norrell, he would like to have her here to share this with him. 3 days before the wedding when Norrell got a call from a woman. I gave him the phone, as I started to walk away I heard him say in surprise mom. At that point it was hard for me to walk away, but I did it. If he needed me I was only a few steps always. He stayed on the phone for a while, then he came into the living room where I was sitting going though some mail. As he sat down beside me, I turned to look at him.

Before I could say a word he said look out my mother will be blowing into town for our wedding. I know that she is only doing it because my grand mother gave her no choose in the matter. You see my grand mother has 3 daughters and 4 sons and no matter how big nor now old they get she is still the one with the last and final word. So if she told my mother, which is her middle daughter to be here with a smile, she will be here, or deal with her mother. As her grand child I know that you do not go against word after she has given it. I asked him if he thought she would be bale to handle the idea of what we were about to do? He could only say that we would have to wait and see.

Miona was out doing some last min things for the wedding. Norrell and I had already gotten our suites, but I was not allowed to see his suite nor miona's dress. The two of were sitting on the sofa talking. Man just sitting there with him was really turning me on. There were some things that I wanted him to do to me. At that moment I desired to have his hard dick inside of my asshole. Before I knew it our lips came together in a kiss. Then we seem to know what the other person wanted. It did not take us long to undress. As I laid there with him slow fucking me. I was feeling so much pleasure. While we were in the middle of our lovemaking when miona walked though the front door. She walked right in on us. Norrell was at the point he was almost ready to cum. So he just kept on fucking me. After it was over the two of us laid there on the sofa together for a few moments nake, then we got up and went in to take a shower. When we came out of the bathroom Miona had started dinner, as we walked in to the kitchen, she looked at us and said hi boys how was your day. The three us shared a kiss before we helped her to finish the meal, so we could enjoy a family meal together. We are truly a real family, one that loves each other. In a few hours will stand in front of the people who are close to us, and devote our love and passion for each other.

As I thought about it in only a few hours I will be married to my wife for two years. Plus we will marry Norrell. There will be no way that she could not top the gift she gave me last year for our anniversary. The next two days went by so fast. It is now only one hour before we say I do. I stood in a room alone waiting to walk in front of our families. Then wait to see Miona and Norrell for first time today. As I stood there I started thinking about much it's going to be once we get to the hotel tonight. I knew it was time for me to take my place, because Tayrone came to the door and told me its time. I walked out in the room where every one was seated. Then Miona and Norrell came into the room. The two of them vision to be held. The room was done up in white and navy, and the both of them had flowers to match. When they enter the room the whole room lit up. Miona's dress was white with peals and lace. While Norrell's suite was different while our suites were made a like his had peals and lace on it. As they walked towards me I felt warmth come over me. I knew that it had to be the love that I felt for them. My parents and Miona's parents along with Norrell's mother and grand mother were each sitting there with our other family members, and our best friends Kayrone and Marzelle, with Kayrone's twin brother Tayrone, and their parents. Soft music played in the background, while the room smelled of roses; we had candles all around to light the room. As we stood there together we exchanged our vows, and rings. When we were told to kiss our partners. I kissed each of the people I loved.

Kayrone and Marzelle hosted our reception; we had all of the trimmings. We even had a photographer taking pictures of everything. The three of us stood there to together as we cut the cake, then we feed each other cake, just before we kissed. Our first dance was one that could not be forgotten. We had so much fun that day. By the time the reception was over I was ready to get the two of them away from every body so I could enjoy them all to myself. We were now starting a new life together and true partners. Before we left Norrell wanted to talk to his mother. The two of them went into another room for a few min, when he returned I could tell that things did not go as well as he may have wanted. On our way to the hotel he talked to Miona and I about his talk with his mother. She was still cold towards him; she was only there because of his grand mother. When we got to the room it had flowers and wine waiting for us. That night we enjoyed each other in every way that we could. The three of us shared our love between each other most of the night. The next morning we called room service to order breakfast. We were going to spend the weekend at the hotel, all of us had to be back to work on Monday morning. We returned home on Sunday evening.

Things were going along great until Saturday night, when I got a phone call. The caller told me that I needed to ask my wife who Michael Ray is, before I could ask any questions, the person hung up the phone. I did not say any thing to Miona about the call. Later that night there was another call, who ever the person was, they really wanted me to ask about this Michael Ray. I did not know why it was so important to them. That time I was able to ask them why they were calling to my house with this craziness. The person asked me, how well do you know your wife? You really need to know this information. Then again they hung up. When I put the phone down. I turned to see Miona standing in the doorway of our bedroom. She asked what was that all about? I told her that it was some crazy person; they seem to want me to ask you about some body name Michael Ray. I watched as her face changed, before I could say any thing else she came over and sat down beside me. With tears in her eyes and her voice so sweet, my wife said something that was like being hurt in the face with a brick. She told me that Michael was the name given to her at birth.

I couldn't really react to what she had said; the only thing I could get out of my mouth was what the hell are you talking about. That's when she went on to say I was born a male. I heard her words, but I could not believe what I was hearing. The person that I thought was a woman was now telling me that it's a man. Her words rang in my ears; I had so many things racing though my mind at the time that nothing was making any sense to me at all.

One thought was now what had I done? I had married some one who I thought was a woman, then the same person brought another man into things. Now I have been turned in to some kind of freak. I was a real man but what am I now? How could this be happening to me? What am I going to do?

I did not know that Norrell had come into the room; he was now sitting on the bed with Miona and myself. She told him that some one had called here and told me about Michael Ray. I looked at Norrell and asked ask Norrell if he knew about this? He looked into my face and said yes I did know, we grew up together. Please do not be mad with her, she only did what she felt was right. When you met her, she wanted to tell you then, but was scared to do so, because she did not want to loose you. Other men she had met had turned on her when they were told. One man beat her up; another made her get out of his car on the side of the road. I did not know if I was mad or just surprised Miona reached out her hands to me and asked me to forgive her for laying to me.

As I sat there I was trying to think. Then I remember something Miona had told me one night while we were talking about having a family. She had said that she could not have children, because of something in her passed. At that time I did not ask for an explanation from her. Norrell said something to me that made me realize how I felt. He said you fell in love with a woman. If you had never been told anything about the name Michael Ray you would have not gotten upset about the matter. That's when I looked at the two of them and said I need some time to think about this. I also told them that I was going to leave for a while. When I walked out of our front door I did not know where I was going to go. As I drove around I ended up at Kayrone and Marzelle's house.

Kayrone was the only person I felt that I could talk to at that time. I knocked on their door. Marzelle came to the door. He asked me if every thing was ok. I told him that I needed to talk to Kayrone. Once on the inside I sat and waited for Kayrone to come down stairs. When he sat down beside me on the sofa. I started to try to explain what had happened. The first thing he told me to do was to call Miona and Norrell to tell them where I was. I did as he asked. When Norrell picked up the phone I could tell something was wrong, because his voice did not sound right. He had been crying, please come home we need you. I told him that I needed to talk to some one. I will be back in a while. It hurt like hell hearing the pain in his voice; I knew that Miona was hurting too.

At this time I just needed to get myself together before I said or did something that would end things between us forever. I stayed there talking to him for about 2 hours. Then he looked me in the face and said fool taking your crazy ass home to the people you love, don't make them worry any more. What dose it matter that she was born a man, you love the person she is now. I couldn't say any thing because he was right. His last words were get the hell out.

As I walked though the front door the two of them ran over to me, with tears in their eyes they asked me to forgive them. At that point I took them in to my arms and held them close to me. That night we went to bed; it had been a long night all I wanted to do was get some rest. When I woke up the next morning I thought about what my wife had told me. And the only thing I felt was love for her and Norrell. As I looked on each side of me to see the two people I loved the most. As the day went on things were getting better until another phone call came in. this call was Norrell. The person on the other end was telling him something that made him upset.

When he got off the phone, things really got a little crazy. He called the two of us in to the living room. He was sitting there with tears running down his face. Miona asked him what was wrong; he said that he knew who had called me, because the same person had called him. The person had tried to him by calling. Then went on to say that it was his mother who had called. She had found out what Miona had done and was going to use it to break us up. She do not want me to be happy, because she is still holding what happened against me. I looked at him and told him not to worry about that any more because I know in my heart that I do love the two of you, and I would never turn my back on you.

What his mother did broke all the ties that could have been between the two of them. From that day on we have nothing else to do with his mother. The matter was never brought up again. I had the family I wanted. And I was a very happy man. Here we are ten years later and the three of us are still together. I am proud to tell every one that I am married to both Miona and Norrell. This is my story all about my world.

Just Another Lonely Night

It was another lonely night in front of the TV. I sat there watching something that did not interest me at all. Time seems to be standing still, and I was feeling down. Maybe I should force myself to be more out going than what I am. Most people have the idea that gay men are these wild guys who are running around trying to have sex with any man they can. Well there may be some people out there like that, but that is not the way I do things. I had been with my last lover for 4 years before he moved away, leaving me alone. At first he wrote a few letters, and called about three times. Then one day he stopped every thing. So I tried to call him, that's when I found out that he had moved on. He had met some else, and they were living together. I was really hurt by that because I loved him with all of my heart. It has been 7 months and I still have not gotten over him. That's one of the reasons I have spent all my time at home alone. I felt that it was going to be a long night.

Just as I was about to get into the shower, before I called it a night. The phone rang, at first I started not to answer it, but I changed my mind. When I picked it up. I said hello, then the voice on the other end asked may I speak to Dee Dee. I replied I'm sorry you have the wrong number. That's when he asked whom am I speaking to? I told him that name is Tee. Which was short for Tyrrell. He said I hope that I did not call you at a bad time. I must have dialed the number wrong or I was given the wrong number. I said well don't worry about that, we all make mistakes. I would never called, but I had met this woman last night, and she gave me what I thought was her phone number. As you can see she gave me the wrong number. I hope that you will forgive me; you seem to be a real nice person. Some people would have gotten very upset. It was funny how we ended up talking for about an hour. It was some thing about the way he talked to me that made him easy to talk to. Once we have ended our phone call I got into the shower, then I went to bed.

The next morning when I got up to get ready for work, I started to think about the man who had called me the night before. I did not know him, but we seem to make some kind of connection. He seemed to be some one that I could be friends with. That day at work was long and hard. Well when I got off I had to pay a few bills with more bills than money. To top it all off while I was in a store, they had to close things down because two people tried to seal some things from the store. I was in no mood for that, but I could not leave out of the store before they finished what they had to do. Then when I got home I was out of it, as I sat down to rest a little before I found some thing to fix for dinner. I must have been really tiered because I found myself waking up when the phone rang. When I answered it I heard aVoice that I had heard before. It was the guy who had called last night. This time he asked for tee. I told him that he was talking to me. He said that you sound a little different. Well I had fallen a sleep, and the phone woke me up. I seem to all ways call you at the wrong time. You have not call me at the wrong time; I need to be in my kitchen fixing some thing to eat. Well what do you have in mind? I replied I don't know. I am so tiered that I feel like I just need to get some sleep. He said maybe I should let you go so you can do what you need to do. I told him that I have time to talk for a while.

As we talked I started to fix myself a little dinner. I don't know what it was but we were becoming friends. He told me that he had found himself thinking about me, and he just wanted to talk a little. We found out that we both enjoyed playing around on our computers. The only thing was that we did not know that much about them. Before we got off the phone he asked if he could call me some times. I told him that he could call any time he felt like it. Then I made a statement you have the ups on me, because you know my name, but I do not know yours. He said my name is Patrick. We talked a little longer before we ended the call. Before hanging up the phone he told me to call him sometimes. Then he gave me his phone number. I asked when would you like me to call, he said anytime; I live alone, so you don't have to worry about calling. We said later, and then we hung up the phone.

As I eat dinner he came across my mind. I don't know why, but I do know that I feel comfortable talking to him. I did not think about the fact that he may not know that I am gay. I wonder if I should tell him or not. Maybe I should play it by ear. That as I laid in bed I had a lot of things running around in my head. One thing was how would he react would Patrick react when he finds out that I am gay. I could tell by the way he talked that he was in to women. So by the time I fell sleep I had made up my mind to talk to him about that the next time we talked. Well I did not had to wait long, because he called me to next day when I got home from work. While we talked I let him know that I needed to talk to him about something. He asked me what was on my mind. I did not know how to bring it up. So I just said I am gay. His reply was what did you just say? I repeated my statement I am gay. Then he replied big deal.

We went on to talk for over an hour about a lot of things. He asked if maybe we could get together some time and talk face to face. I said well if you really want to you could come over here tonight, that's if you are busy. He said I could come over there how if I knew where there is. What is your address? I told him that I live in Hilibrook Court, 436 North Hill Rd. he said that he knew how to get there, I will be there in a few mm. my reply was ok I will be here. Then we hung up the phone. My mind went into over time.

What kind of man was he? Why did he want to come over? It did take that long for him to get there. When my doorbell rang I knew who it was. When I opened the door there was a fine man standing in front of me. I asked him to come in, once we were inside, I asked him to have a seat. We both sat on the sofa. It was very easy for us to talk to each other. Before I knew it we had spent three hours talking. The two of had so much fun that night joking around and being crazy. We did not know that much about each other, but there was something special about him. He told me that he had to go, because the next day he had to take a trip of his job, which meant that he would be gone all day. He also told me that he would call me once he got back home. We said goodnight at my front door. I had just gotten out of the shower when the phone ranged. When I heard his voice it made me feel so nice. We did not talk long because we both had to get some sleep for the next days events. After we said good-night I laid there in bed thinking about him.

The next morning I got awake up call. When I finally realized that my phone was ringing I wondered who could be calling this time in the morning. I reached over and picked up the phone. When the voice said good-morning it was Patrick, he said I hope that I am not calling you to early. I wanted to hear your voice before I got ready to hit the road. I said it's nice to hear you anytime. Once I had said that I almost wanted to take those words back. Why did I say it like? He replied I am glad that you said that, because I seem to want to call you all the time. Our phone call was short, because he had to get on the road. He reminded me that he would call when he got back home. We told each other to have a nice day.

About 4:00pm that afternoon when I got home the phone ranged. Just at that time I got a chill, when I picked up the phone a woman's voice asked if she could speak to Tyrrell. I replied this is Tyrrell. That's when my heart almost stopped. She told me that she was a nurse in a hospital, which was about an hour and a half from the town I lived in. then she asked me to hold on. The next voice I heard was Patrick's, sometime was wrong I could tell it in his voice. He told me that he had been in a car accident. I took a deep breath, and then I ask how bad were you hurt. He said well my leg was broken, and I have to stay in the hospital for a few days. I will be on my way as soon as we hang up the phone. He told me that I did not have to come to the hospital, but I told him that I am going to come. Once we hung up the phone I headed out the door. The drive seems to be so long, I could hardly wait to get there. When I walked up to the desk the funny thing was I did not know his last name. The only thing I could do was to ask if they had a man there by the name of Patrick who had come in with a broken leg, from a car accident.

The woman working the desk look at her computer screen, and said there is a man here by the first name of Patrick, is in room 231. When I got to the door I knocked, he said come in. there he was laying in the bed. I wanted to walk over and hug him, but how would he feel about me doing something like that. Patrick looked at me and said don't just stand come on in and sat down. He told me that he had called his family, and told them about the accident, they wanted to come up here but I asked them not to. I did not tell them about you coming up here. I should be out of here Friday. Before he could say anything I told him that I would there to pick him up. Just as I was able to leave, things went from bad to worst. For some reason his blood presser when up and he was having a lot of pain. I ran to the door and called for a nurse. When one came in to the room he was not looking good at all. She in turn called for the doctor. They had to rush him in to the OR, because something was going on in side of his body.

I waited in the waiting room to find out what was going with him. Over an hour later the doctor into the room and told me that they had found out what was wrong and fixed. He told me that I could see him once he had been brought up to his room. So I waited for a while until he was put into room 338. I went in and there he was laying in the bed with his eyes closed. I walked over to the bed, and called his name softly. He opened his eyes and smile at me. I said welcome back. He asked what happened? I told him that you had been hurt in the accident, and you did not know it. When I got ready to leave earlier your blood presser went up and you were having a lot of pain. The doctor had to take you into the OR. Man you scared the hell out of me. So now you will have to stay here for a few days, or until the doctor feel you are able to go home. I sat in a chair beside his bed, and watched him as he slowly fell back to sleep. As he slept I started thinking to myself that I wanted to do any thing I could for this man even though we are just becoming friends.

I made up my mind to spend the night right there with him. Later that night when he woke up I was still right there beside his bed. I had fallen a sleep, I heard him call out my name. When I opened my eyes the room was dark, and I could barely see. I ask him if anything was wrong he said no. When I woke up I looked around and saw you a sleep in the chair. Why are you still here? I told him that I wanted to be there for him. For some reason I did not want him to go though this alone. He said thank you for doing this for me. It was able 9:00pm, when a nurse came in to the room to check on him. She in formed me that she could have a cart brought in for me to sleep on. I told her I would like that, it was not long after she left the room when an orderly brought it back. That night I couldn't sleep that much. I woke up

It seems like every few mm to check on him. I was like a new mother checking on her baby. The next morning I was awoken when a nurse came in to the room. I sat up on the cart, to see him laying there looking at me. Once the nurse had finished what she had to do, she left the room and he said I enjoyed watching you sleep. I felt that you needed the rest. I asked how long have you been woke? Well I have been woke for a while, I just did not want to wake you up. I looked at my watch to see what time it was; I knew that I had to call in to let my boss know why I was not coming in. I was going to spend the day in the hospital with him. I may leave later tonight and come back tomorrow. When I got off the phone he said I am sorry that you have to miss time off of work because of me. I told him not to worry about that.

When I told of my plans to drive home later that evening, he asked me not to. I told him that I needed to go home and get some clothes and other personal things that I need. Plus I let him know that I was going to come back and spend the weekend with him. Patrick said you do not have to go all the way back home to get what you need. I said well I wouldn't but I don't have enough money here with me to buy what I need. He looked in my face and said I will buy what you need. Then he asked my to give him his wallet. When I handed it to him, he gave me $100.00, go get what you need; there is a mall across the road. First I said I cannot take your money. But he was not going to take no for an answer. So I did take it, and told him that I would be back in a little while. Once in the mall it did not take me long to get the things I needed. I was working fast because I wanted to get back to his room.

I opened the door to his to find him laying there with his eyes closed, he had fallen a sleep, so I just sat in the chair beside his bed and waited for him to wakeup. While I was sitting there his parents came in to the room. I knew that they wondered who I was, but they did not say any thing. He must have heard them talking, so he opened his eyes and spoke to them. With out saying anything I left them alone to talk. I want down stairs to get something to eat. As I sat there at a table I thought to myself what was going though his parents minds when they saw me sitting there in his room like that. I waited for a while before going back to the room. When I walked in his parents were still there, this time he introduce me to them. He told them that I was a friend of his, and that he had called me to let me know what had happened. He also said that I was going to spend the weekend at the hospital with him.

His father said its good that you have a friend that is willing to do this for you. That's when I said I am more than happy to be here for him. His parents did not want it to seem as if they were rushing to leave the hospital, but they did have to get back home because they needed to check in on his Grandmother. Once they had left, he did some thing that never thought he would do. He asked me to come over and sit on the bed beside him. When I sat down he reached out for me. Putting his arms around me giving me a tender hug. My body just melted in to his arms. This was a wonderful feeling. I was thinking that it could not be real. I just wanted him to hold me forever. Well it did not last because a nurse came in to the room to check or him. After she left out of the room, he looked over at me and said I hope you did not mind me hugging you the way I did. I replied no I did not mind at all. With out thinking I asked why should I mind? Well I did not think about how you would feel about me doing that he said. We talked for a while before they brought in some food. The doctor wanted him to try to eat some if he was able to eat, he would be able to go home soon.

While he was eating I went in to the bathroom and took cleaned up and changed clothes.

When I came out of the bathroom it was the first time he had seen the clothes I had brought from the mall. He told me that he liked the outfit on me. His eyes lit up. There was some thing about the way he looked at me. I tried not to think about him in any way but a friend. Why is this happening to me? Why would meet a guy that is straight, but is fine as hell. How was I going to handle this? I know that I could be a friend to him, but it's going to be real hard for me not to notice how good he looks. Right now I must keep my mind on what happening with him. The doctor came in to check on him~ He told Patrick if things keep going in the right direction you will be going home on Tuesday. As long as you can eat and are able to move around a little on your own. We will let you leave.

Late that day 2 nurses came in to help him get out of bed and move around the room. After a few mm of doing that he was ready to sit down and rest. While we were sitting talking he needed to go to the bathroom, so I helped him to get up and walk the best he could to the bathroom. Once he had used it he did his best to make it back to the chair alone. 1 knew it was hard, but he asked me not to help him, he did make it. We spent the day talking. When it was dinnertime they brought two trays in to the room. We eat together then we watched some TV, and talked a little more.

He stayed up as long as he could. Then he felt that he needed to lay down, so I helped him back into bed. I sat in a chair beside the bed and watched TV with him until he fell a sleep. Then I turned the sound down, and watched TV until I was ready to lay down myself. I was able to get more sleep than I did last night. I was woken up early the next morning when I heard him cal my name. I jumped up to see what was wrong. He called me because he needed to go to the bathroom. I helped him to get there and back to the bed. He told me that he was sorry about waking me up that way. I told Him not to worry about it, because I was there to help him. Its Sunday morning and I was going to stay with him, until that evening, and then I was going to head for home, because tomorrow was going to be a workday. I did not want to leave him but I knew that I had to be at work. Plus I will have to get a day off so I could come back to pick him up and take him home on Tuesday.

When I got ready to leave Patrick said have a safe trip, I will call you around 6:00 that will give you enough time to get home. I told him to do what the nurses tell him to do, and I will be back on Tuesday morning. He would let me go before he got a hug. As I walk though the door I looked back at him to see him smiling he waved to me. I waved back then I walked a way. When I got to my car, and opened the door, and looked at the third floor I could not tell which window was his room. I got into my car I started thinking about the last few days. I pulled out of the parking lot and start my trip, which was going to take about an hour and a half. It seemed that almost every song on the radio made me think about Patrick. I about 8 miles a way from my house. And glad to be home. When I walked into the house I put my things down in a chair. It was about 5:45pm and I waited for Patrick to call. Just I sat down on the sofa, the phone rang. I picked it up and said hello, it was him. The first thing he said was I am glad that you made it home ok. I asked what was he doing, he said I am sitting up in a chair. The nurses had me moving around. The doctor told me that I will be going home Tuesday. I said I have planed to be there by 8:30am Tuesday morning.

Before ending our phone call he told me that he will call me tomorrow about the time he think I should be home from work. Ok I will be here. After getting off the phone I went in to the kitchen and found some thing to fix myself for dinner. I had to get ready for work tomorrow. Around 9:00pm I had just laid down when the phone rung. When I picked it up and said hello. I heard Patrick's voice. The first thing I got out of my mouth was is every thing ok. He said yes every thing is all right; I just wanted to tell you good night. Well good night, I had just laid down before the rung. He said that I called before you had fallen a sleep. I will still call you tomorrow when you get home. I said ok, I will be waiting for your call. Good night friend, I replied good night that's when we hung ended our call.

The next morning when the clock went off I thought that I was dreaming at first. Then I knew it was not a dream. It was time for me to get up and get ready for work. That morning when I got to work. A friend of mine wanted to know where I had been over the weekend I told her that I had to go out of town to help a sick friend. Who is this friend she asked. I told that his name is Patrick. He was in a car accident. I went to the hospital where he was and ended up stilling there for the weekend. Wait an mm who is this Patrick? She wanted to know everything. I told her we had met a few days ago. How did you meet him? Well I thought to myself how was I going to explain this to her. So I started from the beginning. One night Just as I was about to get into the shower, before I called it a night. The phone rang, at first I started not to answer it, but I changed my mind. When I pick it up. I said hello, then the voice on the other end asked may I speak to Dee Dee. I replied I'm sorry you have the wrong number. That's when he asked whom am I speaking to? I told him that my name is tee. Which was short for Tyrrell. He said I hope that I did not call you at a bad time. I must have haled the number wrong or I was given the wrong number. I said well don't worry about that, we all make mistakes. He told that he would never called, but he had met this woman last night, and she gave him what he thought was her phone number. As you can see she gave him the wrong number. He told me that he hope that I would forgive him, you seem to be a real nice person. Some people would have gotten upset. It was funny how we ended up talking for about an hour. It was some thing about the way he talked to me hat made him easy to talk to. Once we have ended our phone call I got into he shower, then I went to bed.

Her reaction was, wait a minute, what you just tell me. I told you how Patrick and I met one night over the phone when he called my number by mistake. The next thing she wanted to know was what has gone on between he two of you? I said nothing has happened. We are just friends. Well if hat's what you want to say, then she gave me this look of hers. The man is not thinking about me in that way. You is he is straight, and I know that nothing can happen. I told her that I will have to be off tomorrow so that I am go back up to the hospital to pick him and bring him back home. Yes I see that the two of you are just friends she said with a smile on her face. I mow one thing I though the day would never end. I was ready to get home, so I would be there when he called. When it was time to get off I did not have time to do a lot of talking, because I had to get home. When the phone rung I was there waiting, I picked it up and said hell, Patrick said I ready needed to hear you voice, I asked what's wrong. Nothing I have been missing you. I can't wait to see you in the morning. I will be there around 8:30 ok.

We talked on the phone for a while, and then he told me that he would call me back before I went to bed. I said that I would be right here. Well after we ended our phone call. I got myself some thing to eat, and sat around watching TV. It was hard for me to keep my mind on what was on TV. Because I could not stop thinking about Patrick, I was missing him moreThan I know I should. I know that I will see him in the morning when I go back up there to bring him home. When my phone rung I wondered if it could be him, but no luck it was a buddy of mine's, he was calling to find out was going on with me these days. I told him that I had been busy. Over the weekend I had to go out of town. He asked what was going on? I told him that a friend of mine's had a car accident and was in the hospital, so I went to see him. He asked who is this friend? I replied he is some one that I know, but we are just friends nothing is going on. You are telling me that you were gone all weekend because his guy was in the hospital, and nothing going. It the truth, we are just friends. We met over the phone one night when he called the wrong number. We found it easy to talk to each other, so we kept talking.

Last Friday he had to go out of town for the company that he works for. While he was gone he was in a car accident. Which he broke his leg, plus some other things happened. He is coming home tomorrow. Jokingly he said you real want the man don't you. I said you are crazy, what makes you think that I want this man; he is so straight that he could straighten out a curvy line. The only reason we met that night he was trying to call some woman that he had met the night before. Some how she gave him the wrong number. That was the only reason he called me. Scott said well he is still calling you right. So you got the ups on her. I said it not like that. We ended our call when I got a beep. When I answered it Patrick's voice came over the line saying what's up friend. I said nothing much I was talking to another friend of mine's, when you beeped in. I did not mean to stop you from talking to your friend. Don't worry we can talk any time. I asked how he was doing, he said I doing ok, just ready to get out of here and I am missing you.

Are you still coming up here in the morning? Yes I will be there on time. I know that you are ready to get home. Who will be there to help you out? He said I don't know yet, I will ask some one in my family. Then he asked me what time is now? I looked at my watch and said it's 9:30pm. He told me that he was going to let me off the phone so I could get some rest for my trip. Tomorrow. I will be thinking about you. Until you get here. Good night. We hung up the phone. I got myself ready for bed. I laid there for a while thinking about Patrick I did not have a reason for why, I was doing this. It took me a while to fall a sleep.

It was Tuesday morning and I knew that I. had to get myself together, because. I had a special trip to make. I left my house a 6:45am to go to the hospital to pick Patrick up and bring him home. When I got there I went up to his room, there he was laying in bed sound a sleep. I sat down beside his bed and waited for him to wake up. When a woke he. Looked around the room, his eyes found me sitting in the chair. He smiled and said I glad you made it ok. How long have you been here? Well I have only been just a few moments. Your doctor should be in to see you in a few mm. He said I am ready to get out of here. It wasn't long before the doctor came into the room; I know that you are ready to go home, so I will sign your release papers. Then let you get out of here don't hurry back to see us. You will need to setup up an appointment with your family doctor as soon as you can. He told Patrick that you can start getting dressed. That's when he realized that he does not any clothes up there that he can wear, because they cut his clothes off when he was brought in to the ER. He asked me if I would mind going over to the mall and pick up him something to wear. I said I will be glad to go for you, because I would not want you to have to ride all way the home wearing the hospital grown. He asked for his wallet, which I gave to him. After taking out some money he told me to get him a pair of underwear and maybe a pair of shorts and a tee shirt or shirt, and a pair of sandals. I told him that I would be right back. It only took me a few minters.

When I got back he was waiting to get dress, and leave. The doctor had all ready gotten his paper work done. I had to help him to get dressed; I was trying my best not to think about his body. Which it was very hard for me not to notice it, because he had a very nice body, on top of that he did not mind being nake in front of me. Once he had dressed I went out to the nurse's station to let them know that he was ready to go. An orderly was sent in with a wheel chair to wheel down to my car. Well the guy helped him in to the car, said bye to us. We started on our way home. As we drove the long highway, we talked and had a very good time together. When we got by in town I asked him to show me where he lived. That's when I found out that is place was close to where I live. After helping him to his apartment. I stayed for while to help get things straighten up. He got on the phone and called his brother to ask him to come over and spend the night with him.

Well when I left his place it was later that evening. I fixed dinner for the two of us. I did not want to leave him alone, but I had to get home, and he said that his brother would be there. He told me that he would call me later to say good night. About 9:30pm my phone rung when I picked it up he was on the other end. The first thing he asked me was if! could come to his apartment and pick him. I asked what's wrong? He said that his brother never got for some reason, and he does not want to be alone. I told him that I will be right as slip on some thing. Well I got up and dressed, I was out of the door as soon as I could. It did not take me long to get there. When I knocked on the door I heard him say its open. When I walked he was on the sofa in his living room. Once I sat down beside him, he asked if I would mind if he spent the night at my house I told him that I would not mind at all.

He told me where to find every thing that he would need to take with him. So once I had picked him a bag we made out way out to my car. He told me that he could not understand why his brother did not come over nor did he call. I said you know I am here for you when ever you need me. Thanks for allowing me to spend the night at your house. You should have known that you could have came to my house from the start. Well I did not want to cause you any more trouble, because you I had all ready caused you enough trouble. You have not cause me any trouble, because every thing I have done I did on my own. When we got to my house I helped him into the house. He needed to sit down so I told him to have a seat in the chair next to the door. He needed to rest for a moment or two. As we sat there in my living room I told that I do have a guestroom, but I would need to go in and clean up some before he could get in to bed. Because I use that room to put a lot of things. He looked at me and said you do not have to do that. I can sleep right here on your sofa. Told him no you need to be in a bed. So you can sleep in my bed and I will sleep out here. I cannot kick you out of your own bed. Then he said that blew my mind. He said we could both sleep in your bed, if you are comfortable with that.

I almost fell over. I said the first thing that came to my mind. Which was it's not like I have not slept with a man in my bed before. He looked at me with a look on his face that was so funny. I asked him what's wrong. He said nothing I just was not looking for you to say what you did. I said I will be ok with us sleeping in the same. When we got into my bedroom I showed him where the bathroom was. You see I have a bathroom next to my room, and another one down the hall. Before getting in to bed he ask me if he us the bathroom. I told that he did not have to ask. When he came back in to the room he sat down n the bed, and removed his shorts and tee shirt. I asked him if he needed any thing before we laid down. He said I may need to take one these pain pills so I can get some sleep. I got him some water and his pills; he took it and laid down. When I laid down he told me good night, I replied good night. I laid there next to him in my bed, but I knew that he was not there for sex, but as a friend in need.

The next morning I got up to get ready for work. I went in to the other bathroom to take my shower, because I did not want to wake him up. Before I left for work I left him a note telling him how he could get in touch with me at work if he needed for any thing. Plus I told him to make his self at home. At noon I called back to the house to see how he was doing. He told me that he was doing ok. I asked if he had eaten any thing. He said that heHad found some thing to eat. Then he said I will be all right, I can not wait for you to get home. I would like to talk to you about some thing. I said that I would come straight home from work.

So when I got there he was on the sofa watching TV. As I walked though the door he asked how are you doing. I said I am all right, what about you? He said I just hate not being able to really get around in driving me crazy. I walked over and sat down on the sofa with him. He said I told that I wanted to talk to you about some thing, well I wanted to ask you if! could stay here with you for a while, or until I am able to get around better. The only thing I could get out of my mouth was sure you could. I thought to myself what am I getting myself in to with this fine man staying in my house. Man just looking at him makes it hot in here. We sat there for a while talking, one of the things he told me was that he found that he could depend on his family to help him now. He knew that he could stay with his parents, but he did not want to do that because that would more work on them, and plus they would worry more than they needed to. You how parent are. I said yes I do know how parents are when it comes to their children. I know how you feel, so you can stay here as long as you need to.

So after getting cleaned up I started dinner, it did not take me long to cook. We ate and watched TV. We had a good time talking. The more we found out about each we became more and more comfortable with each other. That evening Patrick started joking and playing with me. I did not know how crazy he was until that evening. He had me cracking up on him big time. We were having so much fun that we stayed up later than what I needed to. Once in bed it did not take us long to fall a sleep. The days passed fast, before I knew it he was ready to go back to his place.

It was a Friday night when we went over to his place to see what needed to be done. While we were there we started talking and he let me know that he really did not want to go back home. But he felt that he needed back to his own place. Well I told him that he was welcome to stay at my house for as long as he wanted to. Well he ended up staying with me a few more weeks. The day be left my house was the day his cast came off and his doctor gave him the ok to go back to work. Well we talked on the phone a lot, and he did come by from time to time.

He came by one time that I remember so well. Patrick came over that evening to tell me that he had met a woman. This time he had the right phone number. And the two of them have been getting along good together. I asked how long had he known her, he said that the two of them met the day he went back to work. She had been hired while I was out. We seem hit it off real good the first day. That means the two of you have been together forover two months. Their relationship did not keep us from being friends. One night about nine months later I was sitting up watching a late movie when the phone rung. I picked up the phone and said hello, the voice on the other end was Patrick. Some did not seem right to me, and I asked it some thing was wrong, he said well yes it is. I waited for him to explain. He took a moment before he went on to say; well I made a big mistake. I had to ask what are you talking about. He reminded me about the woman that he had met, and been with for over nine months. 1 found out today that she that she had been laying to me the whole time. That crazy woman was playing me like a bad game.

Once he had said that he asked if he could come over, because he did not want to be alone. I told him to come over. It did not take him long to get to my house. When he got there I could tell that he was every upset. As he sat there with me he started to talk to me, I saw the tears in his eyes. I wanted to put my arms around him and hold him. Before I could rethink my thoughts, he reached out for me. He laid his head on my shoulder and started to cry. That's when I did put my arm around him. I hate to see a man cry, especially Patrick. I wish that could make all his pain go a way, but what could I do. I know how it feels to get hurt by someone. Once he had cried until he could not cry any more, he looked at me and said I did not want you to see me this way. I said why not we are friends right and friends stand by each other no matter what. One thing you can all ways remember is that I will be here for you when ever you need me. He said I really need you tonight, can I spend the night here, because! Do not what to spend the night alone. Then he looked at me with this look on his face and said I know we will have to share the same bed, right.

Well do you have a problem with that? No it does not bother me at all. You know me better than that. We have slept in the same bed before and things were ok. I just said that joking around. I told him that I knew that, and then we both start laughing. The fact was that I still was not in a relationship with any one at that time, and he was just breaking up with a want to be bitch. I'll friendship had grown stronger. Well that night we did sleep in the same bed next to each other. Again that night nothing happened, there I was in need of a real good man; with a man laying next to me that could be the man of my dreams. I know that we would never be together, because he is a straight man who wants to be with a woman. The next morning we both woke up and looked at each other, saying good morning. That day we spent the morning together at my house. Patrick left around noon to go home and clean his place.

The next weeks nothing changed we called each other every day and we saw each other from time to time. One evening I had gone out to pick up some thing to eat, as I walked in to the place who should I run in to, but Patrick and some woman? We spoke to each other as we all ways have, then he called me over to where they were and introduced me to her. He told her that I was his best friend, and then he told me that the two of them had been dating for about two weeks. I thought to myself why had he not told me about her before now? I had no answers to my question. I went on to get my food. When I got home my phone rung, when I picked it up he was on the other end. His first words were I hope that you are not upset with me about not telling you about her before today. I replied to him what reason would for getting upset about that? Well we are close and I have all ways talked to you about every thing. I wanted to tell you, but I did not because I wanted to wait to see how things turn out. We talked as we all ways have each night.

On Oct. the *27th* Patrick came over to my house because he wanted to talk to me about some very important to him. Well when got there I thought that was ready for any thing, but man was wrong. What he wanted to talk to me about was me being his best man when he marries the woman he had going with for almost a year. It took me a moment to get my self together, but I did how ever say yes to what he wanted, because I only wanted him to be happy. He said thank you then hugged me. I asked when is the wedding he told me that they were planning it for June. Well the months flew past and his wedding was a few days a way. I had picked up my tuxedo, and tonight was the rehearsal. When I got to the church there they were standing in front the arch with the pastor. My heart dropped, but I knew that I had to do this for my best friend. Why was I feeling this way? Tomorrow I would be standing beside him as he takes his wedding vows.

That night when I got home I was ready to get into bed, just as I laid down the phone rung. When 1 said hello Patrick said I am glad that you are going to be there to hold me up tomorrow. I am glad to be there for you was my reply. The next morning when I was woken up by the phone it was Patrick, he said good morning. Today is the day. Remember you have to get me to the church on time. Well I am glad to say that every thing went the way they had planned it. That night I sat at home with thoughts of him running though my mind. This was the first time he had not called me since we started talking. The phone brought me back to the real world. When I picked it up there was a man's voice on the other end, his name was Eddie. I remember who he was. Because he was one of the groom's men. I asked how did he get my number. He replied I got it from Berth, she is my cousin.

Talked I found out that he too was gay, and he like myself was a lone. So that night we talked for a while.

After Patrick and his wife got back from their honeymoon things got by to normal between to two of us. Plus Eddie and

I spending time with each other. Well a year went by and I was not really happy with being with Eddie, because he was the type that wanted to have me and run around with other people as well. I knew that we could only be friends because of his ways. At the same time I thought that Patrick and Berth were happy in their marriage. About eight months after Eddie and I met we ended what we called a relationship. There I was alone again. Over four months past and I had not even tried to meet any new people. Now the weather was now changing and I wanted to go shopping for some new cold weather clothes. As I got the local department store. I almost changed my mind, because I was feeling down. Well I did go into the store, and things seemed to just go down hill. That day I could not find any thing wanted. So as I was leaving the store a guy stopped me. He was an old friend of a woman I knew. He wanted to know when was to last time I talked to her. I told him that it had been only a couple days. He also asked how she was doing. I said that she was doing ok. She was now living with her boyfriend. He told me to let her know that he asked about her.

When I got by home I sat down in front of the TV, wishing that I had some thing to do, or somewhere to go. I needed to get me mind off of some things. Nothing was on TV that I wanted to see, so laid down on the sofa and tried to take a nap that did not work. What was I going to do? Well when my mother called she wanted me to come over to her house to help her with something. I told her that I would be on my way in a few mm. being around my mother helped me forget things for the rest of that day. I think she knew that some was wrong, but she even asked about it. That night she did however ask me to stay with her. So I did, the two of us sat up talking about all the crazy things that I did when I was younger. It was late when we went to bed.

The next morning we got up and like old times she cook breakfast for the two of us. I did not go home until that evening. When I did get home there was a message from Patrick waiting for me. He wonder where I was. He had called more than one time last night but could not find me. So he asked me to call him back as soon as I got his message. I called and Bert answered the phone

I asked for him. That's when she started to act a little crazy, she asked why he was all ways calling and wanting to come over to my house all the time. I told her that she knew that the two of us were best friends. I asked her what was going on? She said that I need to stop puttingmyself in his life. After saying every thing that she wanted to say she did call him to the phone. Once he was on the phone he asked where have you been, I was worried about you. 1 told him that I was at my mother's house. We talked for a while, but I never told him what Berth had said to me.

Well two months past and I got a call one night from Patrick; he told me that he was about to become a father. I was doing every thing I could to show him that I was happy for him. The next thing he asked me was if I would be his child's godfather. I asked him how Berth felt about that; he in turn said well I have not talk to her about it yet. I said maybe you should talk to her, because this is her child too. Before we ended our phone call he thank me for being his best friend. I said you do not have to thank me. I could tell that he did not know how his wife really felt about me.

A few days later Patrick called, and he was not his normal self when I asked him what was wrong. He told me that he had talked to Berth about wanting you to being our child's Godfather. I had a bad feeling about his statement. Well I did not have to wait long before he told me what I knew was coming. He said that Berth did not like the idea at all. Then he said I am going to need a few days alone to think about some of the things he said. He asked if he could come over. I told him to come on over. When we got off the phone I started to think a million things. I hope that I have not caused the two of them to have problems. I never wanted to get in his way of happiness. If I had to I will have to tell him that we need to be long distance friends. Which means that we would not be talking as much.

When my doorbell rung, I rushed to the door. Because I knew that it was Patrick. Well when I opened the door. He was standing there looking as good as the first day we met. He walked in to the living room and sat down on the sofa. After I had closed the door, and turned to walk over to where he was sitting he looked up at me and said can I stay here for a few days. I replied it would be just fine with me. Plus I felt that we needed to talk. It did not take long before he brought what had been said between him and Berth. She had told him how she really felt about me, our friendship. He was very hurt by what she had said, and he wanted to just stay a way from around her, because he did not want to say or do any thing that would make matter worst.

There he was sitting there with me, asking me again to let him stay with me. Well I knew not to allow myself to get carried away on what I thought. He is the type of man that would even think about some one like me. That night we talked more about his wife. When it was about time to get ready for bed, he went out to his car to get his bags. Believe it or not I had just cleaned up the second bed. He carried his things in to the room. He went in to the bathroom to get his self-ready for bed. While I was in the bathroom off of my bedroom. When I came out, wearing my robe. I went to check on him, only to find him in the room crying. I sat down beside him and put my arms around him. I said nothing to him, because I just wanted to comfort him. There he was crying on my shoulder. I did not know what was wrong. I allowed him to just get it all out, and then he lifted his head and faced me. At that point some thing happened that took us both by surprised. We kissed fully on the lips. After it was over, we looked at each other, and then he said I'm sorry, I shouldn't have done that. You were upset, don't worry about it, your emotions just got the best of you. Please let's keep this between the two of us. Ok, but was nothing to tell.

We sat in the room and talked for a while before we decided to go to bed he did sleep in the guestroom. I laid in my bed thinking about what had happened. I told myself not to worry about it because it was done out of his pain. That Saturday morning we got up around 9:00am. I guest both of us were out of it last night. When he walked out of the room we both met in the hallway. We said good morning to each other. Then he went in to the bathroom. I went back in to my bedroom to get dressed. I went in to the kitchen to cook breakfast for the two of us. Well I knew what he likes to eat in the mornings. So there I was standing at the stove when he walked in to the kitchen. The food smells good. I am hungry. Come on and get your food. I need you to serve me. I know now that you have lost your mind. I am in pain plus I am a guest in your house. You maybe in pain but you are no guest. You better get your ass over here and fix your plate. Then I thought to myself what a fine ass too. I knew that I would always think things about Patrick that I could never tell him.

So the two of us sat do at my table and ate breakfast. While we were sitting there he started to talk to me about how Berth had hurt him. He said that she could not handle the fact that I was gay. He could not understand why she felt the way she did. Patrick said that he could not see any thing wrong with him having a gay friend. He did say you have been the best I have had since we met. Before I had been around people who acted like they were my friends, who I found out later were not. Now that I have a true friend I am not going to lose this friend ship over some thing so small as you being gay. Berth needs to try to understand that you and I a close friends, that we enjoy sharing things together. No matter what I want you as apart of my life. To me we are more like brothers than friends. I am going to call her this morning; hopefully we can talk things out. I want us to stay together; not only for my child, but also for the love I have for her.

After waiting to about 11:00am, he called to talk to his wife. As soon as she picked up the phone, she went off about the fact that he was at my house. He tried to talk to her, but she was not willing to listen to any thing he had to say. Once he had hung up with her, he called his mother and talked to her about what was going on. His mother seemed to be an understanding person. She did not want to say any thing against Berth, but she needed to speak what was on her mind. I had no way of knowing what was being said on the phone at that time. When he got off the phone he called me in to the living room where he was sitting. He told me to sat down because he wanted to talk to me. When I sat down beside him, he told me that his mother had talked to him about Berth and the way she is acting. She told him that some thing was not right, and that he needs to find a way to get Berth to open up about her feelings. He asked what did I think about the two of them going to a marriage counselor. I told him to do what ever he felt he needed to do.

He tried to call Berth again, but this time from his cell phone. The first thing she asked him was if he was still at my house. He lied and told her that he had left and was on his way to another friend's house. She was willing that time to talk to him. When he asked her why she felt the way she did about me, she got all upset. So he let it go, then he brought the idea about going to see a marriage counselor. She told him that she needed to think about it. He asked what is there to think about. I am trying to find a way to save our marriage. It seemed that there are some things that we really do need to talk about and work on. So I will see if I can find some one for us to go and see. So I will let you know when and where. They did not stay on the phone very long. Once they had ended to call he looked over at me and said she really does need some help.

He started calling around to see if he could find some one to see him and Berth. After making about 10 calls he did find a counselor would set an appointment for Monday afternoon at 4:00pm. After he had made the appointment he got back on his cell phone and called his wife back. When he told he about the appointment, I could tell that she had said some thing that he did not like. He told her that she did not have a choose in the matter. If she wants to help make things work in their marriage she will be there on Monday at 4:00pm. It was not open for discussion. When he got off his cell phone he said that woman has got to be out of her mind. Now she is saying that the only way she would go to a counselor is that she finds one. I know what she is up to. She wants to find one that will say what ever she pays him to. One thing I know is that one is going to tell me that I have to turn my back on my best friend. Terrell you have been there for me when I needed a friend, will really I needed my family, but you and I both know how that turned out.

I tried to explain to her how you helped me when my own brother was not there for me. Why is so hard for her to understand that you and share a closeness, and that other so call friends turned their backs on me when I was down. Since you and I met you have been here for me. I wanted so much for the baby she is carrying to me my child. The idea of my wife having an affair. What am I going to do? I told him to just wait to see how things turn out.

He asked me how would you handle something like this. I said that I would say a pray and do my best to talk things out with her, but if she did not want to talk, then I would have to go on with my life. Well I never try to tell other people what to do. The truth will come out soon. The baby will be born in a few months. When that happens you can request a blood test. While we were talking his cell phone rung. A friend had called to his house only to be told that he needed to call him at that number. She also told him that he was staying with his boyfriend. He tried to explain to him what was going on between Berth and himself.

The next call he got came from Berth herself. She started in on him about the guy who had called to the house. Then sitting in my living room. That's when she really went off on him. He told her that she need to stop acting that way, because she was only making herself look bad. Why are you so against the two of us being friends? Tyrrell is the only true friend I have. This man took care of me when I got hurt and was laid up for months. My own brother let me down. I don't know your reason for not understanding how we feel about each other. Where did you get the idea that we could be more than friends? I don't know what she said, but he said we need to stop this right here and now before one of use says something that we both may regret.

He turned his phone off and laid it down on the coffee table, than he lowed his head and placed it in his hands. When I turned around I show the way he was sitting. I could tell that he was crying. I walked over to the sofa and sat down beside him without saying a word I reached over and placed my hand on his shoulder. When he felt me touch him, he turned and laid against me crying tears of hurt. I could feel his pain. I also hurt because I felt that I was partly the cause of his problem. When he lifted his face and looked at me he had tears running down his face. The next thing I knew we had kissed. That had been the second time something like that had happened since he him and Berth was having trouble. This time he did not say that he was sorry about doing that. I did not say anything about what had happened. It took him a while to stop crying. Once he was able to talk he said I am so blessed to have a true friend like you. We have been though so much together.

As the day went on he did every thing he could to keep his mind off of what was going on. That evening my phone rang, and when I answered it Berth was on the other end. She went off on me about how Patrick and I should be happy together, two sissies together and how we would be able to mess with each other. He heard me say Berth why are you doing this; I am just a friend to him. Just like I could be your friend if you let me. He came over to where I was and took the phone out of my hand, and started to try to talk to her. She would not say any thing to him, so he hung the phone up. This mad him mad, he was ready to go over to the house and confront her, but I did everything I could to stop him, because I did not want to get in to trouble with her. Finally he did not go over there, but he did call her back from his cell phone. All she did was talk to him like a dog. By the time he got off the phone he could not take any more. He told me that he did not care any more, and that he was going to get an office to go with over to the house to get all of his stuff out. He asked me if he could bring what he need over to my house, and the rest he would that to his parent's house. I told him that he could do what he felt he needed to do.

That night when we were ready to go to bed Patrick ask me if he could sleep in the room with me. I wonder what his reasons were, but I did not say anything. Then he said that he did not want to sleep in the room alone, because he felt so down. I could not turn him down. So that night we undressed and got into the same bed. As we laid there together, he reached over and took my hand saying I am sorry for hurting you. I did not know what to say at that time. I asked him why are you saying that you are sorry for hurting me? He answered; I do not know how to explain it. All I can say is I made a big mistake, and I hurt you. As I laid there listening to his words, he moved closer to me. I could only wait for him to make since of the whole thing for me. I did not know what was going on. His next statement really sent me in to a tailspin. He said I have been trying to deny my true feelings for you. That was the real reason I married Berth. I could not deal with the fact that I was in love with you. When he said my heart slipped a beat, and I lose my breath. I could not say anything for a few moments. While I laid there speechless he put his arms around me and moved closer to me. Before I could react he kissed me.

My mind was going crazy, because he never knew that I was in love with him. How could I tell him how I really felt? I knew that this may not be the right time to say anything, because he was hurting from what Beth was doing to him. As I laid there in his arms I could tell that he was crying again. I forced myself to ask him why he was crying. His reply was I can tell that you do not want me. I should have just done what I felt in my heart, and not married Beth. My first thought was to tell you how I felt when I was right here with you, but being brought up the way I was. Now I have lose you before I have the chance to share my love with you. I had to stop him, the next thing I knew I was telling him just what I felt about him. That night we agreed that we would start a relationship with each other while he is still married to Beth. There was one thing he wanted, and that was to live in my house while he was working things out. I did agree to that. That night we lay in my bed together holding each other. The next morning the phone woke use up. When I picked up the phone, Beth said sissy I want to speak to my husband. So I placed my hand over the receiver and told Patrick that she wanted to talk to him. He waited a few moments before he took the phone from my hand. Then he said hello, it wasn't long before I could a change in his voice. I knew that she up to her same on tricks. This time he told I do not care what you do any more. That he reached over me and hung the phone up. He said I am going over there today and get my stuff out of that house. Once I do that, and she calls to your house, you can tell her anything that you want to. So we got up and dressed. It was about 9:00 that morning when he left the to go over to his house to pick up his things. I was at home waiting on him to come back, because I knew that he had to go over there by himself. However he did take a policeman with him. It took him about two hours to get back.

When he got back I could tell that he was upset, I did not have to ask him what happened. His words were that woman is crazy; she told the cop that I wanted my stuff so I could move in with a sissy. I did not say a word, I just packed up my things and left. The best part of the whole thing is that I was coming back here to you. He asked me if I was sure that he could have all of his things here. I replied to him yes I want you to bring what ever you have right here into this house. Then we went out side and started to bring things from his car into the house. Once inside we just put everything right there in the living room. I was so happy to have him here with me. Things with us had really taken a turn. As we sat there on the sofa he told me that he was going to talk to a lawyer the next day about a devoice. He just wanted to go on with his life, which meant he wanted to build a life with me. This time he was not going to play any games, because he did not want to take a chance on loosing me. We spend the rest of the day together. Between putting away his things to cooking dinner we had a real good talk. He told me just what he wanted out of life. One thing that he made a point of telling me was that he would never hurt me again.

As we sat in the living room watching TV, put his arm around me and held me. I felt so happy being with him. Deep down inside of me I had a fear about loosing him. I had feelings for him, but I could not tell him, because he was saying that he loved Berth. Now I was asking myself if I should tell him my feelings. That's when I told him that had been hiding my true feelings. I started caring about you a little after we first met, but I could not tell you then, because of the way you said that you felt about Berth. There were times when I just wanted to take you in my arms and hold you.

My First Job

I was 18 years old when I graduated from high school. By the time I was 19, and I was starting my first year in college. Like all young men my age I wanted to have a job making good fast and easy money. Well I did find a job, let me tell you all about it. One day I saw an ad in the towns' newspaper. That read jobs opening for young hard workingmen. Please apply at the Royal Inns hotel on Monday and Tuesday between the hours of 8:00am and 11:30am. I did however decide to go down and apply for a job there. The manager interviewed me right then and there.

He told me that if I was willing to work, and depending on my skills I could make some good money. I wanted to know about the job, he told me that I would be doing a number of things around the hotel. The main thing that all of the hotel employees here are asked to do is to make sure that the guest enjoy their stay while they are here. I felt that I could handle working there. Well I started to work the very next day, around 5:00pm. You see he allowed me to set my own hours around my classes, and other school actives. When I got there the manager showed me around. He also gave me the uniforms that I would have to wear. He waited for me to change in the locker room every employee had their own locker to store their personal things. We all wore the same type of uniform, which were black pants, which fit neatly, along with a white shirt and black tie. He told me that I would need a pair of black dress shoes to wear at work. I only worked a few hours here and there, but the job seemed very nice. Most of the other workers were about my age; there were a few who were older. After working there for about three weeks I noticed that only men came there. Well I did ask any questions about it. Because I knew that women have places where no men are allowed. The staff there was made up of only men, which seemed right. The guests could enjoy full room service.

Maybe I need to go back to the beginning of this whole thing. Like I said there I was right out of high school, and miles away from home. I was all alone I didn't know anyone there, plus the place was all-new to me. I was in a dorm room with a guy I knew nothing about. The two of us were both young and new at the game. It wasn't long before I was in need of money. Well you know how that goes; the first thing I did was calling home and asks for my parents to send me some money. They sent me what they could, as always to me it wasn't enough. As the weeks pasted I knew that I would have to do something to make it on my own. That's when I started trying to find a job. It seemed the more I looked, it got harder and harder. Then I came across the ad for the hotel. I was one of those kids that never worked a day in my life. Now what was I going to do? Well I went down to the hotel to see about a job. You see I had been working at the hotel for three weeks. When a man checked in while I was helping out at the front deck. I became his bellhop. I took his bag to his room for him. Once we got into the room he started talking to me. His words were man I've had a long drive and I really do need to relax. Then he asked me if I knew how to give massages. I replied not really, but I maybe able to find someone around who do know how. He told me that he wanted me to be the one to do that for him. What is your name he asked? I said my name is Traidel. Well Traidel I am Walter, he said as he undressed. I watch him remove his shoes, socks, pants and shirt, the only thing he had on was his underwear. Then he laid down on the bed and said I am ready for my massage. Well I knew that the room had a bottle of oil in the bathroom. So I went in get it, then I returned to the side of the bed, not knowing where to start. He must have known that I was nerves he said why don't you start no my back and he rolled over. I started trying to do what he had asked me to do. As I worked on his back he made a statement that surprised me. Looking at me he said why don't you take off those clothes before you get oil on them, no one will know anything about it but us. I didn't know what to say to him at first. I thought about it for a moment, and then it made sense to me. So I did take off my shirt, then I went back to massaging his back, while I was standing beside the bed. Walter looked around at me and said man it may be easier on you if you took your pants off too, and get on thew bed, so you want have to reach or bend the way you are doing now, plus you want get any oil in them. Well I did what he had asked me to.

I got out of my pants and got on the bed with him. He seemed to be very relaxed. I had never done anything like this at all before. Walter knew that I was not use to doing this, because he talked me though everything. When I got to the small of his back he made a point of telling me to please remove his underwear, so that I would not get oil on them and don't forget to do my legs. I took a deep breath and slowly reached for his underwear. I hooked my fingers into the waistband and started to pull them down, he raised his off of the bed so I could remove them. There he laid nake waiting for me to touch his body again. I reached out and touched his right leg. That's when he said you forgot something. I stopped and waited for him to tell me what I had missed. He said I want you to massage my whole body all over that means my buttocks too. Without thinking I asked you want me to touch you butt? He replied that's also apart of a massage my young friend. After waiting a moment I did reach out and put my hands on that man's butt. Once I had finished his legs, it was time for him to roll over. So I could massage his chest and arms. When he rolled over, he didn't try to cover any part of his body. He looked at me and said now please do the rest of my body. You have gone this far you can finish the job. I started to rub oil on his chest and shoulders. I slowly worked my way down to his waist. When I got to that part of Walter's body I did everything I could to work my way around his dick. I had done both legs and was finishing his arms, when he said you can massage that too. It won't bite you or anything. I didn't want to touch another man's dick, but Walter talked me into doing what he wanted. I was glad when I had done with his massage.

As I started to get off of the bed, Walter took my hand and smiled saying it's your turn, I want to give you a massage now. The first words out of my mouth were why. He replied because you did a real good job and you made me feel so relaxed. So why don't you take off your underwear and lay down so I can get started friend. I slowly pulled my underwear down and got out of them. Then I laid down on the bed face down. It wasn't long before I felt oil on my skin. Then his hands followed. Walter knew how to make me relax. His hands were all over my body. Even places that no one had ever touched me like that before. As this went on I fell under his spell. Now you may not believe what happened next. While I laid there with my eyes closed, and my mind was in another world. He got between my legs, and then he put oil between the cheeks of my ass making sure to lub my virgin ass hole. I felt his hand touching my there, but I let him do it without thinking anything about it. The next thing he did brought me back to earth. He was trying to get his dick inside of me. Because I couldn't say anything I felt it pop into place and he lowed his body down on top of me. Walter laid there for a few moments before he started to fuck me slowly. It was my first time. After it was over I found myself lying there in a state of shock. As he got up from the bed, Walter made a statement smiling he said thanks for the room service; it was just what I needed. I'll remember to call for you by name next time. I had no idea what he was talking about. I got up and hurrily dressed, so I could get back to work. When I went back down to the deck one of the other guys was there. He spoke as I walked passed on my way to the employee's locker room. Once inside I went over to the sofa and sat down. I was still in a daze. As I sat there one of guys that worked there by the name of Parker. Came over to me and sat down beside of me and said in a low soft voice it was your first time. The only thing I could do was look at him. I looked into the eyes of an older man, as he placed his hand on top of my left hand. My name is Jesse; I know how you feel, because I have been there. When I started working here when I was younger, I was about your age. And looking for a job. It took me about two weeks to find out what my job was here. Today I go into the rooms, and do what the quest want.

I forced myself to ask him why didn't someone tell me, what kind of place this was? He answered if Mr. Handley had told you what the job was all about, would you have taken the job? After thinking for a moment I replied no. Jesse said just do what most of us do, think about it as a job and do it for the money. Some weeks I make about 600 dollars. Just by doing what I need to do. There are some guys who work here that really enjoy the sex. Man when I walked out of there I leave all of that right here and go home to my woman. She will never know what I do here, as long as I only deal with the right here in the hotel. With out thinking I asked, you got a wife and still do this job. He looked at me and said well where can I work the hours and days I want to, without loosing my job. The men that come here will never tell anyone who they have been with, because they will be telling on themselves, and a lot of them have women. I was able to pay my way though college and have my own place and a nice car. Plus I have always dressed in the best. My woman has been able to live the way she wants to. I have another job working for a company where I work 8 hours a day doing a job that pays just enough to pay the bills. So I work here to really take of my woman and me.

Jesse and I talked for a while before he told me to just go back to work. I told him that I don't know if I can do it. After he got up and walked a way. As he left though the door, I got up and started towards the door myself. When I got to the front desk the guy standing behind the desk told me that I needed to help the guest to his room, which is room 215. As I carried his one bag down the hallway to the room this man followed me. When we got to the door I reached out and opened it. Once we entered the room he closed the door behind us. Then he asked how is the room service here? I answered him by saying it's good. He said why don't you show me just how good it is. He said why don't you show me just how good it is. I knew what he really wanted, but would I be able to handle having sex with this man. Before I knew it I was getting undress for this man.

He told me what he wanted me to do for him. Without telling me his name, he asked me to suck his dick. I tried my best to do what he had asked me. I did everything I could to take my mind to another place while he was doing the things he wanted to do.

After he had finished and had came. I got up and dressed. I left him laying on the bed nake. When I went back to the front desk Parker was on his way down the hallway to take another man to his room. By this time I knew what the job was about. Every time we took these men to a room that they had rented, they always wanted sex.

It had been six months since I started to work at the Royal Inns Motel. One evening I was told to go to room 532, as I walked towards the room I could only wonder what kind of man was waiting for me. When I opened the door the only thing I could see was clothes laying on the floor, as I closed the door I noticed two bodies lying on the bed. The man lying near the door looked at me, and then told me to take off my clothes, and join them on the bed. I stood in front of them and undress. Once I was nake I walked towards the bed. As I laid between the two of them, they kissed and touched my nake body. It wasn't long before the older man started to fuck me, then he pulled out of me, and moved away, and then the younger man got between my open legs and pushed his hard dick inside of my asshole. Both of them took turns fucking me until they had shoot cum all over my body. Once they had finished I got up and went into the bathroom and took a shower. After dressing I left the room and went back to the front desk.

Believe it or not for some crazy reason I found myself getting more and more use to this job. Having sex with man after man was getting easier, and I was starting to not hating it so much. What had I turned into? Was it the job or was it me? What was the answer to the question? When I got to the front desk there was another man standing there checking in to the motel. Just as I went to walk passed him I looked over, and saw that it was Walter. The first man that I had ever had sex with. When he looked at me the first thing he did was to call my name Traidel is that you. I'm glad that you are working this evening. Paul handed him a room key, and said your room number is 328. Walton asked if I could show him to his room. As we made our way to the room, he started telling me that he had been thinking about me. When we got to the room door, he used the key to unlock it. Once in the room it wasn't long before he let me know what he wanted from me. This time I was ready to perform for him. After everything was over he thanked me and I left the room.

After my worked day was over it was finally time for me to go home. Once I got home I got my clothes off and got into the shower. After my shower I sat down to watch some TV. As I sat there I found myself thinking about the things that happened to me at the motel, and the men I had to be with just to make some money. How could I have gotten myself in to something like this? Was it that I wanted money so bad that I would sell my body to men the way that I have been doing for the last few months? This crazy job as made me realize that sex with those men has been more than a job. I know how that I wanted to be with them. Right now I am glad that I am around my parents now because I could tell them what I am doing.

The 11 O'clock news just came, and I knew that I had to get in bed so I can get up and going to work in the morning. Once I was in bed it took me a while to fall asleep. The next morning when my clock went off I didn't want to get out bed. After laying there for a few moments I got up and took a shower, then fixed something to eat. I got to work about 7:45am, and went to the locker room to take a few moments for myself before I had to go to my first room. One of the other guys came in the room. His name was Paul. We spoke to each other, and then Jesse came in and said good-morning whats going on. Paul replied nothing yet. About that time the phone rung. Jesse answered it, and then he said its time to go to work some of the guest wants room service. When we got to the front desk I was told that the guest in room 328, that is Walter's room number.

As I walked to his room I started to think about him. I wanted to be with him for some reason maybe it was because he was my first. Walter was the one who fucked my virgin ass my first day on the job. When I got to the room I knocked on the door he said come in. went I opened the door there he was on the nake. I have been waiting for you. Once inside to room I closed to door and started to take off my clothes. Walter watched me as I undressed; he had a smile on this face. Traidel spent last night thinking about you. That's why I called down to the front and asked for you, I wanted to see you. As we laid there together we started to talk. You have been on my mind a lot that's why I came back to the motel.

Traidel after our first time I went home, and tried to tell myself that you meant nothing to me, but I could not forget you. As we laid there with each other there was something I could not explain, a feeling that was deep inside of me. What was it about this man that was causing me to have feelings that I thought that I could only have for my girlfriend? Walter was an older man who was also my first male lover. Was I now gay? He looked into my eyes and asked if you could change anything in your life what would it be? I did not have an answer for him, as I looked back at him I just wanted to be there with him. I spent along time in the room with him, not only did we have sex but we had a long talk. I knew that I did have to go back to work. I got up and took a shower, and got dressed. On my way back to the front desk I could not get Walter off of my mind. As I went on with my day I did not know that he had made sure that I would not be with any other man. Right before I was to get off of work a call came to the desk to have me to come back to his room, which I was more than happy to do. He did want sex he just wanted to say good night to me. And wish me sweet dreams. On my drive home I started thinking about what we had talked about. Was this really happing? Was he feeling in love with me? What about the feelings I was having about him were they real?

When I got home my girl friend was waiting for me. I tried my best to get Walter off of my mind. She asked me what was wrong I just told her that I had a long hard day at work. As we lay in bed together that night, I found it hard to fall asleep. Things were getting wild to say the lease. Well Walter stayed at the motel for three more days, and we spent a lot of time together. The day he left I felt so alone as I watched his car drive away. Once my stiff was over I went home, and tried to get into things with the girl that I had been with since high school. I did what I could to make her feel that things had not changed between us. The next day I got a phone call from Walter. His word hit me right upside the head. He said that he wanted us to be together and have a real relationship. He also told me that he could not get me off of his mind.

I tried to explain how I was feeling, but I didn't know how to because that was to first time that I had ever felt this way about another man. I thought that I was dreaming, when he told me that he wanted to take me away from what I was doing, and he wanted to love me the way I should be loved. Before we got off of the phone he gave me three numbers where I could reach him at any time. His home number, home number and cell phone number. His words were call me any time that you want to talk to me, I don't care what tie it is. Traidel I know that you can not give me your home number right now because of your girl friend, but I can call you at work. I will try to get back there soon was the last thing I remembered him saying before we stop talking.

After I got off the phone Parker was looking at me smiling. What, was the first words out of my mouth jokily. He you must have been really good to him for him to call you like that. I just said can't explain what's going on. I told him that I was starting to have feelings for this man, and he told me that he can't stop thinking about. While we were on the phone he informed me that he wanted us to be together in a relationship. I don't know what I am going to do, how am I going to tell my girl friend that I have feelings for another man. About that time a deliveryman came up to the front desk, he asked if there is some one here by the name of Triadel Forester. I said that I am Traidel, this is for you, and he gave me a box that I had to sign for. As I opened it there was a note form Walter. I hope that you like this gift; I wanted you to have something special to remind you of me. Love Walter. Down in the box was a gold necklace with a charm on it in the shape of a half noon. As I took it out of the box it was I had a feeling come over me.

My life was about to take a turn that was really going to get wild. Walter was going to come back in to town in about three days and I knew that I had to tell my girl friend that I was falling in love with someone else. It was on a Saturday night and the two of us were at home alone. I started out by telling her that I had to talk to her about something that was going to change our relationship.

There was no easy way to tell her. So I just told her that I had met someone that had brought new feelings into my world. There were a lot of words and tears that night. But I knew that it had to be done if I wanted to be happy. We spent one last night in the house together. The next day I moved out. When Walter got to the motel I was there waiting for him. He checked in, and we went to his room. I told him what I had done, his eyes lit up. I was sitting there in a chair wondering if I had done the right thing. Walter took my hand and said I love you. I want to be with in every way not just sex. All of this was new to me I have never thought in any way that I could be in love with another man.

Walter pulled a necklace from under his shirt; on the necklace I saw that he had the other half of the noon that he gave me. He got up and walked over to me and took the two half moons and put them together. Then he read what was on the charms "Two hearts that beat as one." Without saying a word we kissed each other in a kiss of passion. He held me so close that I could feel his heart beating. It seem that he held me for the longest. When he finally let me go I didn't want to move at all. It felt like I was in a dream, and I didn't want to wakeup. Once I sat back in the chair Walter said I have something special for you. I just looked at him waiting to see what he had. He said I want you to move into my home with me. The only thing I could say was that I would have to stop school. He then followed that with you can stay go to school. It only a 45 min drive from the house to here.

You live that close? He answered me by saying I moved closer to be with you. What about your job? Well I can work anywhere, I am the boss. By the way you can work for me, and we both can work from the house.

I told him that I had to go back to work. That's when he told me that I would not have to work at the motel for muck longer. Please give you notice to the manager. When I got to the front desk I went to my manager office, and told him that I was giving my notice. He agreed with me that it was time for me to leave my job. He also told me that I have also talked to your friend Water, and I know that he is deeply in love you. I hope that you feel the same way about him. I replied yes I do have very strong feeling for him. Well I hope that you and him will be happy. He seemed to understand what was going on with Walter and me. I went back to Walter's room, and told him that I was no longer employed with the motel. Traidell why don't we go and get you things so we can go to our new home. It felt so good to hear those words. Without saying anything he took me by the hand and we left the room.

Once in the parking lot we got into his SUV, and went to my place to get my things. While there we agreed to take the SUV to the house then come back to pickup my car later. As we drove the 45 min to the next town we talked about how we were feeling, both of use had fears, but we were willing to see where things takes. Before I know it there we were pulling into the driveway of a nice big house with two picture windows on the front, and a full glass door. When we stopped he parked and reached into his pocket and pullout a set of keys, then handed them to me. At the front door he told me to use my key to unlock my new front door. Once the door opened I knew that I was in a dream, this house was wonderful, could not have dreamed of a better house. After touring the house we went back outside and got my things. We were going to be sharing the master bedroom. I thought to myself that it was going a great first night in my new home with the man I was falling in love with.

Walter cooked dinner while I was putting my things away. While sitting at the dinning table I thought to myself that I was no longer 17 years old, nor was I the same young virgin that he fucked the first time we met. After dinner we went into the bedroom where we laid on the bed and talked for along time. Before the night was over Walter had me face down with my legs spread, with him in between them. He put oil between my ass cheeks. Then entered my waiting asshole with his hard dick, and fucked me. That night we made love every which way but lose. The next morning we awoke in each other's arms. How could it be that I found love working in a place where men came to pay for sex with guys like me? There was something about Walter he was a special person. I had never had these feelings before and now I just wanted to be him. The next few days things just got better and better. I still went to school each day, and came home to Walter every night. Maybe one day I will have an answer for what happened to change my life.

About a year later Walter and I talked about telling my family what was going on with us. On June 12 the two of us drove to my parent's house and told them about our relationship. Believe me it was not easy. My parents were people who did not want to handle the fact that they had a gay son. After that day it took them over three months to even give me a phone call. The night they called was odd to say the lease. My mother did most of the talking. Still she didn't want to hear any thing about what was really going on. I did everything I could not to upset her. Then it was another two months before we talked again. They called to wish me a happy 21st birthday. Time passed and our love for each other grew stronger and stronger. I finished college and I am now working in a real job. Where I work at one of Walter's businesses.

You know that you are in love when: you feel so along when the other is away. And feel so wonderful when they are near you. You daydream about everything part of your relationship. And wonder if it can get any better. You smile at the little thing they do. You long for a touch or a kiss, or just to hear their voice. That's love.

My Life

My name is Javil Thomson living in my parent's house there was only one rule that each of us had to finish school. Well I did just that, but I waited to do anything about go to college. When I got out of high school I thought that I was all grown up, so I started hanging out with some guys that I knew. Which meant that I was out late at night. Well that's where my story begins.

One night while we were riding around in one of the guy's car, someone started talking about going to get some beer. We went to a small local store. Two of us waited in the car while the other two went into the store. When we left and road some more while we drink the beer. A few days later the police came to my parent's house to arrests me for robbing the store and beating the clerk. I was taken to jail, for the first time in my life.

Once there I was taken into a room where the office told me to strip, after doing so I was searched, then I was given an orange jumpsuit to put on. The office took me to a cell where this older man was laying on one of the bunks. The office told him that he was going to have cellmate for a while. Then he opened the cell door, once I had walked in he closed and locked it. When I heard the key turn I began to feel so alone. I walked over and sit down on the bunk. The older man spoke to me, saying I can tell that this is your first time in jail. Why did you say that I asked, his reply was I can see it in your eyes boy. One thing you don't have to worry about, I will not touch you.

Why don't you tell me why you are in here, he said as he laid on the bunk. I don't know what happened I was arrested this morning for robbing and beating a store clerk, which I had nothing to do with. One thing I can tell you right now, the Judge will not want to hear you crying that sad story of yours about how you did not have anything to do with happened to the store clerk. I did not say anything to him. The next day was going to be the first time I go to court. That night it was very hard for me to sleep.

About 6:30am the jailer woke us up. We had to get clean up for court. There was a shower and toilet in the cell, along with a sink. I was a little worry about doing anything in front of him. He must have known what I was thinking, because he made a statement, you just as well get use to doing a lot more than that when you get to prison. The two of got clean up and eat breakfast, and then they took us to the courtroom. The judge gave me a court appointed lawyer. I was given a half an hour to talk to him before I was taken back to the jail cell. Then next afternoon the lawyer came to the jail to talk to e about my case. He informed me that there were people who were going to testify against me in court, I asked who were they? He told me that each one of the guys with me that night was all turning on me. When I was told that I told him that I did not get out of the car that night. Your case will go before the Judge in a few days. I spent the next few days in that jail cell.

The morning before we went to court Jerry the guy in the cell with me told me that he wishes me luck on my case. Then he look at me and said I know that I am going by to prison, but I am not worry, I can make it. When we got to the courthouse I was taken to a holding cell with all the other guys who were waiting to go before the Judge. One by one we were called to the courtroom. I sat at the table with my lawyer, while the DA called each one of the guys that had once called me friends. All of them told the Judge that I was the one who robbed and beat the clerk that night. The Judge gave me 10 years in the state prison for they said I had done.

Later that night Jerry and I sat in the cell we shared and talked about was going to happen to us from that point on. Well he told me that this time was going to be his third time, so he knew that he was going a way for a very long time. Unlike him this was my first time, being in trouble. Now I was going to prison for 10 years, because of a pack of lies. He told me about the first time he went to prison; he was about 19 years old. Plus he went acted like he was a bad ass. Well that changed when we step off the prison bus.

When a man goes in to prison you have to go though a process. First you taken in to a room that has two walls made of glass. Where more than one officer are waiting to search you. After they unhand cuff you, the office tells you to remove all of your clothing. Then you are told to everything in a pile on the floor. The next thing you are told to do is to get on your knees on a bench, which is against the wall, face the wall, lean over and put your head on the wall. Once the office walks up behind you he will tell you to reach back and pull your ass cheeks apart, so he can sure that you do have anything up your ass.

The officer will had on a rubber glove, and he will put two fingers inside of you and search for drugs, or anything else that can fit up a man's ass. If you try to keep them from doing it you will be held and you cheeks will be opened by another office. The one with the glove will still finger fuck your hold one way or another. Then after they have done that you are taken as a group to another room where a there is a table and a so call Dr. who is going to do an exam, he will touch your whole body as you lay there nake with the officers and the other guys watching. The last thing you do before you go into the prison itself. All of you are taken into a large shower, which is one big stall, and all you will take showers like that everyday. There one thing need to know about what goes on, well as they process you into the prison you are being watched every step of the way by some of the other inmates. They are allowed to watch you nake, and who ever has enough pull he can tell the officers to put you in the cell with him. Sometimes the officers are given orders to put a young guy like you in what is called an open cell with thirty or forty guys who will be waiting for you.

I was sitting there listening to him. Not knowing what was going to happen to me in a few days. At 18 years old I was young and had never been though anything like this before. We would be transferred to prison in about five days. Jerry also told that the first time he went to prison. After being processed in, he was walked though the prison nake fro one cellblock to another until he was put in a cell with a man who was older than he was. When the officer walked up to the cell door the he was standing at the sink with his back to the door, wearing only a towel. The officer called to him, as he turned around the office told him that he as brought him a new friend. The officer gave me a little push, which made me step into the cell door.

There were two bunks in the cell, one of which had his things on it. There the other was bare. The officer said to me, you need to make your bunk kid, and then get dressed. The man was standing there looking at me in a way that made me feel worried. The officer asked me if I had hear what he said, then he told me to put my stuff on the floor and make up my bunk. He stepped in to the cell and put his hand on my shoulder and repeated what he had said. I bend over and put everything in my hands down on the floor. Both of them watched me as I put the covers on the bunk. I was doing this with out having on any clothes.

The officer left out and walked away. The guy was still watching me. When I was about to start putting on my clothes he made a statement, you can make me feel good now or we can wait until later. I stood there speechless I watched this man take off the towel and stand in front of me nake. He reached for a bottle of lotion that was sitting on a self. I had started to pickup my clothes, when I heard someone say man I see you are the one to get the new punk in your cell. I did not like being called a punk, but I thought it was best for me not to say anything, because there were to many men for me to fight all of them. I just hurried to put on my clothes. The man told the other guys I will be lucky to night. Was still nake for a while, and then he dressed, and sat down on his bunk. I also sat down on my bunk with this man watching me.

That day was the longest day to me. When the cells were locked and the lights were turned down, he gave me two chooses. I could become his on my own or he would do what he would have to take me. As I watched him undress in the dim lighted cell. I started wondering what he was going to do to me. Once he was nake he came over to my bunk and sat down beside me. He put his arm around me, and said its time for you to make up your mind. At that point I said please don't hurt me. If you let me have my way I will take it easy on you, but if I have to make you do what I want then it's going to hurt. Then he put his hand on top of mines, he ask what is your name? I replied nursery Jerry, well my name is Russ.

He made sure that I knew he meant business about what he wanted. Its time to get these clothes off, when I tried to move away he pulled me back to him with so force. I said take off your clothes now. He pulled my shirt over my head, and throws it on the floor. Then he rubbed my chest and said you have a nice body. Next he stood up and pulled my to my feet, holding me with one hand and undoing my pants with the other. Once they fell to the floor he pull down my underwear. Feeling his hand on my ass, he turned me around bend me over, that's when he rubbed his hard dick on my ass cheeks. Relax I'll take it easy; I know its first time. I allowed him to get what he wanted that night. He was the first man to bust my ass open. It did hurt because it was my first time, but giving myself to Russ saved me from getting raped or worst at the hands of some of the other men in the prison.

After everything was over we cleaned up. The two of us slept in the same bunk that night. The next morning when we went to the shower he made sure that every man there knew that I was now his punk (female). After we had sex for more than one time I started to enjoy having sex with a man. He was the only I was with the first four years that I was in prison. Then one day an officer came to our cell and told him to get his stuff together, that he was being transferred to another prison.

After that day things changed, I became a bitch for the whole cellblock. Any one and every one was able to do what they wanted to with, or to me. There were times when they used me for their own pleasure, or passed me around like the bitch I was. My last two years was all about pleasing who ever wanted it. When I was released the first time I came back out on the sheet, and tried to find the same pleasure I had in prison. I stayed out on the sheet for about a year, having sex with different men. One day I decided that I was not happy doing what I was doing out here so I did a small time crime so that I could go back in to prison for a second time.

That I stayed for five years. I went in knowing what I was going to do. I allowed myself to be with the men there for the enjoyment.

This time while I was on here on the sheet I tried to find someone who could be here for me, and give me what I really wanted, but I could not find anyone. So here I am again going back to prison for the sex. On Tuesday morning about 4am, the jailer came to our cell and told Jerry and I to get up, and come with him. He took us down to a room where there were six of us. We were all told to strip so we could be searched before the prison bus got to the jail to pick us up. After the search, we were all given our sheet clothes to put on. It was about 5am, when the prison bus got there, we were hand cuffed then loaded on to the bus for the prison to the prisons.

As I took a seat on the bus I started to fear what was faces me. Jerry and I was sitting next to each other, he do what he could to make me feel better. One thing he said was for me to remember what he had told me about prison life. It took a while for the bus to get to the first prison, once the bus pulled inside of the gate, six of the men were told to get off the bus. The officer said come on girls this is your new home, and you will have a lot of new friends.

The next we made was an old prison, this time Jerry and three other men were told to stand and make their to the front of the bus. The office standing on the outside of the bus, said move girls we don't have all day. They got off the bus, and the doors closed, as the bus pulled though the gate I felt as if I had lose a friend when Jerry got off the bus. The sun was starting to come up when we pulled into the gate of another prison; I knew that this was going to be where I would live for the next ten years of my life. I sat that looking out of the window, there were some inmates on the yarn. They were watching the bus as it made its way closer to the building.

The bus stopped and the officers came up to the bus and waited for the doors to open. When they did one of the officers started talking loudly as we step off the bus. Welcome girls to your new home, as long as you stay out trouble your life will be easier for your time here. Step out line and you will pay for it, remember that we are the bosses here. As we walked into the building we walked down a hallway to a room just the one Jerry had told me about. It had two walls made of glass.

We were about to be process into the prison. There were more than one officers waiting to search us. After they unhand cuffed us, the office told us to remove all of your clothing. Then we are told to everything in a pile on the floor. It was step by step what Jerry had said it would be. The next thing you are told to do is to get on your knees on a bench, which was lined up against the wall, one of the officers said face the wall, lean over and put your head on the wall. At that point one of the white guys started to go off, he was not going to let any of the officers search him. Two of the officers forced him down and put the handcuffs back on him and took out of the room.

Then one of the officers walks up behind me, he told me to reach back and pull my ass cheeks apart, so he can sure that I don't have anything up your ass. I did just what the officer told me to do. He pushed his finger into my tight asshole, and moved it around inside of me forcefully. It took everything in me to bare the pain. What was he trying to do to me? Once he had pulled his finger out of me, he made a statement this one checks out ok. After they had finished check each one of you out. All of us were taken as a group to another room where a there is a table and a Dr. who was there to do an exam, he was an older man who was tall and did smile, he told he to get my ass on the table so I can do my job. As I laid there nake with the officers and the other guys watching. He put his hands on almost every part of my body. The white who was taken out of the room earlier was brought in to the room where we were still in hand cuffs.

Then all of us were taken into a large shower, which is one big stall where we had shower in front of each other and the officers, plus some of the inmates who were standing around watching us. That one white was then hand cuffed to a ring on the wall and two officers washed him. The last thing we did was to go into a room where the officers took pictures of each of nake before we were walked around prison nake with the inmates watching, and some of them talking about what they would like to do to us. As we walked around it seemed as if we had toured the whole place. One by one they started to put us each into cells. One of the white guys who was about my size was put into a cell with a who had tats on his arms.

Then the only Hispanic guy was a smaller man was taken to a cell where three guys were sitting around, they seemed to be waiting to see who was going to end up in that cell. The officer call out to one of them, saying here is your new cellie. Then he told the guy to get into the cell. The next person to be put in to a cell was the only other black man, the guy in the cell was an older man who just sit on the side of his bunk and looked at us. The last white guy was put into what Jerry called an open cell; I could see that there were a lot of beds in the cell. This guy was the one who acted as if he was a bad ass when the officers were searching us. When we got to the cell door the officers said welcome home punk. I was the last on left and it seem that the officer was taking the longest route that he could to a sign me to a cell.

As I walked though the prison nake, I felt as if every man there wanted me in their cell, so he could make me perform sex with them. Well when we did finally get to the cell where I was going to be put. As I stood in front of the cell floor, I could see a tall, well built black man sitting on one of the bunks with a pair shorts and no shirt. The officer said, hi Mac here's someone to keep you company. I had a lot of things running though my mind at that point. When I walked into the cell, I spoke to the man, and then I put my stuff down and started to dress. I may up my bunk, and took a seat on the it and waited for him to say something to me.

It did not take him long, before he said my name is Macwell, what's yours? I answered him saying Javil. Well boy follow the rules and we will get along ok. Something inside of me just had to ask, what rules are you talking about? Right now I am talk the prison rules, I don't any trouble. We will talk about my rules later. After he said that I could only wonder what he was thinking. I started to remember what Jerry had told me a bout his first time in prison.

He said that his first day in prison longest day to him. That when the cells were locked and the lights were turned down, he was given to two chooses. He could become his cellmate's bitch on his own or he would do what he would have to take me. He watched him undress in the dim lighted cell. He started wondering what he was going to do to him. Once he was nake he came over to his bunk and sat down beside him. He put his arm around Jerry, and said its time for you to make up your mind. At that point he said please don't hurt me. If you let me have my way I will take it easy on you, but if I have to make you do what I want then it's going to hurt. Then he put his hand on top of mines, he ask what is your name? The man's name was Russ.

He made sure that I knew he meant business about what he wanted. Its time to get these clothes off, when I tried to move away he pulled me back to him with so force. I said take off your clothes now. He pulled my shirt over my head, and throws it on the floor. Then he rubbed my chest and said you have a nice body. Next he stood up and pulled my to my feet, holding me with one hand and undoing my pants with the other. Once they fell to the floor he pull down my underwear. Feeling his hand on my ass, he turned me around bend me over, that's when he rubbed his hard dick on my ass cheeks. Relax I'll take it easy; I know its first time. I allowed him to get what he wanted that night. He was the first man to bust my ass open. It did hurt because it was my first time, but giving myself to Russ saved me from getting raped or worst at the hands of some of the other men in the prison.

I started thinking about what had happened to him, and how I was going to things if this man wanted to have sex with me. I know that I do not want to try and fight him or any one I just want to do my time and get out here. Well ten years is a long time to be locked with no one to help you out. Maybe Mac will not try to do anything to me. Well I would have to wait until later. When it was time for us to leave our cell he told me to stay close to me.

My fears started when the cell doors were closed and locked. I sat on you bunk not knowing what to say or do, because I was scared of what Mac might do. Well he got up from his bunk and went over to the toilet and took a piss. Then he turned around with his dick hanging out of his pants, he walked over to the sink and washed it. After putting it away he went back over to his bunk and started to undress. I could not keep from watching him. He took off thing but is underwear, and then he laid down on his bunk. Are you going to sleep in your clothes or what? Mac asked me. I said no I am not, and started to undress. Once I was down to my underwear and t-shirt, he said come over here so we can talk about my rules.

I did not want to go over to his bunk, because I feared what he might try to do to me. Was he going to rape me, or make sure that he could get what he wanted by beating up then rape. In a low voice he repeated what he had said come over here so we can talk about my rules. I got up from my bunk and walked over to Mac's bunk. He told me to sit down beside him. I sat down on the bunk next to him, and waited to hear what he had to say. He kept laying there, and then he began to talk to me in a low voice. I do not want to hurt you, but I do want to have sex with you. I know that this is your first time in prison, and I can see it in your face that you are scare as hell. Now the facts are if you don't give up your sweet tight ass to me. I will not be able to take some of these men in here from using you as their bitch.

As for me I want to be your friend, I said a friend that want to fuck me in the ass. He said well when I saw you get off the bus this morning something took over me. I watched as they did everything that they had to you, seeing you nake was really good. I did what I had to do to get you put in here with me. After talking to the officer, he let me know that you had not been fucked before. I know that you may not believe this but I really want to be your man. Now if you allow me to I can make you feel real good tonight.

I was watching Mac as he took off his underwear, one he was nake he told me to take off what's left of your clothes, and let down here with me. I stood up and undressed, then I laid down, he slowly turned me over on my side facing away from him, he got right up close to me and put his arm round me holding in place. As I laid there I was getting sleepy, but I was scared as hell to fall asleep, because I thought if he knew I was sleep that he would rape me. I cannot say how long we laid there before he made his move. I felt his hand move under the cover, down to my ass where he put his finger between my ass cheeks trying to find my asshole. Once there he slowly rubbed his finger over it and around it.

In my heart I knew what he wanted to do, I just laid there and let him do what he was doing. He stopped and pulls the covers off of us, and got up from his bunk. I watched as he walked over to the self on the wall he reached up and took something down. He came back to the bunk and turned me on to my back than he spread my legs and got between them. Next he lifted my legs and put them on his shoulders. I felt him rub something between the cheeks; I knew that he was getting me ready for him to fuck. I was partly willing to let him do what he wanted. I did not feel anything for a moment. He was putting on a rubber, and then he found my tight hole with his dick head. It hurt when it popped in, Mac did not push it, he just let it stay where it was. After what just seemed like moments he pushed in more.

Mac took his time before he started to fuck my ass. It was more like he was making love to me and not just fucking to rape me. Believe me there was pain at first, but as he went on with what he was do it started to ease off. After he had finished Mac pull out from inside from my body, he got up from the bunk and went over to the sink where he started to wash up. He told me to come to get and clean my self up, I did. Once we both had finished he put his arm around my waist and walked with me back over to the bunk where he laid me down, then he laid next holding me in his arms. While lying there I started asking myself why did I let this man do this to me? I had never had any gay thoughts before. Did I let my fear take over, and was doing this as away of protection?

Maybe now he will look out for me, and wont let anyone hurt me. I found it hard to fall asleep, while lying here I started to hear cries for help, this went on for a while then it stopped. Mac also had heard it, he said that someone was getting beaten or raped. Then he said now baby boy you wont have to worry about anyone doing anything to you because you belong to me. You have followed rule one in the right way. Now as long as you make sure you follow my other rules I will protect you. I just had to know what his rules were. He said well as long as you carry your self as my woman, and do the thing that a man's wife do for him things will ok. Step out line then I will have to do something about that.

Finally I did fell asleep, the next morning when we were woken up by the officer, and the lights coming on. The officers informed us to get ready for the showers. Mac and I got up from the bunk where we slept the night before. He told me to get my towel and wrap it around my waist. When I did, he not like that, in here when you belong to a man you have to wear your towel in the right way. He walked over to me and took the towel from around my waist, and showed the way I had to wear it from now on. The towel had to be folded in half the long way then wrapped back around my waist. The way it was folded if I bend over anyone could see under it.

Once in the shower Mac let every man there know that I was now his woman and now I was off limit to everyone but him, then he pulled the towel from around me, and without any warning he turned me around so that everyone could see my ass. He made me spread my legs, and then he pushed his finger up my score asshole. Saying this pussy belong to me. After we had gotten back into our cell Mac said I know that you did not like was I did in the shower, but I had to let these guys know that you belong to me or you would have been marked for rape or worst. Guys like you that don't belong to anyone, will be rape or beaten up.

The two of us got dressed and went to breakfast, and then it was time for to get out into the yarn for a while, as we walked Mac told me to stay with him the whole time we are outside. Now Javil don't get upset with me when I do things around these guys, I am only doing it to protect you. While outside we found a table, I had to sit next to him with his arm around me. He lean over and told me to put my hand on his dick, I did what he said. While outside another group of guys came out. One of them was the white guy who had acted like he was so bad when we were being processed in.

Someone in the group started talking loud about what they had done to a punk last night. At first I did not know who they were talking about until one of them pulled the guy out so everyone could see him. He said last night we had the bitch crying while we were breaking in his ass. Then another guy said he could take a lot dick, last night he took thirty. If there anyone who what to try him out today, his is for sale. He is willing to suck dicks and anyone can fuck me. I started think that I could be in his place right now.

Later that night when we were alone in our cell Mac wanted us to have sex again, there was pain at first, but as he went on with what he was doing to me the pain slowly act he was doing to me the pain eased off some, and I some how started to feel some enjoyment from the sex we were having. I most tell you that I have never been gay, but there was something going on that I can't explain. After being in prison for two weeks I found out what happened to the little Hispanic guy that can into prison the same I did. One day while I sitting in my cell some other inmates were talking about how the guys on his cell block was using him as a sex slave. They had raped him and was using him for their pleasure and passing him around to other men. I felt sorry for him just as I did for anyone was being used in that way.

Well I guess some would say that I am being used too, but Mac is not treating me the way that some inmates are being treated. Yes I do things for him, plus I do allow him to have sex with me. As the months passed I found my self-feeling things for Mac that I had never for any man before. We both knew that his time was getting shorter, so we had talked about what he want to happened between the two of us. He said that I had become very important to him, and did not want lose me, but we knew that once he left this prison I would have to be here for another year and a half. He told me that he would understand that if after he was gone I was with another man until my time was done. He also said that he would a way to keep in touch with me until him and I could be together again.

That morning officer came to our cell to tell Mac to get his stuff together, because he was going home. Before he left he told me not to forget what he had told me, then he looked at me and mouthed I will write you as soon as I can. Two days later a new guy was moved into my cell. That first night we sat and talked to each other like men, and I let him know that I was not going to use by him or any one else. A few days after that one inmate from my cell block told him I was not to be messed with because I belonged to someone, and that him and some of the other men on the block was told to watch over me until my time was up.

It was a Monday when I got a letter from a woman by the name of Jolisa Scott, she told me that her cousin had told her about me, so she was writing in hope to get to know me better. At first I didn't know what was really going on until I got to the point where she said that she will be waiting for me to get out and come to be with her. That's when it hit me that Mac was behind the letter. We wrote each other from that first letter until the day before I was released from prison.

I remember that day so well, it was on a Tuesday morning when an officer came to my cell door and told me to get my stuff together because I was getting to go home. As I was getting what I was going to take with me together, and packing. I started thinking about how was I going to get to see Mac, I also thought that he may not want to see me at all, he could have been just telling me what he thought I wanted to hear until he found someone else on the outside. I told that I would taken to the bus station where I could a ticket back home. On the ride I knew that I was going to try and call Mac. I had a phone that Jolisa had put in more than one of the letter I had gotten. When I got inside the station I used the pay phone to cal the number. A woman answered the phone; I asked for Mac, she told me to hold on for a moment.

He came to the phone, hello this is Mac, I said this is Javil I was released this morning and I am in the bus station. Hi baby boy I'm glad to hear your voice, and I am ready to see you, I have been missing you so much. He told me to buy a ticket for the town in which he was living, and then call him back to let him know what time the bus would out, so he could meet me when I got there, I agreed. I went a got the ticket and asked what time the bus would leave. The man told me that it would pull out in about 15 min. I then went back to the pay phone called Mac again, this time he answered the phone, I told him that it would about 15 min. before I leave here, he said it takes 30 min by bus to get here, and that he would be at the station waiting. When the bus was called I got on and sat next to a window. I was happy to be free, but at the same time I had some fear about how things might turn out with Mac. As I road the 30 min to get to where he was I had a lot of things running though my mind. I asked my self was Jolisa really his cousin or was she his woman on the outside.

When the bus pulled into the station I took my time getting off, I don't know why maybe I was scared. As I stepped down from the last step I felt weak or something, then I asked my self was this really happening? Just then I look up and Mac was standing only a few feet away from me. I could not move at it seemed, he was looking the same as he did the day he was released from the prison. I wanted to run over to him and put my arms around him, but I didn't how he would react. Things happened so fast, before I could react he was hugging me, baby boy I have been waiting to get to hold you in my arms again, it's been a long few months without you. Come on let's get out of here, I have a surprise for you at the house.

As we walked to a car that was parked in front of the station, I saw a woman sitting in the driver seat. My mind started to race again, but before I could really start thinking to crazy, Mac said before you get the wrong idea baby boy this is Jolisa my cousin, who I had to write my letters to you. So how he knew what was going though my mind. One at the car she spoke to me and smile, then she said I am glad that you are finally here, because Mac was about to go crazy these last months worrying about you. He open the front passenger said door so I could get in and took the bags I had and put them in the back seat with him.

They lived only about two blocks from the station, when we pulled into the driveway Mac got out of the car first, he open the car door for before I could do it. He carried my bags as we walked up to the front door. Jolisa opened the door and then sees looked at saying come on in and makes your self at home. When I walked in the doorway I started to feel a pressure left from me. Mac put his arm around my waist and said lets take your things to our room. As we walked to the back of the house, we were headed for a door that was closed. Once in front of the door he told me to open it, before

I could move Mac picked me up in his arms and carried me into the room.

The first thing I saw was one bed in the middle of the room, he kicked to door close behind us. He took a few steps then laid me down on the bed; before I could say a word he leaned over and kissed me. When the kiss was broken he looked in to my eyes saying this is our bedroom baby boy, lay right here while I get your things. He walked back to the door and opened it, then he bend over and pick up the bags I had, and brought them into the room. He closed the once again, this he put my bags down in a chair next to the door. He came back and laid down on the bed with me, he put his arms around me, holding for a while without saying anything.

Jolisa came to the door and knocked, she said I am going to work now I will see the two of you later. Mac answered her saying ok. He said that I've better tell this now, when I looked at I must had a worried look on face, because he said don't baby its nothing bad, I just wanted you to know that I also have a job, but my boss gave me two days off since you were coming home. Man I love the looks you do, Jolisa is my boss, and she knows all about the two of us. This morning when you called to let me know that you were out, and that you wanted to come here she told me to take the next two days off to be with you, me and her have always been close since we were kids, when I got out she was here for me, and gave me a job. Plus she has also gave you a job too you will start on Thursday. What do you think about that? Well I am happy to know that I will have a job. Then he said and a place to live, right here with me.

The two of spent most of the day just having fun, and playing around with each other. When we got hungry Mac and I went out and got something to eat, then we came back to the house and spent more time just being free. I was wondering what the surprise was that he had for me. I did not ask him anything about it. Later that night before we got into bed we took turns taking lone showers. When we both got back into bedroom, it felt good to know that we were the only two in the room. As we stood beside the bed he put he arms around me and gave me a kiss. Once we broke our kiss he pulled the covers back on the bed. As I started to walk over to the bed he reached out and stopped me. He would not let move, because he had a plan, which was to undress me, so I did the same to him.

Then we walked over to the bed together, I had idea just how special our first night out side of prison would really be. Because it was going to be the first time that Mac would allow me to make love to him. When he told me what he wanted me to do, I was really taken by surprise. He explain to me that he had a lot of time to think about how he really felt about me, and that he wanted to do everything he could to make me happy once I got out. Well after that night things really started going good for us. I started to work for Jolisa. Mac and I worked together but not doing the same type of job. Friday even when got off of work Jolisa told us that she was going to take us out to dinner. The three of us went home and change clothes, and then we went to eat.

The next morning when we got up Mac asked me if I had called my parents to let them know that I was out, and where I was living. I said no I have not called, he told me to go into the living room and make the call. That's what I did they were happy to hear from me. I did not know how to tell them about Mac, so I just took a deep breath and said I need to tell you something, about the person that I met. My mother was the first one to say what is it. I said well his name is Macwell and he has been very nice to me both in prison and since I have been out. I am living with him and his cousin. She also gave me a job, which I started working Thursday. I will be writing from time to time to let you know I am ok. Mac said you can call them whenever you want.

On Sunday Mac took me to meet his family, which was made up of his parents, along with two brothers and three sisters, plus their families. About two months later we went to visit my family. My family seemed to like Mac and Jolisa. When we got back home, things got better for us as time went on. Now five years later we are still together, but living in a house of our own, and working Jolisa. But of us decided to go to the local community college for two years. Its funny some time where and how love seems to find you. Our hearts does crazy things some times. Going to prison was one of the better things happened to me. That may sound funny to most people, but if I had not gone, I may have been dead by now, and I would have never have met Macwell.

This was is my life, and I am very happy with the way things turned out.

Our Summer Trip

JT and I were young High School students in a small town. The end of the school year was coming up in a few weeks, and we wanted to have some fun over our summer break. As we sat in his bedroom we tried to come up with ideas on what we could do. My Grand father lived near a bigger city, and he was an older man, so I came up with an idea that we could there and stay with him. Then we could go to the city and have some fun. Both of us were big for our ages. JT agreed to that so we decided to talk to our parents about it. The next day we started to work on our parents. By the end of the week we had to ok. My father called my Grand father to ask if we could come for a visit, he said that we could spend the summer with him.

It was two days before the last day of school and JT and I had packed our bags for the trip. We spent a lot of time talking about what we were going to do. The last day of school was on a Wednesday, but we had to wait until Friday for my parent to take us to the bus station. As we rode in my father's van our parent told all the dos and don'ts. When we got to the bus station my father called my Grand father to let him know that we would there about 7:00 that evening, he agreed to meet us at the bus station there. When our bus was called our parents told us to call them when we got there. JT and I both had cell phones so we could talk to them as much as we wanted to.

As we got on the bus we sat beside each other and waved to our parents as the bus pulled off. About two hours later we arrived at the bus station, once we got off the bus and walked into the station my Grand father was sitting there waiting. After we said hello, we got our things and went to his car. We loaded our things in the car then we drove to his house a few miles away. Once there he gave the chose to have our own rooms or we could share a room. We wanted to share a room together. My Grand father smiled and said I know that the two of you will be up late talking and playing around, just like your father did when he had some of his friends to spend the night. By the way I was named after my father, which was named Howard, my Grand father always called me little Howard.

That night my Grand father took us into the city to a movie and dinner. The two of us stayed up late talking with the lights out. One thing that we agreed on was that we would wait until next week before we go in to the city on our own. The next day Grand pa let us sleep as late as we needed to. We got up he was waiting to see to it that we eat, then he took us out to show around his place there was a lot of land, and some animals to see. He told us that he was going to let us be kids, and have fun. JT and I had fun with Grand pa.

A few days and nights passed then we decided that we were going to leave the next night for the city, and then we would come back before we were missed. It was on a Friday night when we waited for my Grand pa to go to sleep before we got up and dressed. We slipped out of the house and started on our way to the city. Well it was a big difference to what we were used to seeing. The two of us walked around and took in the sites. Later that night we went back to the house and got back in the bed. The next day Grand pa didn't know that we had left at all. A week later we did it again, that time was about the first time, there was one thing we did not know. We were being watched. The next weekend that we went into the city a man came to us and asked us how old we were, we told him that we were 18 years old. He told us that it wasn't safe for us on the sheet.

He befriended us and showed us around the city then he took us back to the city limits. We walked back to the house and got into bed. The next night we tried it again, but this time things started out different. When we got into the city we saw the man again. So we spent our time with him. This time we were allowed to drink some beer, we only got high. We told him that we could not come back into the city until the next weekend. That's what we did, this time things went wrong for us. He took us to a house that he said was his. He gave us more beer, after drinking the beer I was really out of it.

That's when things started happening. Another man came in the room where we were, the two of them carried us to another room. There were more men waiting there. I heard some one say it's about time, now we can have some fun. I could not stand on my own, I looked for JT and I saw two men holding him just as two were holding on to me. I watched as JT was being undressed by some one. I felt that I was telling them to stop, but was I? I realized that I was being undressed too. Then I was helped to a cart in the middle of the room. I was placed on the cart face down, I tried to move but I could not do any thing, because my hands were fixed to the cart sides.

I look over and there was JT laying on another cart naked. As I felt some one touch my naked body, I heard him say these two are soft and sweet. Some one asked were did you find these two cuties? I hope they are ready to party. Then the room lit up when they turned on the bright lights. We are going to train them to be men pleasers. I could see some men undressing around us; I was scared of what they were going to do to us. I had a felling that these men were going to hurt us. I tried to move again, but I could barely move my legs. I still could not get off the cart.

I felt someone touching my ass. Then my cheeks were pulled apart and someone said this is the hole of a virgin, this cherry need to be busted. Whose going to be first? I knew that my tight asshole was going to be the target for one of these men. I had never had anything like this done to me before. I felt my legs being sprayed open, I felt someone getting on the cart with me. He was slowly stretching my tender asshole with his hard dick or something. There was a lot of pain. I cried out in pain, he was the first of many men who raped me that night. I could hear JT crying as he also was be raped.

Later that night when they let us go, we made our way to the house. We held on to each once we got into bed out fear. The next morning we agreed that we could not tell anyone what happened to us, because if we did they would say that we wanted it. When we went into the kitchen my grand pa was ready to cook us breakfast. The two of us did do our best to eat something, because we did not want him to think anything was wrong with us. We spent that day helping my grand pa out with some of he work around the farm. That was before he told us to just go on and have us some fun, and let him do the work. JT and I left him to work while we walked around the farm, and talked.

The two of us spent some time talking about what had happened to us the night before. We agreed that we would not go back into the city at night. Later that day when we were sitting in the house with grand pa watching TV some body came to the front door and knocked. Grand pa got up and went to the door. When he walked back into the living room there was a man with him. My heart dropped when I saw who he was, it was the man we met in the city. He was the one who had done this to us, but we could not tell my grand pa who he was. Grand pa told us that his name was Joe, and that he owned the game room in the city. I have known him since he was about 10 years old when his parents moved here from NM.

I watched him grow up. Joe spoke I heard that Mr. Worthington was going have two young guest for the summer. I him that the two of you can come to the game room and enjoy yourself for free. My grand pa said he is here to take you boys to the game room for while today. I looked at JT and he looked at me. I did not want to go anywhere with this man, but if we told my grand pa that we did not want to go he would feel that something was wrong. Little Howard I know that you and JT are like your father was at your age, you love to play any kind of games, so go and have a good time. He reach into his packet to give us some money, but the man said you have to done that sir I will take very care of the boys for you.

He had this big smile on his face as he looked at us. When we went out to his car both JT and I got into the back seat, as we sit there while we drove into the city. Joe said I got some to show the two of you; last night you became starts in your own move. When we got into the city he took us to his business, once we got inside he told us to follow him into his office. When he closed the door, he told us to have a sit. Then he turn on the TV and VCR as we sat there we watched everything that him and the other men had done to us the night before.

As I sat there reliving every moment as I watching the video, I thought that my heart was going to stop beating. JT and I just sat there unable to speak. Once he had turned the video off, he looked at us smiling, what do you think about your first movie boys? JT and I looked at each other and we both started to cry. There is no need to cry, as long as you do what you are told your grand father will not find out what you have been up to. Though my tears I was able to ask why us. Well little Howard when your grand father told me that you and your young friend here were coming to visit hi for the summer. I decided to tell my friends. After talking about I knew that the two of you would be just right for our enjoyment.

Don't worry you are not the first to make us happy men. The other boys used to live around here, but after they got older they moved away, so we had to find someone to take their places. Well as long as you don't tell anyone about our little game, no one but us will know just what you can do. Now its time for you to stop this foolish crying, and get back to work. What are you going to do to us JT asked? We are going to meet my friends and have some more fun like we did last night. I said no, we are not going with you. That's when Joe looked into our faces and said you are going, putting his hands on our shoulders.

He forced us to walk out of the building with him, telling us to get into the car, and don't try anything with you don't want to get hurt. At time another man walked, what took you so long? Well the boys wanted to get ready first. Then all of us got into the car, the four of us road to the same house that we had been taking to last night. This time was worst that the first time because we were no drugged, and the force was more real. Once in the house we were told to take off our clothes, we don't have that much time to do what we have in mind.

JT and I were taken into the room where they had raped us the first time. One of the men said that it is going to be more fun this time because they will have some life in them. Then they grabbed us and forced us down on to the beds face down, holding us down as they raped over and over again. The pain was more that real; each man did everything they wanted to both of us. I don't know how long this went on, but when it was over one of the men show us where to bathroom was and told us to clean up. After washing up and getting dress, Joe took us back to my grandfather house. On the way he told us not to say a word to anyone and he will pick us up tomorrow, by the way you new movie will be ready when I pick you up. Have a good night boys, and get some rest so you will be ready for us.

When we got inside the house my grand pa was sitting in the living room watching TV. He asked did the two of you have a good time today at the game room? JT and I said yes, because we knew that we could tell him what really had happened to us. Then he said I knew that you enjoy yourself, dinner is ready so let get something to eat. We follow him into the kitchen and washed our hands, then we sat down at the table to eat. After eating the three of went but into the living room, and watched TV before we got in to bed. JT and I laid in bed holding each tight most of the night. We woke up early the next morning the two of us laid in bed talking softly so that my grand pa would not hear us.

Grand pa knocked on the door, telling to get up so we could get ready for breakfast. We got out bed, and took turn in the bathroom to wash up, and then we went into the kitchen where my grand pa was fixing breakfast. As we eat breakfast, had a sick feeling that we were not going to be able to stop what we knew was going to happen to us? How were we going to get out of be raped again? The phone ranged and my grand pa got up to answer it. When he did JT and I looked at each other, I could see the fear in his eyes. That's when grand pa turned and asked us are you ready to go back to the game room? I wanted to say no, but I knew that I could not tell him what was really going on.

So I said yes out of fear. He told the person on the phone that we were ready. After hanging up the phone he said that Joe would be to pick us up in about 15 min. there was no way to get out going, because grand pa waited until Joe came before he went to do his work. As we drove into town Joe told us that he was going to take us straight to the house, so that we can get started today. Well our time at that house was a repeat of the day before. I wonder when will this nightmare before over? On the way back to my grand pa's house Joe told us that he was going to pick us up in the morning. That night my grand pa saved us from another day of rape. He told us that he was going to take us with him to get some supplies for the farm.

Once JT and I got into bed we held each other and talked about how happy we were that my grand pa was taking us with him in the morning. As we laid in bed I heard the phone ring. After a few moments my grand pa came to the bedroom door and knocked. Little Howard that was your father on the phone, they are coming to pick the two of you up in the morning. I said ok, then I asked JT did you hear that we are going home, and this will be over. I could feel him starting to cry in my arms.

The next morning JT and I got up early and packed, so that when my father got there we would be ready to go. About 8 o'clock he drove up. Once in the living room he told grand pa that he needed to explain why he had to come and get JT and I up a few days early. It was because him and JT's father was going out of town on a business trip for the company they worked for. On the drove back to home I felt that that things was going to be all right. It seemed that it took a long time to get home, but once we did I asked if JT could spend the night at my house. When JT's parents got there my father ask them if he could stay the night. Well they did agree, and we spent that night with each other.

It felt so good to be miles away from Joe, and the things that he did to us. I did however wonder if somehow my parents would fine out what happened while we at grand pa's house. Weeks passed and school started, on the first day JT and I ended up with all of our classes together. This was our first year in High School, but we could not forget about the trip we took that summer. As the months passed we did what we hade to do to make it though. On the last day of school we found out that we were going on to the 12th grade. That year went by fast, before we knew it the last day of school was at hand, and we were headed to the 12th grade. JT and I spent a lot of time together as we always did. The two of us were as close as any two friends could be; we started to talk about what we might do once we graduated from high school. We both wanted to go to college; we talked about going to the same college.

After our last year in high school JT and I ended up going to different colleges. We wrote to each other to keep in touch. It seemed that we both studied hard, but I found out that JT had been up to a lot more than studying. Though someone I cam to know I learned that he was having sex with men for money. I was told that this had been going on for months before I found out about it.

One night I made up my mind to go and look for him, so I drove for five hours to get to the college where he was going. At first I could not find him, then after waiting for over an hour, he came to his dorm. When he walked in and saw me, he did not speak or anything. The only thing he did was to break down and started crying. Then I watched as he fell to the floor. I went over to where he was sitting and sat down beside him, putting my arms around him, holding him close to me. When he did speak to me the only thing he said was "I'm sorry".

We sat there for I don't know how long before I helped him to his feet, the two of us walked over to him bed where we sat still holding each. I felt that I wanted to cry, but I was doing my best to hold it in. I couldn't the tears started fall down my face. I was hurting for him as well as myself. Plus I was feeling something inside of me that I could not explain. About that time JT looked into my face. The next thing I knew we shared a kiss. It brought out something from deep inside me that made me feel so warm, and happy.

I asked JT to come back with me, so I could help him. "I don't want to be like this," he said in a soft voice. I reach out and touched face, and repeated what I said again, please come back with me. Ok he replied I missed you so much. We packed his stuff and carried it to my car, and we drove back to my apartment. That first night was both crazy and wonderful at the same time. My place had only one bedroom, so I told JT to take my bed, and I would sleep on the sofa in the living room, he told me that he did not want to be alone. Will you please stay in the room with me? I really need you.

JT and I undressed and got into bed together, I laid there wanting to reach out and touch him, but I just laid there. Later that night JT reached out for me, when I felt his touch, it awoke something inside of me, so I rolled over and put my arm around him. I held him for the rest of that night. The next morning I awoke still holding him. I realized what was going on inside of me, I had strong feelings for JT, and I knew it was going to hard for me to hind them from him for long.

As I lay there I had a lot of thoughts going though my mind. When he woke up and looked at me I knew that I could lose him again, I had to tell him how I felt. Before he could say a word, I said JT I love you, and I want us to be together. How can you love me after what I have done? He asked. I said I don't care what has happened; I want you to stay here with me. Please let me love you. I know that most people don't believe in love between two men, but I have to tell you that it can really be for real.

It's been over 10 years, and JT and I are still together and happy. We live in the town where I went to college and we both have good jobs now. The things that happened to us that summer we spent at my grand pa's changed our lives forever. Each night that I hold him in my arms makes our love grow stronger. Maybe I will return to let you know how things are going in another 10 years or so. For now JT and I will say goodbye for now.

Hard Core Prison

A story of private minimum-security prison, and the men who spent years behind its walls, the story came from both guards and inmates. The first person we spoke to was a guard that we will call C.K. he told us that he started to work at the prison when he was 22 years old. Remembering the interview he had with the warden/owner of the prison. Once inside the office, he was asked to take a sit across the deck from the older man who was going to make a decision to hirer him or not. It started out the way that any other interview would have, but then things changed, when the warden asked C.K. to stand up and remove all of his clothes. He asked the question why; the answer was he wanted to see everything that C.K. had to afford. With out saying another word he did as he was asked, he stood there nake in front of this man.

The warden got up from his seat and walked around C.K., so he could see every part of his body. Once he had done that, the warden told he that he was now an employee of the prison. He was to start on the following Monday. His first day on the job was very different from what he had thought it was going to be. After being taken into a room with three other men who was there for their first day. They were told all the rules that they had to go by. There was one rule that he found hard to understand; we were told that we had to have sex with the inmates and/or with each other. C.K. said that he told it as a joke, thought no more of it for a while.

After that meeting we were taken on a tour of the prison, were we show the inmates walking around in only white briefs and t-shirts, I remember that one of the other men asked why didn't the men have on their clothes? We were told that in this prison the inmates only allowed to wear their underwear, until the warden allow visits from family members. Then they can wear the uniforms that they had. As we walked pass a cell there were inmates having sex openly. They did not care that they were being watched. As we toured the prison we show some inmates in their cells laying on bunks nake, and playing with themselves sexually.

There were other men who walked around nake all together. The guards nor the other inmates seemed to mind what was going on. When we go back to the office we were told that you new guys are going to get the chance to see how new inmates are taken though the intake process. They took us to a door, then one of the officers opened it, there were six fully nake men and two guards. We watched, as they were lead down a hallway, passed other inmates who stood around watching them, and making comments. As we walked in to the room, we watched as each man was told to bend over and spread their ass cheeks, then one of the officers who had on a pair of rubber gloves greased the man's ass. After that they he reached for a hose which he in pushed into the man's hole, then the water was turned on to flush him out. He was told to set down on the toilet, the office reached between the man's opened legs and pulled the hose out.

Once the man was flushed out he was told to get on a table, and lay down. Then open his legs wide so that the office can access his hole. Net to the table was a TV monitor, the office picked up a equipment which was connected to the monitor, he slowly push it into the man's hole, and watched the monitor while he slowly fucked his hole. After a few moments he pull it out, and told the new inmate to get off of the table. Another one took his place until each man had been done the same way. This was done while we were in the room, along with the other guards. Plus on the other side of a glass wall other prison inmates were also allowed to watched what was going on.

The six new inmates were then walked out of the room and down another hallway, into a room were the prison Doctor was waiting. Each of the men were asked to get on a table where he touched their bodies sexually from head to toe. After the doctor had finished the men were walked down to a big shower room to take a shower. Then they were taken into another room where each man was measured for his underwear and uniform. Before being walked around the prison they were given a set sheets, pillowcase and a bar of soap, washcloth, and jar of lubrication and a box of rubbers, which they were told to use. The six men were lined up in a row on a wall while the warden told them what the rules of the prison were. One 1 thing that he said really made me wonder he said you have 24 hours to get your asses fucked on your own, before it will be done for you. Don't worry no one is going to rape you.

After being given a tour of the whole prison, each new inmate was put into a cell with two other inmates. Whom they would share the cell with for their time in the prison. That was my first day on the job at the prison.

Next we talked to a guy who was an inmate at the prison, who we call W.P. can you tell us what you went though while you were in the prison. Well it all started on the day that I went in front the judge, and he gave me 10 years in prison. I remember taking what seemed to be a long trip from the jail I was in to the prison where I was going to spend 10 years of my life. As we got out of the van the guards walked us up to a door, where he pushed a button, then the door open by a guard would worked at the prison. Once we walked inside a small room, the guard closed the door behind us. He told us to take off our clothes. The room was small with only one window, which was in the second door. We were each told to place our clothes in brown paper bags and write our name on it. Then we had to pass it to the guard behind a counter.

Then the second door was opened, so we could walk though it. As we stepped into the hallway we saw a lot of men standing around in their underwear. We had to walk pass them to get to the next room. Once in that room each one of us was told to open our legs and stand over a toilet, bend over and spread our ass cheeks. A guard greased our asshole, the guard pushed this thing put our ass, then turned on the water. It filled my inside up, it hurt some. I was asked to sit down on the toilet, once the water was turned off, the guard pulled the hose out of my asshole. I felt my body emptying out.

When I was told to get on the table, I did as I was asked. I had to hold my legs open like someone who was about to get fucked. Well that just what happened. One of the guards pushed something up my ass and slowly fucked my hole with it. When he finished what had to do, he pulled it out. I was told that could get off of the table. We stood there until each man was done, then we were lead though another door this time we walked pass more men until we got a room where a man stood waiting for us to be brought to him. This man played with my nipples, nuts dick and ass like he was enjoying what he was doing.

The last room we went into a guy made sure that we would be wearing tight fitting underwear, and uniforms. As officer C.K. told you we were walked around the whole prison, then we each placed into cells. The cell I was carried to had two other men. One was a younger man the other was an older one. As I walked into the cell the younger one was laying on his bunk nake, and the older man was standing next to his bunk in his underwear. I knew that the only bunk left was going to be mine's for next few years, so I walked in and said hi. Then I put my stuff down and started to make up my bunk. While sitting on my bunk I asked them when would I get my clothes. The older guy name T.D. told me that I might get them sometime tomorrow.

We then started talking about the other things that happens in the prison. T.D. asked if the warden had talked to us about how to follow the rules here. The number one rule is that each man here had to get fucked within 24 hours after they come in to the prison. Well my first time was with the doctor when he was doing my exam T.D. said. Then went on to tell me what happened to the younger guy. His name was J.J. his first time was the day he got here and they turned him in to a porn star for every one to watch. The guards took him in to a room where six other inmates were used to turn him out sexually.

After T.D. talked to me, I sat on my bunk nake thinking about what he had told me. Trying to make up my mind on what I was going to do. I was a full-blooded man, and I had never had sex with a man in my life. Now I was sitting in a prison where warden makes sex one of the rules that you have to follow. Well that night I made up my mind that I had to do it my own will, or be forced later. I watched as J.J. laid on his bunk and fingered is ass hole. I got up and walked over to his bunk, and sat down beside of him. Then I reached out and touched his chest. T.D. was sitting on his bunk; I knew he was watching what was happening between J.J. and myself.

I allowed him to suck my dick until it was hard, then I put on a rubber and had sex with him. Once it was over I knew that it now my turn to give up my ass to one of them or get fucked by someone else that is picked out by the warden or a guard, or maybe it may be more than one man. I was still laying on top of J.J. when T.D. came over and touched my ass. I knew what he had on his mind. I just laid there waiting to see what was he was going to do. I did not have to wait for long. He parted my cheeks and pushed his finger into my ass, slowly finger fucking my tight hole. He wanted to fuck me, and I knew it. J.J. put his hands on my ass cheeks and held them open for T.D. He slowly pulled his finger out. Then he told me to spread my legs, I did what he wanted. Only moments past before I felt the head of his dick against my hole. The pain was red hot; I did what I could to relax.

There I was being fucked by a man, it seemed as if time was moving real slow. Finally it was over, and the three of laid there for a while then we got and took turns cleaning up. I had no idea that the next day every one would watch what happen all over the prison on TV. It was the next afternoon when we were sitting in our cell when there it was a movie of T.D. busting my ass, while J.J. held me for him. I knew I was willing, but seeing it on TV was not what I had wanted. I was sitting still nake, because I had not been given any clothes as of yet. I could hear some of the other inmates talking, saying things like I can bet that the new ass was good. I wish that I could get some of it. That hole should be still tight and wet. I would like to get him alone long enough to stick my dick up his ass.

My heart started to racing and mind was reeling, I looked over at T.D. who was laying on his bunk, just looking at the TV. It must have felt that I was looking at him. He turned his head and looked at me. He said you know if you want to be with any of these men in here you can, cause no one belongs to any one, that's the rules in here. The warden wants it to be a free for all, that's his way of making us pay. Even the guards fucks us, and we can fuck them too, so you better get use to the way things are around here. About that time a guy walked up to the door of our cell, and stood there looking. Then he took off his shirt and underwear right there in front of us, and said who wants to have sex? Then he walked over to me and stood in front of me with his dick right in my face. Why don't you suck on this for a while?

I reached out and took his dick in my hand and rubbed. Then I did allow him to put it in my mouth. It got hard and I knew what was going to happen next, he was going to want to fuck me. When he pulled out of my mouth, I looked up at him. I could see the look on his face, so I laid back on my bunk and waited for him to put on a rubber and get on the bunk with me. He got just what he wanted with J.J. and T.D. right there. I didn't know that some other inmates had come to the cell to watch the show, but when it was over and he got up. I saw the others standing on the other side of the bars playing with their dicks and smiling. It was not over yet, he told now it's your turn to fuck me. We changed places, and I did fuck this guy while the other watched.

Once it was over the two of us got up from my bunk, the guy picked up his underclothes and walked out of the cell nake. Some of the other guys left too. There were one or two guys still left standing in the doorway of the cell. I did some thing that was new to me; I walked over to J.J. and laid face down on the bunk next to him. He put his hand on my ass, I spread my legs, and so he could put his hand between my ass cheeks. I allowed him to fuck me. That was the start of my sexual life in this prison.

Welcome to the interview we are going to call you W.S. how long were you a guard there? I was there for over 20 years. Tell us about when you worked there. Yes I did the sex thing while I worked there just as the other men there. We all did what the warden wanted us to do. Maybe I should tell you about my first time. I was 22 years old and it was my third day on the job, but it was the time having my ass fucked. The warden sent for me to come to his office. When I walked in there were three other guards already there. Plus there were two inmates, who were standing in the room nake. The warden told me to remove my clothes. I didn't want to, but I knew I did not have a choose. So I took off my clothes, and waited to see what he was going to tell me to do next. That's when he let me know that the two inmates were there to fuck me. I knew that the guards were there to hold me down if it was needed. I gave in to what he wanted, and let the two fuck my tight ass.

I spent the next few years having sex with both the other guards and the inmates. How can I explain what it was like to work there and see all those men every day walking around in their underwear, or nake? Knowing that I could have sex with any of them whenever I wanted to. When I worked at night I could do things like go into a cell while the inmates were sleeping and wake one of them up to have sex. On day shift I could do what ever I wanted to. Some times I would go to a cell and ask the inmates to have sex so I could watch, from time to I would join in and have sex with them. I had even done things like finger fuck an inmate while he jacked off. Walking around the prison and seeing guys having sex with each other was a turn on. Then when the warden showed the in house porn on the TVs it was another turn on for me.

Now we will call you R.L. you were also a guard at the prison. Yes I worked there for about 14 years. And like everyone else there, I was used as apart of the warden's sex games. No matter if we worked there or if you were an inmate, you had to take part in what the warden wanted. I had sex with the other men you talked to as well as a lot of the men who was in the prison, the guards and inmates. Plus I was one of the men that the warden fucked for the first time. It was only hours after I started work at the prison. The warden called to his office where he informed that he was going to fuck my ass. Well one day while I was working I did something that really was wild. I went to one of the cellblocks and got nake so that I could have open sex with most of the men there. Did anyone make or tell you to do that? No, I just wanted to, so I did it. Did you get in to trouble over doing that? No, it was all apart of the whole thing. The next day I stood in the hallway and watched each one of those me fuck me until my ass hole was red and lose. I enjoyed what had been done to me. I was not the only one watching the TV, everyone was seeing the same thing I was. Later that day three of my coworkers got me into one of the bathrooms and let me know that they wanted some of my ass. They wanted to fuck me like the inmates had done the day before. I gave into them; I got nake and let them have their way with me. After they had finish fucking me. We had to go down the hall to shower, once there I had some fun too. I told the three of them to bend over so I could get some of their ass. I enjoyed each of them. C.K. was the one that got me off.

R.W. was a young white male when he came into the prison. Yes, I was 18 years old. And like all the others the warden had plans for me. He wanted me to be turned out real good, because he had some men from the out side that he wanted to fuck me, so he had me put in an all black cellblock. He told the leader of the block that I was to be fucked by him and his boys. It was going to be my first time. When the guard walked me to the cell, he told me that the inmates were going to throw a party just for you. The guard told the guys in the cell that your party boy is here and the warden wants him ready by in the morning. The older guy said he would be ready.

When I walked into the cell, the inmates got up and walked over to me, and started to touch my body. I had my own ideas what was going to happen to me. I looked over at the door the guard was still standing there watching. Then I heard a voice that I had heard before, when I look over it was the warden. He told me that you are going to be fucked and I am going to watch, I need you opened up for a job you are going to do in the morning. I did as the warden had told me, and I let the men he ordered to fuck me. He stood right inside of the cell with us as they did me. That night I laid there nake wondering if one of the two inmates might come over to my bunk and have sex with me. They let me sleep, but the next morning when our block went to the shower, the same men had sex with me that did it the day before. After it was over the guards pulled me from the shower, and told me to dry off. Then I was taken to the warden's office, where he had some men waiting there for me. He told me it was time for me to make all of them feel good. Well I spent 8 years in prison. Once I was released I used the thing learned in the prison to get into male adult movies.

The next person we talked to was a guard who we will call R.P. He was also interviewed by the warden. Please tell me about that interview. Well I was 21 years old when I applied for a job at the prison. I was called two days after turning in the application. Once at the prison I was taken to the warden's office where he told me to have a seat across from his desk. He asked me a few questions, and I answered him in return. Then things took a turn, when he asked me to stand and remove my clothes. I did as I was asked at the same time I asked what that had to do with the job.

The warden looked me right in the face and said, I want the guards that work there to have strong bodies. So let me see how strong your body is. In moments I was standing in front of him nake. As he looked my body over I saw a smile come over his face. He told me that I was hired, and I was going to start to work that next week. On Monday I went into work for training. It was my first day, and I had no idea what was going to happen to me. The day started out I think like any first day on any job, but about half thought the day. The guard that was training me took me into a room where he made his move on me. There was something about him that made me feel comfortable with him. I had been with another guy before that day, so it was easy for us to have sex.

I had no I did that we were being taped, the next when I went to work I had no idea that what we had done was going to be movie of the day. There I was standing with him in one of the hallways when it came on the TV. There I was having sex with this man for every one to see. Everything that we had done in that room was now an open book. After that day I learned that every man there was having sex with who ever they wanted to. It only took me a few days before I was doing it too, I also enjoyed it. Well I work there for 16 years. Unlike other people I really like going into work every day.

Sitting beside R.P. was an ex-inmate that we will go T.W. I ask him to tell his story. He said well it started when I was 16, and I got into drinking and drugs. This went on for a couple of years, then when I was about 18 years old. I decided to break in to a house and steal some things that I could sale to get money to buy more drugs. That night I road around looking to find a house to break in to. About 1:00 am I drove pass this one house, were all the lights were out, and there was no car in the driveway. So I felt that on one was going to be home. I forced the back door open and went in, the house was dark.

As I was going some draws in the dinner room a guy came in and I beat him up and left him there. So I was arrested for breaking and entering plus beating the guy up. I got 10 years in prison. I was sent to the prison that is knew as the sex prison. Once there I was turned out, that was done a few hours after I got there.

After I was fitted for my clothes I was then taken into a room, where I waited for the guard to come back and get me. The door opened and three men walked in on me. Each of the men were nake, I begin to fear what they were going to do to me. Before I could say anything an older man came into the room, he told me that he was the warden. Then he told me that the men were there to break me in. Lay down boy and take this like a man. The three men took their turn having sex with me. Once it was over I was taken to the shower room, and told to clean up.

A few days later I met R.P. and some how we became friends. It was something about him that made me feel good when I was around him. One day while I was laying on my bunk nake I felt someone's hand touching my body. When I rolled over to see him standing next to my bunk. I watched his he took off his clothes, and got on the bunk with me. That was the first time we had sex, but it would not be the last time. The two of us started something that we could run away from. The next few years were hard but we made it though.

The last day that I was in the prison was the best day of my life. R.P. came to me and asked if we could find away to get together on the out side. My second night of freedom spent with the man I was feeling in love with. We made love that night in so many ways. The next morning we made decision to move in to his house together. R.P. and I had been together for the last few years now.

A lot of the men who spent time in the prison did not want to talk to us at all. Many of them were trying to forget the things that they did while they were there. Some of them had families who did not know what went on inside the prison, and others just wanted to go on with their lives, but there was one more person who was willing to tell us all about the prison. You will never guest who that person was.

On our last day of interviews the warden came in and sat down with us. He did not mind telling all about why he wanted to run a prison like the one he owned. Well I wanted to have the enjoyment of man on man sex, and bodies that I could look at and control. Men with big dicks and nice asses, plus tight ass holes that I can pop or watch them being pop. Knowing that each of them was there for my enjoyment.

The next chapter: what happened to the men after they got out of the prison known as the hard core prison. Well a few of the men went on to a half way house that was also owned by the warden, and they are willing to talk to us about the things that went on there. While some others went back out on to the streets, The half way house was only miles away from the prison, but not all of the men who went to the house came from the Hard Core Prison. One of the first men that sat down with us while we gather the information for his chapter, was W.P. who spent 10 years in the prison then he was sent to the halfway house for another year.

W.P, On the day I was released from the prison there were two men there to pick me up, and take me to the halfway house. The first thing I had to do was strip nake in front of them. Then redress, Once dressed I was lead to the van they had waiting. We drove just a few miles from the prison to the halfway house. When we got there I was taken to a room on the second floor. I was told that I would be sharing the room with another guy, who I had not met yet. One of the men went over the rules of the house with me. They were almost the same rules that we had in the prison, like walking around in our underwear and tee shirts, or nothing at all, because it was all about sex there too. He also told me that we were not allowed to close the doors to our rooms. At night we had to sleep in the nude just like we did in the prison.

It wasn't long after the man left me alone in the room that a nice looking black man walked into the room and sit down on the bed across from. What's up man my name I guest you are my new roommate. Yes, my name is W.P. I replied. Then he said well my name is P.J. as we talked I open up to him and told him that I was just getting out of the prison everyone calls the hard-core prison. He informed me that he had spent 8 years in a prison some called the hell house. I sit on my bed and watched this man as we talked, his body was smooth and sexy while is face was very nice to look at. There was something about his that made me feel good inside.

This was the last of my interviews, but story did not end here. Maybe one day they will let you in on what happened after this story. As of today the prison is still going strong, and turning out inmates just as it has been for years. Will you be one of them?

ANOTHER LOVE STORY

I was a 29-year-old man who worked 6 days a week in an auto repair shop, owned by my uncle. He was the oldest of eight, his parents worked hard to make it in their day and time. As him and his brothers and sisters grow up they learned how to work at an early age. I started working at the age of 18 after I finished High School, but I didn't go to college because I am the oldest of 5, and being the only out of two boys, and three girls. I went to work to help my mother with our family's expenses.

This story started on July 9th, a few days after the 4th of July. A red SUV came into the shop that morning. My uncle asked me to check it out. About 10 minutes later I went to the office and told him that it seemed that the SUV needed to have a tone up and an oil change. I wasn't sure if that would fix what was going on with it. So my uncle told the owner that he would have to keep the truck for a day or so to make sure it's fix. I never saw the owner until the day it was ready to be picked up from the shop.

On July 11th about 2:15 pm, my uncle came to me and asked me to bring the red SUV around to the front door of the shop. When I did carry the keys into the office there was a man sitting at the desk with my uncle. As I walked into the door they both looked at the door when I opened it. I walked over and handed the keys to my uncle. He told me thank you. I turned and spoke to the man sitting there, he smiled and said hi. For a moment it seemed that time stood still, as I looked into his eyes. Then I broke the spell and walked out of the office, and went back to work.

For the next few days I never thought about that man again until about a week later I was on my way home, when I stopped at a local store to pick up something to drink. As I was standing in front of the cooler someone said if you can't make up your mind, you have to but one of everything on the self. I turned to see who was talking to me, as I did there he stood behind me. It was the man who owned the red SUV that I worked on at the shop. Before I could say a word he said, thanks for doing a good job on my truck. The only thing I could say was your welcome. Then he said my name is Carvell Davis. As I looked at him I told him that my name is Marcus Jones. After that I turned back to the cooler and opened the door, and reached for a soda. I went to the counter to checkout. Just as I walked out of the store, he was standing next to the door.

By the way is there a number where I can get in touch with you if I need to. I gave him my cell number. He reached into his packet and pulled out his cell phone and keyed in my name and number. Then he told me that his number is 326-0740, so I keyed his info into my phone. Later that night I was sitting at my computer when my cell phone started to ring. I picked it up and looked at the caller ID (Carvell Davis 326-7040), I answered it; he said I was sitting here wondering if this was really your number, so I decided to call. With out thinking I said what do you mean you were wondering if I had given you the right number? Well sometimes people have been known to give out a false number to keep the other person from being able to call, because they didn't want to talk to that person.

Well I gave you the right number in case you needed my help with your truck. Then he asked I hope that I am not calling you at a bad time or something? I was just sitting around relaxing before going to bed, I replied I am just sitting here at my computer, checking e-mail, trying to relax after a long day at work. Carvell said I've better let you go back to what you was doing before I called. You don't have to rush off I can do both things at the same time. I didn't want him to feel that I didn't want to talk to him.

After talking for a while he said we both better get off the phone if we are going to get any sleep. That's when I noticed that it was about 11:30, and I needed to be up about 5:00 am. At that point Carvell and I decided to end our phone call. Once that happened I went into the bathroom to get ready for bed. The next morning I woke up about 4:50 am, and by 5:40 I was on my way to the shop. I got there about 5:55; my uncle was already getting ready for the day's work. We had a number of cars to work on, and by 6:00 he was ready to close up when a woman drove up, she wanted her car checked out, because it was going running funny. I had never seen her before, my uncle checked out the car for her. After closing he told me that she had said that her boyfriend had told her about the shop.

I didn't hear from Carvell for over two weeks. Then one night after work I was lying in bed watching some crazy show that was really off the chain. My cell went off, I was wondering who was calling that time of night. It was Carvell, I hope that I am not calling you to late. No I was just watching TV. I didn't tell him that I was already in bed. He told me that nothing was wrong; he just wanted to talk to me. We talked for a while, and then he asked if he could meet me the next day after I got off of work. I agreed to meet him at a little restaurant down town. We ordered dinner and talked while we were eating. He told me a few thing about him self, like the fact that he was 24 years old. He worked for a used car lot. I was 29 years old and as you know I worked at a car repair shop.

Let me tell you what I noticed about him, he was between 5'9" and 6'0" tall. The reason I said that is because I stand at 6'3" and he was a little shorter than I am, I also know that he was a little smaller than me. There was something about him that I could not put my finger on. He was a friendly young man neatly dressed. Once we left the restaurant we both went our on way. When I got home I turned on my computer to check e-mail. Then later I got into bed, because I had to go to work the next morning. For some reason I thought about Carvell off and on for most of the day. Just as I started to drive home he called. He too was getting off of work, and then he told me something that made me wonder. He said that he had been thinking about me since we had dinner together the night before. Why was he thinking about me, or better yet why had I been thinking about him? Well I've better tell one of the reasons that I was thinking about him. You see I am a gay man, and I he was a nice looking man. The only thing is that I have always been attracted to men who were older than I was. Plus at that time in my life I was trying to get over a man who had really hurt me.

I was not ready for another relationship, plus I did not feel that he was gay or any thing like that. He asked if there was any way he could maybe come over to my place that night? I didn't know if I should allow him to come over, but I did give him my address, and we again to meet around 7:00 that night. So I went home to make sure that things had been picked up, and put away. When he got there we went into the living room, where we watched TV and talked. That night something happened that change everything. Carvell told me something that I was not looking for from him. As we were sitting there together he looked in to my eyes and said for some reason you had been on my mind a lot, Then asked if there was any way we could be more than just friends. I asked him what did he mean? He said that he had never thought about another man in this way, but there is something about you, I don't know what it is.

As we were sitting there he took my hand, and said let's give this a try. I agreed to try it for a while. He left that night about 11:00, and when I got into bed I laid there for a while thinking about him, wondering if he really knew what he really wanted or was it just something he was going though. The next morning as I was getting ready to walk out the door to go to work Carvell called, he just wanted to say good-morning, and wish me a good day. He told me to call him back later. He was on my mind all that day. When I got off of work I called him, asked if he could do something for me tonight, I asked him what? He told me that he wanted to cook dinner for me at his place. What should I be there; he said you could come over now. Well I need to go home and get cleaned up. Don't worry about that you can do that here. I said the only thing wrong with that is I don't have clothes to change into at your place.

Well you can always use something of mine's. Okay if you say so, what is your address? He told his address, it took me about 20 minutes to get there. I knocked on the door, and a few moments later he opened the door. Come in he said with a smile on his face.

Once on the inside of his place he closed the door, and said come with me so I can get you something to change into. I followed him into his bedroom, where he gave me apart of shorts and a t-shirt. Then he showed where his bathroom was. I closed the door and undressed, and then I got into the shower. After taking a short shower I got out and dried off, then put on the shorts and t-shirt he had gave me.

As I walked back into the living room, I could see Carvell standing in the kitchen. He turned and looked at me smiling, that looks good on you he as he walked towards me. You can have a seat. dinner is almost ready. I sat down on the sofa, I tried to watch TV, but I couldn't keep my eyes off of him. It was just a few moments before he came back into the room, saying dinner is ready.

I got up and walked over to the dinner room table, where he had sat up two place settings. He went back into the kitchen to fix our plates. He returned with our food. As we started to eat I told him that he was a good cook, he said thank you. After we finished eating, he told me that he had planned something else special. When he came back out of the kitchen he had two bowls of stew berries with chocolate and cool whip. Why don't we take this into the living room, where we can watch some TV, so we did just that? We sat on the sofa and eat. While we were sitting there we talked. He said I hope that we can really become better friends. Well we can see where this goes. That's when I felt that I should tell him that I was gay. Carvell looked at me and said I know that, that's why I've wanted to be around you.

That's if you want to spend time with me. Yes, I said in replied. Then he smiled. That night we must have forgotten about time because the next thing we knew the 11:00 news was coming on.

I said well I've better get out of here so you can get some sleep. He said wait have you thought about it, we don't have to go to work tomorrow, and I don't have any thing to do in the morning. So you don't have to leave unless you just want to. Well in the back of my mind I really did not want to leave. He took my hand and asked me to stay with him. Before I could answer him, we kissed. That was the only answer he needed. Then without saying another word he stood up and pulled me up with him, leading me to his bedroom. As we stood there next to his bed, he begins to undress me. The two of use stood there naked only for a moment, I watched as he leaned over and pulled back the top sheet on the bed.

We got into bed and laid there together holding each other. That night was so special between the two of us even with no sex. When I opened my eyes the next morning, he was watching me as I slept. Good morning Marcus, I glad that you got a good night sleep. Do you want breakfast? Well a little something wont hurt. Carvell started to get up, and so did I, but he told me to stay in bed. I laid back down and waiting for him to return to the bedroom. When he did, he had two plates of food. We had breakfast in bed. After eating, he took the plates and put them on the drawer, and got back into bed. We held each other for a while with out saying anything to each other.

That day we spent most of it at his place. About 3:00 that afternoon we went out to the park near his place. Carvell and I walked around for a while, then we sat near the lake and watched the water. Later we went back to his place for dinner. After dinner I let him know that I was going home, because I needed to get ready for work the next morning. He agreed with me, he walked me to my car. Just before I got into the car he told me to call him when got home. I thought about him as I drove from his place to mine. When I got into side and locked the front door, I used my cell phone to call him and let him that I was home. When he answered the phone, I told that I was at home. He said that I'm glad that you got home safe. We talked for a while before we got ready for bed.

The next morning when I got to the shop Carvell was outside waiting for me, good morning, I got you something for breakfast, then he handed me a bag with some food, he had gotten on the way to see me. He told me that he needed to get to work. So he left, and headed for work. I went into the shop and eat the food, and then I started working on a car that was in the shop. I spent that morning working, at lunchtime I decided to call Carvell. Hi there I've been wanting for you to call, how was breakfast? I like what you brought this morning, but it was not breakfast in bed, I said. He said that

I can tell that you are smiling. If you let me I will make it up to you. What do you have on your mind I asked? What about a special dinner in bed, followed by breakfast in bed the next morning?

How about a date Friday night? After we get off of work. My reply was I like that idea. My place at 7:00, you don't have to bring any clothes this time, Carvell said. Ok that was really funny I said back. He I will talk to you later, I need to get back to work. We ended our phone call, and went back what I was doing. It was just Monday I had four more days to go be the date we made. He called me back around 6:30 after we both got off of work. When he called he wanted to know if I had any plans? No I don't, what are you thinking? Well what you say if I said that I am right outside of your place, and I would like to come up.

Bring it on I replied, not knowing what was going on with him. A few moments later he was knocking on my door. When I opened the door there he was standing there with a bag in his hand. Have you had dinner yet? No I haven't been here long before you called. Well here's dinner he said as he held up the bag, I hope you like Chinese? Yes I do. Why don't you come on in and bring the food. That statement made him smile. As he walked though the door he lead over and gave me a kiss. That took me by surprise, but not for long, I kissed him back. I pushed the door closed, made sure that it was locked.

You can have a seat on the sofa while I get us plates and folks so we can eat. So I went into my kitchen and got what we needed, when I returned to my living room Carvell had really made his self at home. Where is your bathroom I need to freshen up. It's this way as I lead him down the hallway to the open door to my darken bathroom. I reached around him and turn on the light. I stood at the doorway as he walked in, he turn on the water and washed his hands, you just want to stand there and watch, or maybe you want to come in and help me. What do you want me to help you with I asked, what ever you think that I need help with he said with a big smile on his face.

That's when I walked in and stood next to him, reaching over and groping is dick though his pants while I looked into his face just to see what kind of reaction he would have. Looking back at me he placed his hand on top of mines and smiled. We better see about eating before the food gets cold. Still holding his dick I started to back out of the bathroom, I held on until we made it back to the living room I let go only when we got next to the sofa. Why did you let go? He asked. Because we wouldn't be able to eat that way I said. Why not, we could fees each other right, Carvell side as he sat down. I sat down next to him; he opened up the bag and started to take the food placing everything on the table in front of us.

Reached for the TV remote and turned it. Do you want something to drink I asked as I turned to look at him. I have some juice, soda and water. I'll like some soda please. I got up from the sofa and walked toward the kitchen. I returned with two glasses of soda, here you are, as I handed one of the glasses to him. As he took our hands touched for just a moment. Once he had taken the glass, I sat down beside him, and took a drink. Then I placed the glass down on the table, started to eat again. After we had finished eating Carvell asked me if he could take a shower.

I told him to go a head; you know where the bathroom is. There's a clean towel hanging on the shower door. As he walked away he said, I need help washing my back. I did not think that I had heard him right, so I asked what did you just say? A few moments passed before he replied, I need your help with washing my back. I looked up to see him standing there wearing only his underwear, and a smile. Now are you coming to wash my back or not? Are you asking me to take a shower with you? Do you want me, I asked? Come on man, how much plainer can I say it. I want you to get in the shower with now.

I jumped up and headed for the bathroom behind him, taking off my clothes as fast as I could. Once in the bathroom I open the shower door and lead over to turn on the water. As I did he moved up behind me pressing against me. He reached in to test the temp of the water. It ok to me, lets get in. the two of us got in and started to wash each other's bodies. As we faced each other he pulled me to him and kissed me. After our shower was over we dried each other off. Carvell ask me if he could spend the night. I said that would be ok with me. We were standing there with the towels we used in our hands; I realized that he didn't have any to sleep in, that's when my mind went back to the night spent at his place. We both slept naked, I most have started to smile, because he asked what are you smiling about? Nothing I replied. It had to be something to put a smile like that on your face. Why don't you tell what's going on. Well I realized that you don't have anything to sleep in here. Maybe I forgot to tell you I like sleeping in the nude. Plus when I'm at home alone I don't wear clothes at all.

Let's get out of here, and maybe go back into the living room and watch some TV, or something. I took the two wet towels and hung them over the shower frame to dry. As we walked out of the bathroom, I got two dry towels out of the hall closet, and took them into the living room with us. I laid them out on the sofa so we could seat on them. Once we had sat down he moved as close to me as he could get. Our naked bodies were warm against each other. He put his arm around me, and I laid my head on his shoulder. It was very hard for me to keep my mind or my eyes on the TV with him next to me naked as the day he was born.

When the news came on, we went to bed. My alarm was set for 5:30 am. The next morning when my clock went off it was time for us to get up and get ourselves ready for work. Carvell dressed then told me that he was going by his place to change, and then he would pick us up something for breakfast, I'll be at the shop by the time you get there. Ok I'll see you in a few. When we got to my door he gave me a kiss on the lips. He walked down the hall; I closed and finish getting dress so I could leave.

I got to the shop about 20 minutes later, and he was there waiting for me. I parked, and got out of my car, and walked over to him. He turned and reached in to his SUV and picked up a bag. Then he turned back around and handed it to me. Thank you, I said as I took it from his hand. Your welcome he said with a big smile on his face. I've better head for work; we'll talk later ok. Ok I said as he got in to his SUV. I watched as he drove off, then I went inside. I sat down and eat before I started to work.

At lunchtime my cell started ringing, it was Carvell. I answered it and we talked about last night. We also talked about our date on Friday night. After talking for a while we both went back to work. I finished out the day, and then I went home. Later that night he called me again, and we talked for a long time. Before we both knew that we had to get some sleep, because we had to go to work the next day. The last thing that he said to me was that we have three more days to go before our special date. Then he said get a good night sleep. I replied you too.

The hours went by so fast that it seemed that I had just closed my eyes when it was time for me to get up. When I got into the shower each tie I touched my body it felt that his hands were touching me, what was going on, why was I feeling the way that I have been? I know that Carvell is too young for me, was only 22 years old. Just as I stepped out of the shower my cell phone started to ring. Well I know that you don't have to guess who was calling me. Yes it was him, and he was sounding real good to me. What was this man doing to me? He was turning my world upside down, and we have not even had sex yet. He was calling to say good morning, and that he was going to stop by the shop to bring me breakfast.

After dressing and driving to work, there was Carvell standing in front of the shop waiting for me. Once parking I got out of my car, and walked over to him. Hi there, here's your breakfast, handing the bag of food. We had a short talk, before he left to go to work. After eating I started my day. By lunchtime we were on the phone talking again. He wanted to see me tonight; I agreed to see him, because I felt that I needed to talk to him about what I was feeling. When I got home he was waiting for me. Once inside we had to clean up, I went into the kitchen and started to fix us some thing to eat for dinner. Once I had finished cooking I brought the food back into the living room, where we sat down and ate.

While sitting on the sofa watching TV, I told Carvell that I needed to talk to him about some thing. We turned to each other, and I started to tell him how was feeling. I told him that my world was turning upside down. I also told that I felt that he was too young for me. He looked at he as if I had hurt is feeling, and then he said what's wrong with my age. Well you seven years younger than I am. I asked him if had ever had a relationship with a man before. No, I have not, but it's something about you that I really like. You will be my first. That's when I asked to big question what do you think your parents feel about this? Well why don't we find out what they will have to say. I didn't know what to say, then he went on to tell me that if I wanted to that we could go to the family house on Saturday night. I agreed to go with him even though I had a feeling that it might be hard.

Carvell left about 11:00 o'clock to go home. Once there he called back to tell me good night. To next morning I decide to do something that would surprise him. Once taking a shower I hurried to get dress, so I could go and pick up some food and take him breakfast. When I called him I told him that I would meet him at his job, when he drove up I was waiting with food in hand. When he got out of his car, and walked over to me. I said here's your food. That put a smile on his face, before I knew it he had given me a kiss that I was not looking for. It was fast but good. I didn't know how to react, because we were sitting right outside the building where he worked. I knew what I really wanted to do, I wanted to put my arms around him and kiss back, but I didn't.

Just before I left he side tomorrow night is our big date, I have everything almost ready. I asked what do you have in mind? He replied you will just have to wait and see, with a big smile on his face looking a child who was up to something. Then he said don't forget I am taking you to meet my parents on Saturday night; they are ready to meet you. I knew that I had to leave so that I could get to work on time, plus I wanted to have time to eat. When I got to the shop I went in and eat my breakfast. Just as I finished up my uncle came over to me, Marcus can I talk to for a moment about something. What is it that you want to talk to me about, what's going on I asked. Well I noticed that you have a new friend coming around, he is the owner of the SUV that we worked on a few weeks ago right? Yes, he is that's how we met. Me uncle asked he's a little young isn't he? I replied we have talked about that fact, and he is taking me to meet his parents on Saturday night.

Well as long as you two is ok with it. I guess it is fine with me. Just let me know how things turn once you meet the parents. I will let you know on Monday. After that I started on a car that the owner was coming to pick up later to day. Just as I was finishing up my cell phone went off, I knew by the ring tone that it was Carvell. I answered it saying what's up. He replied thinking about you. The food was good this morning, but I wish that we could have eaten together. How are things going with you at the shop? Well I just finished up a car that is to be picked up later, and you I asked, well we just got out of a meeting that I will tell you about later ok. I have a few things to doing before I go home so I've better get to work, I'll talk to you later.

When I got off the phone my uncle was standing in the doorway looking at me with a smile on his face, I don't think I have to ask you who that was do I. Looking at the big smile on your face I would say that it was your friend. Yes it was, he just called to tell me thanks for caring him breakfast on his job this morning. I'm to see that you are getting over that SOB that hurt you. He has managed to make me feel better. He stayed on my mind for the rest of the day. When I got home Carvell was outside of my place waiting on me to get there. Once inside we sat down on the sofa together, because he said that he wanted to talk to me about something. I asked him what was going on. He replied I got some good news today at work and I wanted to share it with you. I told you that we had a meeting this morning, well our boss made the announcement on the promotions in the company, and guess who's going to be moving up. I'm going on to the next lever, congratulations on your promotion I said as I put my arms around him to give him a hug. He hugged me back and gave me a kiss.

I in such a rush to hear what he had to tell me that I didn't noticed that he had a bag in his hand. I stop and got us some take out before I came over here. Let's cleanup so we can eat. We went to wash our hands, then came back took out the food, I was happy for him, and I didn't mind showing him. He left about 10:00, because he said that he had to go home and put the final touches on things for our date tomorrow night. I didn't him anything about it I remembered what he had said the late time I asked him. I stayed up and watched TV before going to bed. Just as I got into bed he called to say good night. He also told me that he was going to work early in the morning, because he wanted to get off early and get home so he will be there when I get off of work. I want you to come over when you get off.

Friday morning was here and I could hardly wait for our date. I got up and got ready for work; before I left I picked a gym bag to take me over to his place. I knew that I wouldn't need it; I just wanted to take a change of clothes. At work my mind was going little wild wondering what he had in mind for our date. The day went by a little slow, but at about closing time he called to tell that he was at home waiting for me to get there. I asked him if I should bring anything? No everything is ready just waiting for you; I hope that you are ready. I'll be there as soon as I leave here. Ok I'll see you in a little while.

I got to his house about 5:30, when I knocked on his front door, he came to the door wearing only a pair shorts and no t-shirt. The shorts he had on fit just right in all the right places if you know what I mean. Carvell took me in his arms and gave me a kiss, and then he said I know that you want to cleanup, why don't you go and take a shower. He had a look in his eyes that he had something on his mind. As I walked towards the bathroom I started to remove my clothes, I didn't realize that he was walking behind me pick each peace up. I was down to my underwear, when he let me know that he was right. He softly stop let me do that for you. I did just as he had asked; I turned around slowly to see him standing there with a smile on his lips. He generally pushes me backwards into the bathroom. Once we both together in the bathroom he dropped my other clothes on the floor then he reached for my underwear, pulling them down slowly. The whole time he was looking into my eyes.

I couldn't stop myself I started removing the short he had on, once they were down I noticed that he was not wearing any underwear. Baby let me wash your body, he said as I stepped out my last peace of clothing. He leaned over to turn on the water in shower, and then he took my hand and stepped into the shower. He slowly pulled my hand towards him. I step in, and he took me in his arms holding me close as the water ran over our bodies. Once we were wet, he reached for a bottle of body wash that he had in the shower, and then he rubbed his hands all over my body. The all I could smell was coconut. I closed my eyes and let him handle my body. I opened my eyes to find him down on his knees, rubbing my legs up and down slowly, while he was looking up at me.

I reached for the body wash, putting some in my hand; I wanted to touch his body so bad. Once I had put the bottle down I took my other hand and pulled him to his feet. Rubbing my hands together, then I started to rub his neck slowly working way down his young manly body. My hands touched every inch of his skin. It took so much for me not to do what was going though my mind at time, but I had no idea what he wanted. Rinsed off we dried each off, and then he took me by the hand and led me towards his bedroom. The room was dark, he told to close my eyes for a moment, why I can't see anything I replied. Just do as I ask please he said softly in my ear. I complied with what he wanted. I heard to light switch click, then he said open your eyes baby.

When I opened my eyes I saw there were white rose buds everywhere. As he led me to the bed he said I hope that you're ready for a very special night. Once at the bed he pulled back the top sheet, get in bed. I promised you dinner in bed he said with a smile on his face. I did just as he asked, pulling the sheet over me to my waist. Carvell turned and walked out of the room. He returned moments later with two plates of food; he sat the plates down on the nightstand next to me, then he walked around to the other side of the bed and got in to bed next to me.

Once he had gotten in to bed, he asked me to pass him one of the plates of food. By the way I forgot one important detail he had soft music playing. After we had finished eating, he got up and took the plates back into the kitchen, and brought back sliced stew berries and dripping chocolate. Now it's time for some sweets. He pulled the sheet off of me, and got back on the bed with me. As I laid there he took a slice of stew berry and dripped it into the chocolate, and feed me. Then I did the same thing for him. We did that for a while, he placed the bowl on the nightstand on his side of the bed.

Before I could react he was on top of me, touching and kissing. That was the first time that he made love to me. After wards we cleaned up, then got back into bed where he massaged my body. He pulled me close to him and put his arms around me and held me as we slept. The next morning I awoke in his arms, with him still asleep next to me. I just laid there trying not to wake him. I don't know how long it was before he woke up. When he did, he lead over and said good morning baby, I got something else planned for this morning. Then he kissed on the cheek before getting out of bed. I watched his naked body as he walked out of the room.

He returned with more fruit and whip topping for breakfast. After we finished eating we went into the bathroom and showered together. The two of us sat around and realized. Later that afternoon he reminded that we were going to his parents' house that evening. About 6:00 he said that we should start getting ready, as I was standing there in his bedroom naked, he had finish dressing, so I asked him to go out to my car and get the clothes that I had brought with me. He went outside, and came back with the bag from my car. I dressed as he sat on the bed and watched me. When we got ready to leave, we got into his SUV, and headed for his parents' house. I didn't know to expect, but I was trying to get for anything. We talked all the way there. When we drove into the yarn there were other cars parked there. My heart started to beat a little harder, my mind was racing, to whom does all the other cars belong to?

Once he had parked his SUV, we got out and walked towards the house. When we got to the door he opened the door, and we walked into the house where his family was sitting. We spoke, and then he started telling each person's name. Like me see if I can get this right, there was his twin brothers along with one brother's wife and the other one's girlfriend. Three sisters two of them were with their husbands, and the other one was with her boyfriend. At the table were their mother, and their father along with his wife (their stepmother). I didn't know how much of a night I was really in for until his father did something that got me off guard. Once Carvell told him my name, he was like you don't get away with just speaking to me, come over her and give me a hug. Carvell told me to go on and do it. I walked over to his father and gave him a hug. As I walked back over to where Carvell was sitting on a love seat in the family room. His father made a statement; I think I've found my new girlfriend. It was a big joke to everyone in the room, I didn't know how to react to what was said. Carvell looked at me and said baby he was just joking, that's his way of doing things. He loves to joke around.

We all had a good time that night. it was wild. His family was nice to be around. He told them that him and I were dating, and that we had been for a few weeks. Their father got up and put on some slow music, and then almost everyone was up slow dancing with their partners. He got up and took me by the hand and pulled me to my feet. Pulling me to him, holding me close as we started to dance. Their father was dancing with their stepmother, when their mother walked over and cut in, then he took her in his arms and finished the dance with her.

When the song was over everyone but sat back down. One of his brothers asks him why we were still standing. Carvell did not say anything, but I knew the reason why, he still holding me close to him because he had a hard on. He said do not move right he said softly in my ear. So we stood there for a few moments, then once his hard had went down we walked over to the love seat. I sat down first; before I knew what he was going to do he sat in my lap. His mother told him to get up off of me; he should be sitting in your lap. Oh mom he replied, and then he stood up and took my hand pulling up. Once he had sat back down he pulled me on to his lap.

It was late when everyone started to leave the house and making their way home. Two of us also left, and drove by to his place, where I was going to spend the night, we talked about how things went at his parents' house. He was happy that his family knew that we were dating. He told me that he could tell that his family all liked me. It late when we got into bed, we fell sleep holding each. The next we were awoken when he phone started ringing. The first call was from his mother, as they talked he told her that he was still in bed. I don't know what she asked him, but what he said really got me. He told her that he was not alone. The phone calls kept coming in everyone that was there that night was calling him.

It was so funny to me the way they kept asking him about our relationship, about me. His daddy was the funniest of them all. One thing about the way he talked to his family made me feel really good, because he told them that there was something special about me.

After he had gotten off the phone we had a long talk about was going on with us. He told me that really wanted things to work out with us. We started the next week on a very happy note, talking to each other three or four times a day. On Thursday morning while I was at work something happened, I got a call from Carvell's mother, she wanted me to know that he had been in a car accident. When she told me, I wouldn't say much, the only thing I could do was to ask her if he was ok. She told me that he was in the hospital an hour way. She also told me that he was asking for me. I went to my uncle and told him what was going on, and that I needed to leave to go where he was. He told me to go and do what I needed to do.

I left work and headed for the hospital. When I got there I went to the front deck and asked what room he was in. the woman at the deck told me that he was in ICU 2, then she asked if I was a family member. I had to tell her that I wasn't, that's when she told me that I could not go up unless a member of the family came down and gave their ok. She said that she knew that some of the family was in with he. She called up to see if someone could come down for a moment. I waited for what seemed to be an every long time, but it was only a few moments, then his mother came to the deck.

She gave me a hug, then she said come on with me, he really wants to see you. We went upstairs to where he was, as we got to the doors she called into the ICU and asked them to open the door. I took a deep breath just I walked inside the doorway, because I didn't know what I was going to see. We walked passed the deck and turned; his room was the second one on the left.

As we got to the door of his room, I could see the lower part of his body covered in a hospital blanket. His mother walked into the room first, then I followed. His father and stepmother were sitting in the room with him. When I walked in I looked at him lying there with wirers and tubes connected to his body. Just as they spoke to me, Carvell opened his eyes and looked at me. Hi baby I am glad that you're here. As I moved closer to him, he reached out his hand to me, and I took it in my hand. What in the world did you get yourself into? I asked.

I was driving on my way home, when this car ran a red light, I didn't even see it coming until it hit. The next thing I remember is waking up here. I had to have an operation, don't worry I'll be ok. The doctor said that I would have to stay in the hospital for a few days. How did you find out I was here? Your mother called me. Thanks mom for calling him for me. Well you were asking for him, so I knew that you wanted him here, so I called.

The three of them left us in the room alone. Baby-sit here on the bed with me for a while. I did as he asked, doing my best not to get on any of the wirers or tubes. I was glad that he wasn't hurt real bad, or worst. As I sat there we held each other's hands, while he laid there and tried to rest. He looked into my eyes and asked if I could spend the night here? I replied I will have to call my uncle and let him know what is going on, and ask him if I could have the time off. Later the nurse came in to check things out. She looked at me and smiled, not saying a word. After a while his parents came back into the room. When he heard them come in he opened his eyes. At that time I was about to get up from the bed, but he held my hand tighter and said don't move. So I stayed there not to him.

About 8:00 that night I called my uncle to ask if I could have sometime off. He told me that I could have the next two days off. I thanked him for understanding. I stayed at the hospital with Carvell. I left on the third evening to come back home, so I could go back to work. That night after I got home we talked on the phone for a while, before he felt sleepy. That next morning I went to work, It hard enough being Monday morning, but it was also hard for me not to think about him. Then about noon I got a cell phone call that made me very happy because it was him. He wanted me to know that he was coming home. He wanted me to come to his place after I get off of work. I told him that I would be there. When I got there his mother was there with him, but she had to leave, so asked me to stay with for a while. I was happy to do that. Later that night he asked me to spend the night, I told that I could stay, but I would have to leave in the morning to go to my place to get ready for work.

He said since you only live just moments away why don't you go home and get some clothes or what ever you need and come back. I was worry if he would be ok while I was gone, but he assured me that he would stay in bed until I got back. I went home as fast as I could and returned. He had given me a key so I could lock the door, and get back in. when I got back I went to check on him. He was lying in bed watching TV. I stayed in the room with him until 11:00, then he took his meds, I knew that he needed to get some sleep, so I asked where I could find some covers so I could sleep on the sofa. He said I want you to sleep right here in the bed with me. That sounds good, but I don't want to do anything to hurt you. Marcus, I don't worry about that just get into bed. I told him that I was going to take a shower, and then I'll come to bed. Ok baby I'll be right here waiting. When I returned I dropped the towel that I had wrapped around me, then I walked over to the bag that I had brought back with me to get some underwear to put on. Just as I was about to do that, he asked me not to put anything on just come to bed. As I laid down beside him I told him that if he needed anything just wake me up.

Later that night he had gotten out of bed without me knowing it, because he had to go to the bathroom. As he was getting back into bed that's when I woke up, I asked him if everything was ok. Yes I just needed to go to the bathroom. Plus the Dr. said, that I need to start doing things for myself. Once in bed he kissed me and said you can go back to sleep.

The next morning my alarm went off, and I knew that it was time for me to get up and get ready for work. When I was about to leave, I asked him if any one was coming over to stay with him. He told me that his mother was coming, and that she would have came back last night, but he had called her and told her that I would be spending the night. So I went to work, later that morning I called back to his place to see how he was doing. His mother said that he was taking a bath, and that she would tell him to call me back. A few min. later he did call my cell phone, and we talked for a while. He asked me if I would be coming back to his place after I got off of work. I told him that I would. I spent the next few nights there with him.

About three weeks after his check up with his Dr. he was told that he could go back to work only if worked for half of days at first. Carvell agreed to do that, and he went back to work. The car company did allow him to work for half days. Things between us were getting stronger each day. Then one evening while we were having dinner at my place, he got a call on his cell phone. I didn't know who was on the phone, but I could tell that it was someone that he did not want to talk to. Because he asked whom ever it was why they were calling him. Then he told the person not to call him again. Once hanging up the phone he said I'm sorry about that, but some people don't get the massage when you tell them that you do not want to have anything to do with them. I didn't ask him whom he was talking about.

A few nights later I was at his place when someone knocked on his door. He called to me from the kitchen will you get answer the door please. I got up from the sofa and went to the door. When I open the door there was a young woman standing in the hallway. The first thing out of mouth was who the hell are you? And where is Carvell? Before I could say anything, she pushed pass me and walked into the living room calling his name. He walked out of the kitchen, and asked what are you doing here? Her reply was since you won't talk to me over the phone I came to see you in person. Well you can leave now he said. What's going on here she asked with anger in her voice. It's none of your business he replied. That's when she turned and looked at me, and asked did he tell you that he has a girlfriend? You are not my girlfriend he said with a more forceful voice, and I want to leave and don't come back.

He took her by the arm and walked her to the door and out into the hallway, the he closed the door. When he turned around he had this look on his face. Marcus please let me try to explain what just happened. He walked over to me and reached out his hands to me. I placed my hands into he's as he started to tell me that the girl was someone that he had tried to date months before we met, and he had broke it off with her, but she just want let it go. I hope that you won't end stop seeing me, because of her. I really want to be with you, and I hope that you feel the same way that I do. Look we can make it though this one step at a time.

Week passed and that girl was showing me and everyone in his family that she is crazy has hell. She calls all the time, and it seem that when we are trying to spend time together she finds away to cause some kind of trouble. I was trying to stay in the back ground until one day when she showed up at my uncle's shop and start go off about me trying to still her boyfriend. Like I told her I can't what don't belong to you, if he don't want you. You need to walk leave him along, and stay out of my way, because you don't know me and you don't want to know me, not like this. That's when my uncle step in a said that you need to leave my business now and never come back. She left and my uncle talk to me about what had happened, he said you need to talk to him about, I told him that he had told me about her, and now he had broke it off with her, but she has been doing everything she can to make thing hard for us.

Marcus you need to let him handle whatever going on between the two of them. Well I was trying to do that, but now she has crossed the line, and she about to bring out a side of me that she doesn't want to see. About that time Carvell call me on my cell phone, I started to tell what she had done, and he said she wants to talk to me well she got it. I asked what he was going to do. He said I am going to call her, but she is not going to like what I have to tell her. We got off the phone, and I was worried about what he was going to do. After getting off of work that night Carvell and I had a date at his Father's house with the family. While we were about to have dinner someone knocked on the door. His stepmother got up to answer it, you wouldn't believe who was standing on the other side. That bitch just doesn't seem to give up.

What are you doing here his stepmother asked? I came to see Carvell she said. That's when his three sisters got up and walked over to the open door. She was told to leave, but she wanted to run her mouth, and that was a big mistake on her part. The sisters really got hot, and they let her know that she was in the wrong place and it was the wrong time. One sister said I know what my brother told you when he called you. So it will be to your benefit to get the hell out of here before you get your feeling hurt real badly. Once she saw that she wasn't going to get though the four women standing in front of the door. She turned and stormed away. A few moments later we heard her car start up and drive out of the yard.

Once she had gone and everyone was seated again, his sister eased my mind even more by saying that Carvell had talked to that crazy child on three way so that there would be a witness to what was being said. Marcus I can tell you right now that you don't have anything to worry about, because your number one in my brother's world. He told her that he was with someone now and she needs to move on. She wasn't too happy about it at all, as we all could tell by the way she acted when showed up earlier. I was sitting in a room full of people trying my best not to show what I was really feeling. I didn't want anyone to know that I was happy to know that Carvell was really into me.

So many things had been going on that I had forgot that my birthday was right around the corner; I didn't know that Carvell had not forgotten it. I had only eight days to go before I was going to turn 30 years old. On our way back to my place he was doing his very best to reassure me that there was nothing going on between himself and the girl that been trying so hard to break us up. I told him that he did not have to worry, because I wasn't going away, and if she pushed to hard that I will start to push back and she would not like me at all. I have aside to me that I really don't any body to see. He told not to worry about it her, because he has away to handle things with her. What are you going to do? I asked. You don' have to really about it. Plus my family likes you a lot.

A few days passed then his stepmother called me and asked me if I would able to come out to the house on Saturday night. I agreed to come out there at about 8:00. When I talked to Carvell later that same day he had no idea that she had called, or why she would have called. I asked him if would go with me to their house on Saturday night. He said that he would be glade to. So the next few days went by kind of fast, on Saturday morning when I went into the shop my uncle gave me a card and told me happy birthday. Then later that morning a florist deliver man brought two dozen white rose bud, with a card that said happy birthday to a very special person that has my heart. The flowers were from Carvell.

After work I went home and cleaned up and found something to wear on our date that night. I didn't know just what was going on. He came to pick me up about 7:30, and then we drove to the house. As we drove into the yard I noticed that there were some cars there. We got out of his car and walked up to the house. As we walked in the door, the only the thing heard was surprise, it was a surprise birthday party for me. I turn and looked at Carvell. He was standing there with a smile on his face. he said got you baby. There members of my family and some of my friends along with his family. The party was great; we had a lot of fun.

The next year was brought many surprises and good times. It was coming up on the 4th of July, and his was having a family reunion. I going to meet some members of his family that I had not met yet. On that day things were going real good until on uninvited guest showed up with trouble on her mind. When she got there things took a turn. She was acting crazy like she always does, but she had to deal with the family and believe me it wasn't easy a lot of people there did not like her, and they let her know that. One of his cousins was a police officer who told that she was going to be arrested if she did not leave. She left, but she was mad about everything. After she had left Carvell did some that really made me happy. As I stood there I watched him walk over to the to DJ to make a request, then when the song started to play I heard him started to sing with his brothers and sisters as back up. I didn't know that they could even sing.

No one knew that it was going to be the last 4th of July for his stepmother. A few months later she would in the hospital, and she would never recover. While the family was planning her home going service, they were planning to have everything in the colors of ivory and purple. The family was going to wear those color, with the women wearing ivory dresses or suits with purple tops and the men would be wearing purple suits with ivory shirts. On Thursday I got a call from his mother, she wanted to know if I was planning to be at the service. I told her that I was going to be there. That's when she asked if I knew about the colors that the family was going to wear. I told that Carvell had told me that he was going to wear his purple suit. That's when she asked if I had an ivory suit and a purple shirt. I told her that I did. Ok we will see you at the house; I told her that I would meet them at the Church.

Marcus you have to be at house so that you can take your place beside Carvell in the family line. He had been spending his night at my place, because he didn't want to be alone. That night when he got there I told him about the call I got from his mother. He looked into my eyes and said I'm glad to see that they are doing their best to make you apart of our family. Plus I do want you by my side. On Saturday morning the two of us got up and had breakfast, then we got into the shower. Once out of the shower we got dressed, we had to be at the house no later than 1:00.

We got to his father's house at 12:30, once parking the car we made our way into the house where his father was. Each member of the family was dressed in purple and ivory. At 1:00 the people from the funeral home arrived, when we walked outside there were seven limos parked in a row. The director asked that the family gather around so he could help them to line up in the other in which we would go into the Church.

The order goes as followed his father and mother, then his stepmother's sisters along with their husbands, brothers with their wives. His stepbrother and his wife and his stepsister, and her husband. Then his sisters' and their husbands and boyfriend, next was the twins with their wives, Carvell and I were behind them. The group that followed us was the grand children and step grand children. The rest of the family followed them. After the pray, we started to get into the limos. We got into the fourth limo with the twin and their wives and his oldest sister and her husband. Once at the Church we lined up again before walking up steps to go into the Church. We made our way in with the Pastor leading the way. In front of the alter was cover with ivory and purple flowers around the ivory casket. The service was very heart felt and warm. Everything took about an hour, and then went to the gravesite, after which we went back to the house where we were going have dinner.

Later that evening Carvell did something that surprised me, and most of his family. He asked me to come with him into the dinning room where he had asked as many of his family members to also come in there too. Once we got into the middle of the room, he took my hand and dropped down on one knee, then placed my hand over his heart and said, "Marcus I have something very important to ask you, and I want my family to be a witness to just how much I love you. So will you make me a very happy man and share the rest of my life with me from this day forward?" then he reached into his packet and came out with a ring box, when he opened it there was a beautiful diamond ring. It didn't take me long to give him an answer to his question, my answer was yes. He got back on to his feet and pulled me close to him and gave me a hug and a kiss. Thank for making me the happiness man in this whole house.

At that moment he may have been the next happiness person in the house, because I was so happy that I felt like I was on cloud nine. Not everyone was for us, one of his stepmother's sisters let it be known that she did not think that two men should be even think about getting married, she said that it wasn't right. That's when another one of the sisters told that she should stop being so hard headed, you need to come out of the dark and start living in here and now. His mother came over and told how happy she was for us, others who wanted to tell so how they felt followed her.

After the dinner was over we went back to my place where he spent the night. Once there I asked him about the ring he had given me. He said that he had talked to his mother, father and stepmother about how he felt about me, and that he wanted to have me in his life for as long as time would allow. Then before my stepmother died she told me that she wanted me to give her ring to you. They knew that I love you with all of my heart. As we talked I shared with him my dream of what kind of ceremony I have always wanted. I know that we could not have a real wedding, but he told me that we could have a commitment ceremony with our families and friends there to see it.

I know that this may sound crazy to other people, I have dreamed of a wedding with a real wedding party. I would use the colors rose and ivory with a touch of gold to sit everything off just right. When I told him about it he agreed to do what ever I wanted. The only thing we had to do is set a date, and find a place to have out ceremony. Later that night we went to bed and before falling sleep he made love to me. The next day we both had to go back to work. When I got to the shop I went to my uncle and told what Carvell had done last night. He looked at me and asked what was your answer; I told him that I had said yes to him. Then he asked when are the two of you going to get married. We have not set a date yet; maybe we will do that tonight.

That night we got together for our date, while we were having dinner he brought up the fact that we had not set a date. I had been thinking about the end of June. I asked now the only thing that we will need is a place to have it. After dinner we seat back and watched a movie, when the movie was over he asked me to spend the night at his place, and I did. As I laid there in his arms I had a dream about what our ceremony could be like. I saw a number of dresses in the color of rose, and two dresses in gold, while I would be wearing ivory. All the men would also be in ivory tuxes. The flowers would be tiger Lilly's and roses. The next day we both just spent most of the day resting, and enjoying being with each other.

About 3:00 his mother called she wanted to come over, so he told it would be ok. When she got there we all set down and talked about the ceremony. He told her that we had talked about the end of June. She told us that she had an idea, he asked her what her idea was, she said why don't you get married on July 4th while the family will all be together that way they will only have to make one trip. He looked at me and asked what do you think about that baby? Well it will ok with me. Now where we have I asked? His mother said what about your father's house? The whole family will be there for the family reunion, and Marcus can invite the people that he wants to be there. Carvell called his father and told him what ideas we had about the ceremony. He agreed to have it at his house on the 4th.

Once his mother had left I started to make notes on what I wanted the ceremony to be like, I basely wrote down everything I had dream about the night before. I had gotten up to go to the kitchen to get something to drink. While I was out of the room he read over the notes. When I came back into the room he let me know that he had read what I had wrote, and that I really like the ideas that you have. Now we have to start getting the people that we want to have in our wedding. I know who I wanted to be my maid of honor, my youngest sister, my matron of honor my close friend. Now I have to come up with the other ten women. While I was trying to think of some women that I think would do this for me. His sister call and she wanted to talk to me. Once I got on the phone she told me that she, and the other two sisters along with the two sisters in laws wanted to be in the wedding. I told her that I would be happy to have them as some of my bride's maids. She said just get back with us on the details. I agreed to do that once I knew just what I wanted. Now I had to come up with five more women. I thought about some people that I could ask, and I started making calls. After about two hours I had the people I needed. Three of my cousins and two other people I knew. I told Carvell how many women had on my list as members of the wedding party. Then he would need to come up with the men. He told me that he was going to ask his brothers, and his brother in law along with his two sisters boy friends. He also was going to ask some of his cousins and some friends that he knew.

I ask him who was going to be his best men? He said that he was going to ask his father to be one of them, and his stepbrother.

Later that evening he called his father back and asked him to be one of his best men. Then he called his stepbrother they both said yes. Now that we had everyone, now it was time for us to start making plans. Now I would have to pick out the dresses and shoes along with the other things I wanted to be used.

A friend of mine's owns a clothing store down town, so was going to go by there tomorrow to see if she has any books that I could bring home to look over to see what I could find. Plus I would to bring back books for Carvell to look though, because he will have to find tuxes for him self and the other men. The next afternoon I went over to my friend's clothing store to get her help. She gave loan me some books that I could take home. While there I told her what colors I had thought about using. She told me that she could get the colors that I wanted, I would have to order the dresses four months before the ceremony to make sure that she could get them back on time. I agreed to make sure that the order would be placed no later than April 1st.

When I got home Carvell was there waiting for me to get home. After dinner we sat down and went though the books to see what we could find. As we sat on the sofa we looked though the books. I found dresses for the women. The ten bridesmaids were going to dresses made with an empire cut bodice, and a slim skirt that has a back walking vent, and spaghetti straps and a lowered back. While the maid and matron of honor's dresses would be gold with spaghetti straps that criss-cross the back of a princess seamed bodice, with a slim shirt that has a flirty side slit. All of the women shoes will be gold and clear sandals that has criss-cross straps across their feet with side adjustable buckle, and 2 ½ inch heels, they will also wear gold jewelry.

He picked out an ivory ¾ tuxedo coat with matching pleated pants, ivory pleated wing collar shirt, and matches ivory shoes. Carvell, the ring bearer and my escort would wear an ivory fullback vest and Windsor ties. The two best men would be wearing the same tuxedos as Carvell and the other men but with a gold fullback vest and Windsor ties to match the dresses of the maid and matron of honor's dresses. The ten groomsmen would be wearing the same tuxedos, with a rose fullback vest and Windsor ties to match the ten bridesmaids dresses. I had decided that I would be wearing ivory, but I wasn't going to let any one know what I was going to be wearing I wanted to surprise Carvell and everyone else.

After we had finished picking out the dresses and tuxedos, we started make out a list of the full wedding party for me to give to my friend so she would have it when they came in to her store to be fitting, and pay their deposit so thing could be ordered. Later that day after I had gone to drop off the list his aunts called me to talk about the ceremony. One of his aunts does flowers and the other one does wedding cakes. They told me that would be willing to do what they could to help. We were going to get a wedding cake big enough to feed over two hundred people, and all the flowers for the ceremony for free. And his mother said we would not have to worry about the food. That evening we started making calls to everyone to let them know where to go for their tux and dresses. They agreed to make it their point to go by the store before April 3rd. That night while we were in bed he asked me what I was going to wear on that day. I told him that I wasn't going to tell him or anyone else.

The next day we spent most of the day laying around and relaxing. We had a lot of fun with each other. That night after he went home to spend the night at his place, so he could be ready for work tomorrow morning. The next few weeks seemed to go by kind of fast. The next thing I knew it was March, and I was working on my idea for what I was going to wear for our ceremony. It was the last week in March I had my finished produce locked away so no one could see it. One night while we were at his place we got phone call from everyone in the wedding party to let us know that they was going to get together that Saturday morning to go to the store to be fitted and to pay their deposit. So we agreed to meet them down there. That next morning we got our self together and went to the store, everyone was there along with our mothers. By the time we left all the dresses and tuxedos were ready to be ordered.

Our Invitations read as followed

Mr. Marcus Jones
And
Mr. Carvell Davis
Along with their parents, and families
Request your present
On Fourth of July, one thousand nine hundred ninety eight
At
The home of Mr. Jonathan Davis
3927 East Highway 211
Cheswick, North Carolina
At
Three O'clock in the afternoon.
As they celebrate their love for each other.
A reception will follow.

We were about a month away from our big day, and things were almost finished. One of his aunts' had done the flowers, and the other one was going to do our cake. The food was going to be done by members of both of our families, because that day was also going to be a family reunion for the two families. The women's dresses were back and each of them had been into the store for their final fitting. What I was going to wear that day was hidden away ready to be wore. One of his cousins, one of his uncles' were going to build a stage to be used that day for us to stand so everyone will be able to see us. The days seemed to be going by fast, and I was ready to become his partner in life. Each night that we spent together was a sign of his love for me, he made love to me, but I didn't know what was yet to come.

A week before our ceremony Carvell and I went to his father's house to talk to his mother and aunts, his cousin who was going to perform the ceremony. We wanted make sure that all the plans for our ceremony. After leaving the house we went back to his place to move the rest of his things into my place. While we were putting away his things he was trying to find what I was going to wear for our ceremony, but he didn't know that it was not anywhere to be found, because I had moved it somewhere to be safe from everyone's eyes. I told him that he would have to wait a few more days. That night we enjoyed a night of talking and watching TV. When it was about time to go to bed he took me by the hand and pulled me to my feet, and lead me towards the bathroom where he undressed me. Then he undressed himself, after that he turned on the water in the shower. Once he had stepped in he held my hand and lead me in. we washed each other's bodies, before making love in the shower.

The night before our ceremony he spent the night at his mother's house. Because we were told by his mother that we could not spend the night together nor see each other the next day until the ceremony. I got to his father's house about noon along with the women in the wedding party. Because we had to get dressed. By 12:30 Carvell and guys came to the house. He tried his best to see me but his mother kept him from coming into the room.

About two thirty other family members started to arrive. By two forty five the yard was full of people, it was almost time for our ceremony to start. I was in the room with the women, but I had not gotten dress yet. I was waiting for them to leave the room, because I did not want to see what I was going to wear. Two fifty his aunt came to the door and told the other women that it was time for them to get into place so that things could get start. As they went out to line up I started to dress.

Three o'clock the music started and our mothers made their way to take their seats. The two of them dressed in ivory suites, and ivory courage with touches of rose and gold. Then Carvell and his two best men along with his cousin who was going to perform the ceremony took they places on the stage, and the ten groomsmen wearing ¾ length tuxedos with rose fullback vest, and rose color rose buds boutonnieres to match the dresses of the bridesmaids lined up one behind the other at the bottom of the side door steps where the women will be coming from the house. The first woman made her way down the steps and to the first groomsman who was going to escort her place then he would also take his place. Each of the ten bridesmaid carried arrangements of mostly ivory roses with a touch of rose ribbons. Their dresses were rose, and made with an empire cut bodice, and a slim skirt that has a back walking vent, and spaghetti straps and a lowered back.

My matron of honor made her way down the steps and start slowly walk towards the stage. My maid of honor followed her. Their dresses were gold with spaghetti straps that criss-cross the back of a princess seamed bodice, with a slim shirt that has a flirty side slit. All of the women shoes were gold and clear sandals that has criss-cross straps across their feet with side adjustable buckle, and 2 ½ inch heels. The maid and matron of honor carried arrangements of mostly ivory roses with a touch of rose and gold ribbons.

Carvell was standing on the upper level of the stage waiting to see me he was wearing an ivory ¾ length tuxedo coat, with matching pleated pants and a ivory wing collar shirt, ivory fullback vest and Windsor tie, and ivory shoes, with an ivory boutonniere tipped in gold. His two best men were standing beside him dressed almost in the same thing that he was, but they had gold fullback vest and Windsor ties, with gold color rose buds boutonnieres to match the dresses of my maid and matron of honor. The ring bearer was next person to make their way down to the stage he was dress just like Carvell and he carried a ivory pillow with two gold rings on top, and rose and gold ribbons.

After everyone was in his or her places. The music for the wedding party stopped and the song that I was going to make my way down to the stage on was about to start, the song title was Always and Forever. When Carvell saw me for the first time his reaction was the one ever, damn baby you look! He said with out realizing how loud he was. Picture me in a hand made ivory satin grown covered in ivory lace with a low cut V back, and a front-side slip which reviled my left leg each time I made a step. The grown fitted with spaghetti straps and a long train made of lace that followed me. I carried ivory tiger lilies and rose, and gold roses with mostly ivory ribbons with a touch of rose and gold. My escort was dressed just like Carvell and the ring bearer.

I slowly made my way to the stage, as I took to the bottom level of the stage Carvell step down and took my hand to help me step onto the upper level where we will be standing for the ceremony. Standing there beside him I turned to look in his eyes, there he was looking so handsome, his eyes were filled with tears that he was doing his best to hold back. I love you with all of my heart, he said. His cousin said today we are all gather here for a special day for our families. The two people standing before us are here to commit themselves to each. As we also come to together here once again for our family reunion.

I ask of you Carvell Davis do you hereby promise to commit your self fully to Marcus Jones as your life partner from this day forward. Carvell answered yes I promise to take marcus as my life partner. Now I ask of you Marcus Jones do you hereby promise to commit your self fully to Carvell Davis as your life partner from this day forward. I answered yes I promise to take Carvell as my life partner. At this time both Carvell and Marcus has something that they wish to say to each other.

Carvell will you please start, He started by saying over a year ago I met you and some how fell in love with then a few months ago I got down on my knees and asked you to sure the rest of my life with me. On that day you made me so happy. Now today you are not only making me happy, but you are filling my heart with so much joy, that I promise to do the very best I can to make you happy each and every day until the day I die. I love you with all of my heart.

Now Marcus will you please start. I started by saying over a year ago I met a young man that touched my heart in so many ways, and like you some how I fell in love. The day that you asked me to sure the rest of your life with you it made me so happy. Now today I stand here in front of both of our families I want you to know just how much I love you.

Now with everything said and do Carvell and Marcus you may now kiss your life partners. After I our kiss he asked us to turn and face our families, then he said today for the first time I introduce to you Mr. Carvell Davis-Jones and Mr. Marcus Jones-Davis, please welcome them in to your family and into your hearts. We were the first to step down from the stage followed by the ring bearer, best men and the maid and matron of honor, then the groomsmen and bridesmaids. The ceremony was now over, and it was time to start reception/family reunion.

His aunt had made a wedding cake for us that was to say the lease wonderful. The cake was sat up in the dinning room of his father's house. The main cake had a 12-inch tier on the bottom with 4 pillars and a lighted fountain in the middle. A top of that was a 10-inch tier with 4 shorter pillars, next there was an 8-inch tier with 4 pillars the last tier was a 6-inch which was top with our special topper, there was two grooms standing side by side before a floral arch of roses and peals on a base adorned with soft lace. On the right side of the main cake were three more cakes, which stood stair stepped one in front of the other curved toward of the front. Each tier were decorated with rose colored roses with green leaves, and gold colored ruffling trim. Each of the smaller cakes were done with one 8-inch tier topped with a 6-inch tier.

That after noon we had a lot of fun. There were a few people there that were not happy about what we had, but it didn't matter because we loved each other and we wanted everyone to know. After followed the order of the reception, and his mother had made sure that plates were fixed for us to take with us on our trip. Before the family reunion was over we left to start on our trip. We were going to V.A. for what could be called our honeymoon. We had booked a room at a motel for the weekend. Carvell drove to the motel from his father's house. Once there we went to the room and got ourselves ready for the night ahead.

I went into the bathroom to take off the clothes that I was wearing, and he was in the room undressing. When I opened the door he was laying on the bed waiting for me. He was wearing only a white thug and nothing else. Well I too was wearing a thug that day under my clothes. I walked over to the bed and sat down on the side of the bed next to him. He reached out for my hand, and said I have a special gift for you. As he looked into my eyes he said I want you to do something tonight that will make me yours. I asked him what he was talking about; he said I want you to fuck my ass for the first time. The only thing I could get out of my mouth was, are you sure that's what you want? Yes, he replied I want you to burst my ass, I know that it is going to hurt, but I am yours now and this is my gift to you.

You can unwrap your gift when ever your ready. I got on the bed, and pulled the thug he had on off. Carvell said come on baby do what you have to now, I have been waiting for you to take my ass. I asked when did you come up with this idea? I had been thinking about this for a while now. He pulled the thug that I had on off, then I got the lube that we were going to need, and lube us both up. I got between his legs and lifted them into the air, I slowly worked my way into his tight ass, once my dick head popped in I heard him let out a loud moan because of the pain that he was feeling. I took the time to let him get used to having my hard dick in his ass. Without pushing or anything it went in the full length. I laid there waiting for him to let me know that he was ready, his words were fuck me baby I am ready for you to take what yours. I did just what we both wanted I fucked his tight ass slowly until I couldn't hold back any longer. Then I knew that I was hurting him but I was to far gone to stop. He was holding close to him tightly and we both were wet with sweat. I could hold back any longer, and I shoot my hot load into his wet ass hole. This was the first time that he had ever allowed me to fuck him. From the first time we had sex the only things he wanted was to have me suck his dick, and he fucked me when ever he want to.

Then one night while I was sucking his dick I tried to ease my finger into his tight hole, he stopped me. After a few times he would let me finger his hole, but I couldn't go that deep. He has always been the real man in our relationship from the start. So what would make a man like that to change his mind? That night as we laid in the motel bed holding each other, I asked him to tell me why he wanted me to fuck him? He said I had been thinking about our relationship, and how much I loved you. That's what made me realize that you deserved to have all of me in every way. Then he went on to say I had been very selfish since started having sex. I was only out to get what I wanted, which was wrong, but now I know that you have needs too. Marcus you are the first and only man to ever do anything like this to me.

We fell asleep in each other's arms, the next morning when I work up I found Carvell holding my hard dick in his hand. When he knew that I was woke he told me that he was ready for it again. I didn't move or say anything, that's when he asks me, baby did you hear what I said? I replied yes I heard you, then I asked are you sure that's what you want to do? Yes, that's what I want; I enjoyed that big dick of yours inside of me last night. Plus you don't have to wait for me to ask you, you can fuck me any time that you want to, I'm yours now. So we did make love, then we got out of bed and took a shower together.

We went out to have breakfast and to do some shopping. While we were out I was feeling pretty good knowing that the man with was mine's, no one could change that. While we were in one store, I was looking at some t-shirts and he was looking though another rack of clothing when a young woman walked over to him and tried to talk to him. She didn't know that we were together. But Carvell didn't wait to long before he told her that he was shopping with his husband. She looked at him in a funny way, that's when I walked over to where they were and put my hand on his lower back. He looked around at me, and said hi baby did you find anything that you want to take back with us. I showed him the two t-shirts that I had in my other hand. Is that all you want? He asked with a big smile on his face. well I had thought about trying to find some shorts to match them, if that's okay with you?

I'll be glad to wear an outfit like. I had to ask him if the color was okay? He replied why not, well they are pink I said as a joke. Baby I like pink, why wouldn't I want us to dress a like? Lets see if we can find some pink shorts, then we walked over to a rack where some shorts were hanging. We did find some pink shorts that were the same color as the t-shirts. On the front of the shirt was V.A. is for lovers, when got to the counter he asked the guy standing there if he put something on the back of the shirt. He said yes we can airbrush what ever you want on it for you. Carvell told that he want to have the words we belong together for ever. So that's what he did while we waited. Once he had finished, we were told that it was going to take a few hours for the print to fully dry, and then put each shirt on a hanger, so that we could hang them up over night to dry. We still have another day before we go home, so by the time we get ready to leave we will be able to wear them home.

While we were out we got food to take by to the motel with for lunch. After we got back to the motel things heated up between us again. Believe watching him walk around the room with a pair of string bikini underwear, and nothing else can make things react. I was seating in the chair trying to watch something on TV. I guest you know what got hard, it didn't help having him standing next to me, where I could reach out and touch his ass.

We had one more day in the motel. The two of us were going to check out on Monday afternoon to drive home. After having sex that night, we slept nude in each other's arms. The next morning we got breakfast and spent the day enjoying the sites and shopping. He did everything that he could think of to make sure that I had fun on our trip. Our last night there was filled with dinner and dancing, then we went back to the motel room to get some rest for our trip back home. The following morning we got up to take a shower, and ended up having sex. So we had to clean up before packing up to head home.

Once we had gotten on the road, Carvell cell phone started to ring. He told me to answer it for him. I said hello to the person on the other end was one of his cousins; he wanted to talk to him. I told Carvell who was on the phone, I gave the phone to him, but I couldn't hear what his cousin was saying. He told him that he was on his way back from V.A. and that he would call him when he gets back in town. That's when ended the phone call. I did ask him what was said but I could tell that he was upset by it. Next thing I knew he had reached out and placed him hand on top of mine's. He said some people just don't give up, even when they know it's the best thing to do. I didn't as what he was talking about, I just said don't worry about it. the drive took us about six hours to get home, once we got back he wanted to let his mother know that we were back, so we went by her house. Her first words were what are you doing here? You should be somewhere enjoying each other. Carvell said believe me we have enjoyed out honeymoon. He had a big smile on his face, his mother looked at him and asked what is that smile about, I know you, something up.

Well mom I have something to tell you, I looked at him not knowing what he was going to say, my heart started to beat faster. She said what is it, well something happened on the first night we were in V.A., he put his arm around me then he said I gave myself to Marcus all the way. She looked at us with a puzzled look on her face. I held my breath for a moment, waiting for him to drop the boom. That's when he said I let Marcus fuck me in the ass. When he said that I wanted to go though the floor. She replied was that what you wanted to do? His words were yes that's what I wanted. At that moment I felt something come over me. His mother started to smile, and then she said as long as your happy, I'm happy for you.

Mom believe me I am happy with Marcus. I have found what I had been missing. What I did was thought out carefully. It was hard for me to wait until after our ceremony. Now that I have done it, I feel good about it. Well all I have to do now is tell my brothers and sisters. You know that they will be behind you no matter what, his mother said with a smile. About that time his cell phone started to ring, when he looked at the caller id, he said why don't he gave up. She asked who is it? Its little J. he called me earlier and I told him than that I would call him back when I got home. I just don't why he can't seem to understand that I want to be with Marcus. Every else he found out that I was dating him he has been trying to come between us. Don't worry about him; just do everything that you can to make your relationship work.

While we were sitting here his mother's phone, when she answered it, one of his brothers was calling to see if she had heard from Carvell. She told him that we were back in town, and that we were at her house right then. He asked to talk to Carvell. She asked him to hold on, then she gave the phone to him, what's up man, we got back in town a little while ago. I needed to talk to mom about something, so we came over here before going home. They didn't talk very long, after giving the phone back to his mother. She hung it up. We said our good night, because we needed to go home to get some rest.

Once getting home we got our things out of the car, and carried it into the house. We weren't going to unpack the bags, so we just left them in the living room. We didn't stay up for long because we both were tried from our trip. Once in the bedroom we took off all of our clothes and got into bed. Laying there for a while holding each other, the only thing I member was waking up the next morning still in his arms. He was sleeping with his nude warm body almost on top me. I was willing to let sleep, but his cell phone rung, and that woke him up, he reach for the phone, half asleep he answered it hello, man I was tried when we got back last night, so we came home and got into bed, where we are right now. What is so important that you have to talk to me so bad?

Look try to understand that I need to get so more rest, and plus I am laying here with my baby. I promise that I will go you back later. After hang up the phone he pulled me closer to him, and started to kiss on my neck and shoulder. Believe me he knew that he was turning me on. My dick started to react to what he was doing, and my breathing changes. I want you right now he said. Let me make love to you, and then you can do the same to me, he said as he ran his hand down my back and then he rubbed my ass. I was ready for anything that he wanted. He got in between my legs and raised them into the air, after lubing us both up he slowly eased his hard dick into my waiting ass hole. He made love to me slowly. Don't hold back fuck me, I said. Could tell that he was at the point of no return, he was about ready to cum. He pulled out of me, said now it's your turn; I want you to fuck me. That's just what I did his moans told just how much he was enjoying it.

After we had finished, we got up and went into the bathroom and got into the shower. Our hands were all over each other's bodies as we washed. Once we had dried off we didn't put on any clothes for a while. I enjoyed looking at his nake body as we walked around in the house. About 3:00 pm his sister called and wanted to come over. He asked me if I would mind if he asked his brothers and sisters to come over so he could talk to them. I told him that it would be ok with me. Called the other brothers and sisters to tell them that he wanted to see them. The two of us got dressed, and waited for them to get to the house. We dressed in our pink t-shirts and shorts; Carvell was the picture of a real man. He was well built, with the ass of a black man. Plus he was a very handsome young man. A lot of both women and men wanted to be with him, and I knew it, but he was all mine. A little over an hour later our house was full of his brothers, sisters and their other halves.

As everyone sat in our living room Carvell and I sat together with holding me close to him. Well I know that you want to know what I have to talk to you about. Last night I told mom something that I need to tell you. Then he took a deep breath and said on the first night of our honeymoon I gave my body to Marcus. One of his brothers asked what do you mean, you gave your body to Marcus? Well I allowed him to fuck my ass. After saying that he waiting for one of them to say something in response to what he had said. His oldest sister was the first one to say what ever makes you happy. You are still our brother no matter what. Then one of twins (brothers) asked how did it feel? Carvell said it was my first time, it hurt, but I liked it. The rest of the time they were there with us, they joked around about it.

A few days later his family got together at his father's house. His cousin little J. was there. While some of us was standing around talking he walked over to us and wanted to get in on what we were talking about. One of Carvell's brothers made a joke by asking him how do your butt feel today? The reply was it feels good after this morning. That's when little J. made a statement why don't you stop talking like a fag, and be a man. I know that you are not a fag. The brother that made the joke said man why don't you stop acting like a dope. Why can't you see that Carvell is happy? Carvell said man I love because you are family, and now Marcus is apart of this family. So you need to get us to it. That's why little J. got mad and walked away.

Little J's sister Brenda was standing there, she said I don't what's wrong with him. He is acting like jealous about Marcus being apart of your life. She went on to say I'm glad that you have found some one to make you happy, and I glad to have him as a part of this family. His brothers started to play around like a group of young kids. Some of the kids of the family got into the games too. The next thing I knew Carvell pulled me into what was going on we were having so much fun. Later that evening we went home and spent some time alone.

One day while I was at work I got a call on my cell phone, the person on the other end asked to speak to Marcus Jones-Davis. I replied this is Marcus. He went on to tell me that something had happened at the dealer ship, and Carvell had been taken to the hospital. I thank him for calling me. I went to my uncle and told that something had happened to Carvell at the dealer ship, and he had been taken to the hospital, and I needed to go and see what was going on. He told me to go a head, and check on your man. I got into my car and drove to the hospital's ER. When I got there I gave the woman at the desk his name. She asked me if I was a member of his family I said yes I am. Then she asked what is your name? I told that I am Marcus Jones-Davis. Take a seat and someone will be with you in a moment. A nurse came to the door and called my name. I got up and walked towards her, she come with me. We walked to a small room were Carvell was laying.

I said in a soft voice Carvell I'm here baby. He opened his eyes and said I'm glad you're here. Then I asked him what happened? He said that someone hit him with a car. Just as he told me that the doctor came into the room to exam him. While he was doing the exam, he found that Carvell could not feel his legs. The doctor told us that he needed run some test to see what's going on. You will have to stay in the hospital for a few days. When the doctor left the room I called his mom and told that he was in the hospital. It wasn't long before they came into to take him to have x-rays done. By that time his mom and some of his brothers and sisters had gotten. When they brought him back to the small room, I let them come in and see him.

Later the hospital had a room ready for him. It was going to be on the third floor, Room 314. The orderlies took up to the room.

I went up with them, and his family followed. The next few days the doctor did a lot test, but he couldn't any reasons why Carvell could not feel his legs. So he released him and let him go home. His mom said that she would help me take care of him, and she did. For a few months he had to us a wheel chair. Then one day when he went to rehab things changed he was able to take his first steps. The doctor told him that he had to take it easily for a while. After a couple visits to the doctor we were told that he was not going to be able to go back to work. Because his legs may give out on him again. After getting that news he talked to the owner of the dealer ship about was going, and he told him that he would not have to worry, because he was going make sure that he would be looked out for. Until he could get some other income coming in. the doctor was going to paperwork to help him get disability.

It took about three months for the disability to come though. Also the head office of the dealer ship sent Carvell a letter telling him that they were going to make payments to him once a month for the rest of his life, because what happened to him. He told me baby I am going to be able to take care you in the way I really want to. Well if he only knew the truth about the way I really feel. I would love him even he didn't have a dime to his name. I am happy that he was able to walk, but if for some reason he never walked again I would be right by his side.

One day he called me at work to tell me that Little J. wanted him and one of the twins to ride with him to V.A. to take care of some business, and that he would be back home by the time I get off of work. That evening when I got home Carvell was not here. I tried to call his cell phone, and got no answer. I also tried to his brother's cell. That night seemed to be a real long night for me not knowing what was going on. I got into bed about 11:00 pm, but he was still not at home. About 12:30 I heard a car door open and close. As I laid there hoping that it was him and that he was ok. When I heard the front door open I made up my mind to lay there in bed as if I was sleep. He came into the bedroom and undressed, then he got in to bed beside me softly calling my name, but I didn't answer him. As he put his arm around me I could tell that he was crying. After a few moments I let him know that was a wake, I turned over and put my arms around him, holding him close to me.

Carvell said I know that you mad with me, but you need to know that Little J did everything that he could to keep TJ and me from coming home early. He wouldn't let us our cell phones. When we tried to make call he talked to us as we were less than men when we wanted to let the people that we love know what was going on. I know that I have learn my lesson, from now on I give up on him, I am going wash my hands of him. Please forgive me it will never happened again no matter what. I said I was worried that something had really happened to you. The next I got up to go to work, while he was still in bed asleep. About 11:00am he called me, the first thins he wanted to know why didn't you wake me up this morning? Well I felt that you needed the rest after your late night. His reply was that's not a good joke, the next time I still late its going to be with you. I am going to call Little J and let him know that what he did has messed up the relation ship with me.

After work I came to find him laying on the sofa waiting for me to get home. About the time I walked in to the door his call phone started to ring. When he answered it, once he found out who was on the other end, he said Little J I don't know why you are calling me. We have nothing else to say to each other. Then he hung up the phone, he just as well stop calling me. I don't want to talk to him. By the way baby I got something in the mail today that I think you will be happy about. He reached on to the coffee table and picked up a letter. When I opened the letter I read that there was a check enclosed in the amount of $1,675.00, which is your payment for this month. This letter was from the dealer ship. Then he handed me some papers, these papers was from his bank showing that has opened an account with most of the money. The last thing he gave me was $500.00, and told I want you take this money spend on yourself. I tried to tell him that I didn't need to take his money, but he informed me that it wasn't just his money, but it belongs to both if us.

Marcus can you take a little time off of work to go by the bank and sign some paperwork, so your name can be put on all of my accounts. Plus they are going order ATM cards and checks. From now on all of my money will be going into the bank, and I want you to be able to handle my money too. After dinner we went out to do some shopping. Carvell made sure that I spent every cent of that $500.00 on me. I had thought about spending it on the two of us, but he would not let me do it, every time I tried to pick up something for him he would tell me to put it back.

When I got to the checkout I had spent the $500.00, there was $35.00 tax, which he paid himself. After getting home he wanted to see everything that I had brought. The next day I took a little time from work to go to the bank to sign my name on his accounts. While we were sitting there he made sure that the woman knew that I would have all rights to the accounts. That's when he said now you have all of my money. That evening when I got home we talked about we were going pay the bills we had. He told me that he will pay all the bills, but I told him that I would not let him do that. That's when he said well how about me paying half of all of the bills. So we did agree to that.

About a week later he wanted us to going out to pick up a few things, when we got ready to go to the checkout, he told me to us my bankcard. I don't think I have that much money in my account, who said anything about your account he said. You do have the card to our accounts. When we got to the checkout the system asked for ID for some reason. When I gave the young woman my ID she wanted to know who was Carvell Davis. He spoke up and said I am, but my partner has all rights to use that card, plus he has the right to write checks on the account. She went on and up it though. But he still ask her why did the system ask for ID when both of our names are on the account. She said maybe it was because there are two names on the account.

After putting what we brought away, we went into the kitchen and fitted dinner, and then we sat in the living room and eat while we watched TV. Once we had finished eating he had other things on his mind, and he started to let me know what he wanted by kissing me on my neck, then pulling my t-shirt up and over my head. He then started to lick and suck my nipples, which turned me on. The next thing he did was to take my shorts off. The only thing I had left was my underwear, but I didn't have them on for long. We made love right there on the sofa. The two of us did everything that we could do to each other. We licked and kissed each other's bodies, then did 69 so we could suck each other's dick. Before things were over we fucked each other. After that we went into the bathroom and took a nice long shower, washing each other's bodies, then we licked each other dry. That night we held each other's nake bodies all night as we have done every night.

On one Saturday when I got home from work Carvell told me to pick us a bag, because we were going to V.A. until Sunday evening. I asked what's going on? He said we are going back to motel where we spent our honeymoon. So I got us a change of clothes, and we got into car and drove to V.A. well that night after we had gotten in to the room his cell phone started to ring it was Little J. Carvell did not answer it. So he turned around and called my cell phone, which I didn't answer. You may not believe what Little J did. On Sunday when we walked out of the motel room to get ready to come back home the V.A. police was waiting for us. An office came over to us and asked our names. Once we had told him who we were he called another over, and that office told me to come with him. When I did he walked me to a police car, where he told me to turn around and put my hands behind my back. I asked him what I had done? The only thing he said was you need to come with us for questing. About that time Carvell started to go off he wanted to know what was going on? I could not hear what the officer was telling him.

Carvell pulled out his wallet to show the office the card he had that would show that we were life partners. Once the saw the card, and what was on it. The officer called the other officer and told him to let me go. That's when we found out who had called the police, it was Little J. when he saw that the police was letting me go little J started to act like a real fool. He was trying to tell the police that I had forced Carvell to come to V.A. with me. He wanted them to think that Carvell was not in his right mind or something. The police arrested little J for make a false report. Then officers told that they were sorry for putting us though that, and wished us a safe trip by home.

On our way back little J's girlfriend called Carvell cell phone going off on him for having little J arrested. Carvell told her that he didn't have anything to do with his arrest; the police was the one who made the call on that. Then he hung up the phone on her. After that call little J's mother called. She said that she was not upset with him about what had happened. He told her what little J had tried to do to me. He told me what she had told him, told him that little J had no right to do what he did.

About a week later we had to go back to V.A. to testify in court. Little J was still trying to make everyone think that I was forcing Carvell to do things against his will, but no one would believe him. The judge gave him 90 days in jail for filing a false police report, which made him mad as hell. His mother and girlfriend were there in court too. His girlfriend was very upset with the judge and us; she was running off at the mouth really loud. The judge told her that she would have to be quite or leave the courtroom. When we walked out she started to go off on us, little J's mother tried to get her to come down. Carvell told her that he had done to himself. The two us walked out of the courthouse and drove back home. Later the night little J's mother called us to tell us that she was sorry about the way Joyce Ann had acted at the courthouse.

It was different having Carvell at home waiting for me each day when I come home from work. He couldn't work, but he was becoming a very good househusband. He some time have dinner ready, there were days when he couldn't do much because of his legs. From time to time they would get weak and he had trouble walking or doing other things. In the mornings he would get and go into the bathroom and take a light bath. Then in the evening he would say that he wanted to take a shower, knowing that he did not get into the show alone because he was worried about his legs giving out and falling. So whenever he said that he was going to take a show, he meant that we were going to take a show together. Most of the time we would end up having sex.

One day a box came for him, and I wanted to know what was in it. So as we sat on the sofa he opened the box. He pulled out little clear packages I asked what they were, he said just wait a moment and you will see. The box was filled with what I found out with sexy underwear in many colors. He had order some underwear for us both. Things like low rise, bikinis, and see through, along with thugs. The underwear was the kinds that he likes to wear. I noticed that some of them were too small for him, when I looked in side of a pair I noticed that they were my size. That's one thing that loved about him, he like to wear his little sexy underwear. And his pants fit him just right, and when he wear shorts they make his body look so good.

While we were sitting he got up and started undressing, once he was down to nothing, he picked up a red thug and put it on. How do you like this he asked as he stood there in front me? I smiled and said yes I do like what I see. I glad that you like it, because I want to dress as sexy as I can to keep you turned on. I'm only doing this for you and only you. I want you r dick to get hard every time you look at me. After that I got up and took off my clothes so I could try on a pair of the underwear had brought me. I picked up a pair of sheer white bikinis and put them on, now what do you think? His replied I like the way they fit you, but I want you to turn around and let me see how they look on your ass. So I did just what he asked. His reacted by saying wow baby your ass look good enough to eat.

At that point he reached out put his fingers in to the waistband of the underwear and pulled them down, then lead over and kissed both of my ass cheeks. Now bend over and let me have my snack baby. I did just what he wanted, and he licked my asshole until it was wet. It taste so good baby. After doing that he let me know that he wanted me to make love to him. Before going to sleep we went into the bathroom and took a shower together, because we really needed it after getting sweaty and dirty from the sex.

Starting the next morning and every morning after I would pick out the underwear that we both would wear that day. One weekend we at his mother's house with his other brothers and sisters along with their other halves. While we were sitting there someone started a game where we had to answer questions about our other halves to see how well we knew each other. Someone put the question out there, what kind of underwear do your wife or husband have on right now? Carvell and I were the forth couple to answer the question. I said that he had on a pair of sheer blue bikinis that match the shirt he had on. His mom said now we have to check to see if Marcus is right. Carvell stood up and undid the to of his pants and gave them a peep at the underwear he had on. I was right because I was the one that picked them out, plus I was also wearing the same type and color. After buttoning his pant back up he sat down and gave me a kiss. Once the games were over we went into the dinning room and eat dinner there was a lot of food, because his mother had cooked put the rust of us brought dishes that we had cooked.

Sending time with his brothers and sisters was a fun time, because they love to have fun with each other. We also found time to spend my family. We sometimes went out to a club for a night of dancing and fun. One night we went out with is brother and sisters along with their other halves. Let me tell about one night that we went out; the guys had gotten up from the table to go to the bar to get drinks. While they were gone a woman tried to come on to Carvell, but he didn't respond to her. When they got back to the table he told me about what had happened.

The DJ started to play good dance song, so he asked me to dance; our whole table got up and headed for the dance floor. The girls and I looked at each other, and then we started to dirty with our men. We danced up very close to them rubbing our bodies against them. The woman that tried to come on to him got really mad, and started running off at the mouth about it. The women made sure that she found out that she was making a big mistake. The next song that the DJ played was a slow one; he put his arms around me and danced with holding me close to him. We didn't care about letting people know that we were together. There was one love song were the guys took us out on the dance floor and got down on one knee and sung to us.

When we got ready to leave the woman was out side of the club, and she let us know that she was not happy. Just as I was about ready to say something to her Carvell stepped in and told that I was his husband and that he was very happy with the man in his life. At that point we walked away and got into our car to leave. She wasn't the first and I knew that she was not going to be the last to make a play for my man. Though the years there were many things that the two of us went though, but we made and our love grew stronger over time.

One our tenth anniversary we recommit our relation to each other in front of our family and friends. On that day we used the same color that we had used ten years before. The dresses and tuxedos styles were different. I also had a very different dress; I wanted to make him weak in the knees. When he saw me for the first time he had a one of kind reaction. We had a lot of fun that day, and then we went to V.A. for our second honeymoon just as we had done for our first one.

A few months later his father got sick and dead, on the day of his home going service, I took my place beside Carvell in the family line, I stood by his side though it all. When my father dead he did the very same for me. We took very good care of each other, and we shared a love that unbreakable. Today we both are older, and still in love with each other. Love can stand the test of time; we have found that out the hard way. Some people ever thought that a gay couple could love each other until death. Maybe now our families will see that love like ours could last.

About Carvell was not only did he not only like to wear his clothes neat. I have told you that he also likes to wear sexy underwear, and sometimes when we are at home alone he has some short shorts that he puts on; the best of all is when we both walk around nake. There has been times when I have been sitting at our computer checking e-mail. He would come into the room with nothing on and stand in front of me, and then he would bend over. I knew just what to do first I would bite his left butt cheek then I went to the right one. From there I would lick his sweet juicy ass hole just before I made hot love to him.

We also had an agreement that when I came home from work he would meet me at the door with a hug and kiss. While we were doing that I had to grab his ass though his pants or I would put my hand down his pants. Plus there was another part of the agreement if one of us was sleep and the other one got horny the one that was horny could remover the other ones clothes and have our way with then. That also included when we were in bed at night sleep. Say if the two of us were asleep in bed, and I woke up in the middle of the night with a hard dick, all I had to do was put on a condom; lube it so I could slide it into his hot hole. There were a few times that he had laid down to take a nip, as he laid there I walked into the room to find him wear only his underwear, so I eased them down and went for what I wanted. Some people may say that what I did to him was rape, but to him it was just the person that he loved enjoying him.

Don't get me wrong he also did the same things to me whenever he wanted to make love to me. One night we were sitting in the living room watching TV, and I wanted to have some fun, so I started taking off his clothes. Once he was nake I pulled him close to me, he laid his head on my shoulder. Then he pull my t-shirt off, he tenderly kissed my chest. Next he undid my pants and pulled them down. Once they were down at my feet he took them all the way off, my underwear followed. We laid on the sofa nake, in each other's arms. Our hands touching each other's bodies, soon we were lost in time and in the warmth of sexy body heat. Whenever we did something like that we became one in passion, we will always be one in love.

One Sunday morning we slept late, and when we got up we showered and put on just enough to walk around the house in., which meant that both of us had on a t-shirt and a pair shorts. While we were in the kitchen I walked over to where he was standing and pulled his shorts down pass his knees. He wasn't wearing any underwear so I got a good look at his fine ass. That's not all that I did, I ran my finger up and down his ass crack stopping to play with his asshole. Before it was over we both were nake and having sex right there in the kitchen. After our sweaty fun we had to get cleaned up again. Later that day while we were laying on the bed. There was a knock on our front door. I got up and went to the door, when I opened it there were his two brothers standing there. They asked for him, I told them that he was in the bedroom. One of them called out to him saying boy you need to get your ass out here now. When Carvell walked out of the bedroom, one of them put his arms around my waist and said I was just getting ready to take my girlfriend out for some fun. They loved to joke with him about me. The four of us sat down in the living room and talked for a long time. Carvell got up from the sofa to go into the kitchen to get some sodas for every body. I reached out and grabbed his ass. He looked around at me with a funny look on his face. Then he turned and walked in to the kitchen. When he returned he handed each of us a soda. Then he sat down beside me as close as he could get.

After his brothers left we both were ready to eat dinner, so we went into the kitchen and found us something to warm up. We spent the rest of the evening watching TV and having fun with each other. When it was bedtime we went into the bedroom and undressed, and got under the covers where we held each other all that night. When my clock went off I knew that it was time for me to get up, so I eased out of bed hoping not to awake Carvell. Well he had always told me not worry about waking him whenever I got out of bed. But I just wanted to let him get his rest. While I was in the bathroom taking a shower, he came into the bathroom and slipped into the shower with me. After our shower we went into the bedroom to get dress. Once I had dressed I went into the kitchen to get something to eat. He gave me a kiss right before I got ready to walk out the door.

That evening after work I came home and was greeted at the door by my man wearing only a towel and a smile. He gave me a kiss and I removed the towel from around him. While holding him I grabbed his ass and held on tight. At that time I was wishing that I was also nake so I could feel his hot skin against me. I wanted to jump out of my clothes right then and there. I knew how his skin felt by what my hands was touching. At that point my dick started to wakeup and I knew that he could feel it too. I could feel him trying to unbuttoning my shirt, as it opened he kissed the skin on my chest. Then he undid my pants, and let them drop to the floor. As we stood there holding each other, I started thinking about having hot sex with him. I had just gotten off of work and dirty; I needed to take a shower. Carvell broke our hug, and then he finished undressing me. Then he took me by the hand, turning and started walking toward the bathroom, leading me by the hand. Once in the bathroom he leaned over to start the shower, we stepped in, he washed my body tenderly and slowly.

Once we were out of the shower we dried each other off. Then we put on our robes, and walked into the dinning, where he told me to take a seat. He went to the kitchen and fixed our plates. Carvell and I shared a loving and wonderful night together along with so many more wonderful years with each other.

College And Beyond

In just a few weeks I will be leaving for college, and this will be a scary time because I will not know anyone there. I guest when I get there I will find out who my roommate is going to be. I hope that we will be able to get along. My parents are trying not to worry, but I can tell that they are doing so. I am going to have to say good-bye to my girl friend, along to other friends. It maybe a while before I will get to see them again. I really hope that I will make some friends on campus. I am counting down the days until I leave the town that I grow up in. this is a small town where most of the people here know each other, and most of my family are here. As I lay here in bed tonight I can't help but think about being alone there.

I woke up this morning and started my day off with breakfast, then I took a shower, I hope to spend time with my girl friend today. So I called her to find out what she wanted to do. After getting dressed I went over to her house, where we sat and talked for a while, then we went out to get something to eat. The two us walked in the park around the lake. I took time to talk to her about my going away to college in just a few weeks. She took what I had to say real well. We said that we will call and write to each other, and I told her that I would be coming home before to long, then we would be able to get together then. It was getting later in the afternoon, and she had to get home, so I took her home. We said our good-byes in my car. I waited for her to get into the house before I backed out of her parents driveway.

I did not go home myself because I had to go to the mall to pick up some things to take to college with me. On my way home I started thing about what path I wanted to take to get the degree

I wanted. I remembered that I had to drive to the school Friday morning to talk to someone there about the classes I will need to signup for. I am going to be making the trip alone, so I will have to leave very early that morning. In the back of my mind I feel that it's going to be a little scary, I know I can handle it. After getting home my parents wanted to have a talk with me about my trip. They told all things that most parents would tell their child who is about to take a trip like this.

The days went by fast and Friday was only hours away. I had to go to bed early Thursday night because I had to be up at four Friday mornings to get dressed and eat something before I started on the drive. As I was sitting at the table eating mom walked in she had gotten up to see me off. Dad was still sleep because he had to get up later to go to work. You know how moms are, no matter how old we get we will still be their baby. It doesn't help really be her youngest child. I told my mother that I would see her and dad later tonight when I get back home. As I pulled out of our driveway mom was standing in the doorway, we both waved to each other, when I turned onto the highway I started wondering about how things were going to go once I seat down with Mr. A Battle in his office later this morning. The hours and miles seem going by kind of slow, maybe it was because I had never taking this trip alone before. When I cam to see the campus my parents came with me. When I pulled onto the campus I was trying to read the signs that were around telling me which way I needed to go to find the admin building that's is where Mr. Battle's office is located. I was able to find the building that I needed there was a lot of cars in the parking lot. I found a parking pace on row 6 in the middle of the row.

After getting out of my car I made sure that I had every thing I may need before I locked the doors, and walked toward the building. When I enter the building there was a big counter area where four women sat at their decks. I went up to the counter, and one of the women as if there was thing she help me. I told her that I was there to see Mr. A. Battle this morning at 10:00. She told me have a seat and that she will let him know that I was there. I turned around and walked over to the seating area where some other people were already sitting, I sat down and looked around the room to see what was there. While waiting some of other people were called into offices. Then a tall middle aged black man walked up to the counter and talked to one of the women, when he turned to face the seating area, he called out my name, I stood up and started to walk towards him, as I stood in front of him he reach out his hand for a hand shake.

After that we went into his office where we sent about two hours talking. He seem to understand that I was lose on which way I should go for now college was going to be something new to me, so he helped me to see what my first steps were going to have to be if I wanted to make the next four years work for me. When it was over I felt good about what we had decided. I walked out of his office and headed for the parking lot so I can start on my drive home. Hours later I pulled up into my driveway it was about 6:30 by that time, and I was ready to get inside and change clothes, plus get something to eat. I got out of my car and went into the house and just what I was thinking. After I finished eating my parents wanted to find out how things went at the meet this morning. I explained everything to them, and I hoped that they understood what I was trying to tell them.

Once I had rested some I called my girl friend to let her know that I was back and to talk to her about my meeting with Mr. Battle. I told her what he had talked to me about, so the next two weeks is going go by fast for me. I talked to her about time we should send together. After talking to her, I laid back on my bed and watched TV until I started getting sleepy. I turned off the set and went to sleep. As I slept I dreamed about my girl friend and going to college, the dream started out with her sitting together with me on the sofa at her parents house, we cuddle up with each other. Then it went from that to me heading off to college.

The next morning when I work up it was hard for me to remember much about the dream. I could only see parts of it in my mind, so I did not try to remember it so I decided to get up and take a shower, then get dress. After breakfast I called my girl friend to see if we could spend the day together. She told me that had to stay home and baby-sit here little sister, but I could over to her house. Well I did go over there, and the two us spend the day doing things with her little sister, there wasn't very much time for us to spend alone. Once their parents got home, we left and went for a drive to the park, where we sat in the car, and held each ours' hands.

As I held her hand I lead over and gave her a kiss. Before long we had to find us some else to go, because we wanted to have sex. She knew of a place where we could go, she had a cousin that had a house on the other side of town; she called from cell to ask if we could come over for a while. Her cousin told her that it would be ok. So we went on our way to her house, once we got there we got out of the car and walked up to the front door. She knock on the door, then her cousin came to the door, and opened it, and told us to come in. she must have known what was on our mind because she told us to go into the other room where we could be alone.

We went to the room and closed the door, where we took off our clothes and had sex. Once it was over the two of us got redressed. Then we sat there for a while talking about me going off to college. She told me that she was going to miss me once I left, about a half an hour later, we decided that it was time for her get back home. So she went into the room where her cousin was and told her that we were getting ready to leave. Then she walked us to the front and we all said good night, after getting into the car I took her home, once there I kissed her good bye, I waited for to get into the house before I backed out of their driveway. When I got home I got off of my car and went into the house, and went into the kitchen to get something to eat.

After eating I went to my room, so I could take off my clothes to take a shower, once I had dried off I went back into my bedroom and watch TV for a while before getting into bed. The days flew by and the time was getting close at hand for me to leave for college, I needed to pack up what needed to take with me, an I want to see y girl friend before I left. So I called her to see we could get together, she said ok. So I went over to her parent's house to get so we could spend this tie alone, because I was horny and wanted to have sex with her. When got off to ourselves I made my move and she shoot me down when she told me that it was time of the month, and we could not have sex. So ever though I really want sex I was welling to set and talk. Then I took her home where we said good night. I only had two days left before I was leaving, and sex was out of the question.

I spend all the time that I could with my girl friend but still no sex. Here was Thursday and I would be leaving in the morning for college, my parents are going to also drive to the school so I can take all my stuff with me, and they want to see where I was going to be staying. Well being an 18 year old I tried again to get her to have se with me, but she still couldn't. So I was going to be leaving without sex, and it was going to be a while before I would be back home. I was going to do my best not to think about it. That night I went to bed early so could be able to get up at three am to get ready to take the drive to the college and move in to the dome room with a roommate that I was going to meet for the first time. I fell a sleep kind of fast, and did a little dreaming about my girl friend and going off to school.

First morning my clock went off at three am, and got up so I could go into the bathroom to get ready for breakfast before the long trip that I was about to take. After getting dress I into the kitchen where my parents were, my mother had breakfast already done, so all I had to do was sat down and eat. She had fitted all of my favors. Once we had finished eating we got ready to leave. Everything was already loaded into my father's SUV and my car. All we had to do was take for the drive. I followed my father to the school. When got there we had to find the dome where I was going to living for the next few years.

We pulled up into the park lot of The Harrison Ward Build, where my dome room was located on the forth floor, room 410. We took the elevator from the first floor to the forth floor with the first load of my stuff. When I got to the room we walked into the room, where a young black male was standing in the room. After we spoke he told me that his name was Warren Evans, and I told him that name is Timothy James, then said that he had waited until I got there before he decided where to put any of his things.

Because he wanted to be respectful to the person whom he was going to be sharing a room with. I think him for doing that, and then I introduce him to my parents Mr. And Mrs. James. He told us that his parents did not up with him. Didn't ask him why? My parents and I went back down stairs to get another load of stuff to bring back to the room. It took about three trips back to the cars to get everything up to the room.

After helping me move in my parents said their good-byes, they left for their drive back home. Now that all of my stuff in the room, my roommate and I started talking and made up our minds on who was going to get which side of the room. Then we started working on putting of things away. There was good thing about the room, it had it's own bathroom. Well about three o'clock the dome counselor came around and told that there was going to be meeting for the house at four, to tell about the rules and a few other things that we need to know, the meeting was to be down stairs. So about four the two of us went own to the meeting.

The counselor was telling about things like what time we had to be in the dome, and what time our meals would be every day. We find out that in a while little dinner was about to be serviced. So all the students were shown into the dinning room, and we formed a line to get our food, then we found a table to eat. After Warren and I finished eating we went back to our room to finish putting our things way. About ten o'clock we went to bed, but we did not go to sleep right away so we laid in our beds and talked. The next morning we got out bed around eight. We knew that we had to see about finding The William Jones's Build where we were going to get our classroom assignments for the classes. Warren and I found out that we were going to have a couple classes together on Monday and Tuesday mornings each of those classes are going to be two days.

Well after everything was over, the two of us went back to the dome and got lunch in the dinning room. I got a cheeseburger, fries and an iced sweet tea. Warren got a burger, onion rings and a soda. After eating we up stairs to our room, where we sat and talked about our first class on Monday morning. The class is going to be PCN 110, which is pubic communications network. The class meets on Mondays and Wednesday at eight o'clock in the mornings, and on Tuesdays and Thursday mornings Warren and I have another class together that morning at eight o'clock, the class is CCT 115 computer communications technology, which means the skills of written communications using the computers, and typed forms. Then Tuesday night I have a class at seven o'clock in the evening until nine thirty. That class is OPN 126, office processions network. Friday morning at eight o'clock, MAT 213 math for the work place. Then next class I will have is on Thursday evening at six o'clock, PHY 101 physiology for the work place. The last class for the week will be Friday evening at seven o'clock, CCM 100 counseling for case managers. I am a full time student with a full class load. Warren is also has a full class load too.

The weekend went by fast Warren and I spent most of our time in our dome room talking and getting to know each other better. I leaned that the reason his parents did not come with him to the school. Was because his father had died and his mother could make the trip. He is the youngest of six kinds and the first to go to a four-year college. Being the youngest child in our families is one thing we have in common. Sunday night we took turns taking showers before we got into bed, hoping to get some sleep for out first class in the morning. Some time during the night we fell asleep, the next morning the alarm clock went off five thirty and the two of us got up so we could get showered and dress, and get something to eat before going to class by eight o'clock.

Once they got into the classroom they saw that our professor is an older woman. She introduced herself as Mrs. Scott and this is PCN 110 public communications network. This is your first day, but now on this class will start at eight o'clock each morning that we meet. You will be learning the tools of public communication within the network systems and how deal with the different networks that public and private agencies use to handle their cases and caseloads. Hopefully you will start this course as young students and leave it twelve weeks from now one step closer to being case managers who will be able to communicate with each other within the network, and handle the networks' in and out. This class is three hours long and it is an interactive class.

Warren and I spent the next three hours all the things that we did not know about communication, and how much work we though we were going to in for, after leaving class we talked about it as we walked back to our dome room. It was only our first class and we both that we were no longer in high school any more. Once the class was over we walked back to our dome room where put our books and other things down, so we can go back down stairs to get some lunch. We talked about the class along with some of the other students in the class. When we got into the dinning room we got us something to eat, then we went back up to the room and did some studying. After that we watch some TV. Later Warren and I each went in took showers so we could get ready for bed. We have another day of classes.

The morning seems to come early. It was Tuesday and we had another class together. The class was eight o'clock in the morning. It was CCT 115 computer communications technology. When we got into class that for this one we have a male professor. He introduced his self as Mr. Parker, and he started telling us about the class he said that we were going to learn how to use computers to communicate with other public and private agencies though forms, fax and e-mails. When you work in offices you have to be able to talk to other case managers. Also you will need to create the forms and paper work for your files. This class was three hours long and it was going to be some real work to it.

After this class was over I had a few hours before my next class that evening. Once we had lunch the two of us spent time in our room reading and talking. I had to be in my evening class at seven o'clock. The class was OPN 126 Office Processions Network. When I got in class I found that I had another male professor his name is Mr. Harrison. He told the students in the class that we were going to learning how the process within the office networks systems work. Each student was required to have their own laptop when they came to the college. Both Warren and I both have a laptop and all in ones. So we can do our schoolwork. Well this class ended at ten o'clock that night. When I got out of class I straight to my dome room I am glad that I have some things to sack on in the room. As I opened the door Warren was sitting there watch TV. When I walked in the door I spoke to him, he replied by saying hi, how are you doing after your class?

Well after I got there we both talked a little then we started to get ready for bed, by each going in to take showers. Warren and I took a turn doing just that, and then we got into bed. We both have a class in the morning together. It is one of our two classes. We have Mrs. Scott's class Public Communications Network. I hope that I am able to get to sleep so I will be rested for the class. I don't know when I fell asleep but the next I heard was the alarm clock going off. So we got up and started getting dressed, so we could go down stairs to get something to eat before we go to class. We made to class to on time and was ready for what ever she had in store for us. We spent the next three hours doing and talking about how to communicate in an office setting. When it was over we had the rest of the day to spend doing class work and relaxing. Warren and I are getting closer as friends as time goes on, and getting to know each other the more time we spend with each other.

Once we got back to our dome room the first thing we did was get out books and net books so we could do our assignment form the class. We work for a while then we went down to get something to eat for lunch. Warren and I spend most of our time in the dome room because we don't really know any of the other students in our dome building or on our floor. Some may not understand how we feel about stepping out and meeting new people. As time goes on we will make a few know friends along the way. We have four years to do so. After lunch we were back in the room working again. We worked for a while once had finished we just sat back and relaxed we decided to listen to the radio, doing that time we talked and we had gotten to know each good enough that we were able to start playing around with each other as friends.

Before it got to late we went down and got us some dinner, then we back to our room and this time we watched TV until we got ready for bed. We had another class together in the morning;

it's going to be CCT 115 Computer Communications Network, with Mr. Parker he had us doing some things sample forms on the computer. We had to learn how to fill them out and print along with filing in the client's folder. Each student was given printer paper work with client information and we had to type everything into the right forms, if we made mistakes the computers would let us know by high lighting the mistake in red. The information was not listed in order so we had to read over the paper work to find what was needed. The class got out at eleven o'clock. Warren and I went back to our dome so we could get lunch. I had to be in my evening class at six, so I had a little time to work on our class assignment and do some reading.

I left our dome room to go to my Thursday evening class, which was going to start at six o'clock. When I got there I found that I had a female professor by the name of Ms. Williams, the class was PSY 101 Psychology for the work place. She said that we were going learn how to use psychology in the work place with both clients and coworkers within the work place, and also when dealing with other agencies, and client's families. The was over at nine o'clock, and was on my back to my dome room so I could try to relax and do some reading, we had no take home assignment for this class, but we was told to do some reading. When I opened to door to the dome room Warren was just coming out of the bathroom only wearing a towel wrapped around his waist, he had just gotten out of the shower, he walked over to his dresser to get something, when opened the drawer he pull shorts that he was going to sleep in. I closed the door behind me, and I went over to my desk and put down my things. We spoke to each other, and went to what we had to do. I guest it was good that Warren and I had become enough that we felt comfortable while sharing a close live space.

After doing some reading and trying to relax, I went into the bathroom to take a shower so I could get ready for bed. Warren had a morning class the next morning, but did not. My last class for the week was going tomorrow evening at seven o'clock, so I had some time to make sure I had all of my work done for my classes, and to maybe rest a little. The next morning the alarm went off and we got up, Warren went in to the bathroom first, then once he came out I went in and took a shower then dressed. The two of us went down stairs to get breakfast. I went back up stairs to the room while Warren headed to his class. He came back to the room about eleven thirty; once he put his stuff down we both went down to get lunch. After eating we headed back up stairs for a while before I had to go to class.

I left about six thirty to go to my Friday evening class, this class was going to start at seven o'clock, which I had another female professor her name is Mrs. Pittman, the class is counseling for Case managers. We were told that this class was going to teach us how to counsel our clients and their families. To help them make any decisions about their case. She told us that we would handle sample counseling client cases, along with other class activities about how case managers should handle themselves in the work place. I got back to the dome room about ten o'clock thirty; I wanted some to eat on. I was glad that I had something to sack on in the room. It wasn't very long before we both ready for bed even though we did not have any classes tomorrow we both had Saturday and Sundays off from classes, we had to still read and make sure that our class assignments were done for the next week.

As we laid in our beds the two of talked about glad we both were that our first of college was over. Now can look forward to the weekend, we did not have any plans. On Saturday morning we woke up a little later than we have the passed few days, because we did not set an alarm to wake us up. I was glad that we did how ever wake up in time to go down stairs to get breakfast. After eating we headed back up to our room, where we found something on the radio to listen to for a while. We were in no rush to do anything, because I guest that both of us just wanted to rest and relax. Later we did do some reading, and watched some TV. Warren and I talked about if we where going to Church services on Sunday morning. The campus has its own small Church. About ten o'clock decided to take a shower. So I undressed down to my briefs and went into the bathroom., after taken a nice warm shower I dried off, then I thought to myself that I had not brought any clean briefs into the bathroom with to put on, so that meant that I to go back into the room and get some out of my drawer. Just as I walked out of the bathroom a crazy thing happened, my towel dropped to the floor, at the very same time Warren was headed toward the bathroom, he only a few steps from me when it happened.

Warren couldn't help but to see me nake, I went to get my towel and cover up, but it was really to late for that. He made a commit by saying you just wanted to show your stuff, and laughed about it and walked passed me to go into the bedroom. While he was in there taking his shower I went on to put on a pair of briefs, then I folded the towel and placed it on the closet door knob. As I was walking around the room I heard the water for the shower stop running, I knew that it was not going to long before Warren came out of the bathroom. I had made it over to the my bed and was sitting on the side of it when the bathroom opened and he was standing in view, with his towel wrapped tightly around his lower body.

He walked over to his bed and picked the shorts that he had laying there, which he was going to sleep in. he took off the towel and put on the shorts, with his back to me so that the only part of his body I could see was his back side. As I watched him I wonder why he always slept in those type of shorts, when he normally wear briefs the same as I do. I don't know what ever made me ask the question, I asked what with the shorts buddy? Warren turned and looked at me, saying well one thing is that they keep me from getting so many underwear dirty plus it feels good to have on something lose fitting when I sleep. We both got into our beds and we talked for a while before I fell a sleep.

Warren and I woke up on Sunday checking the time; it was about seven o'clock in the morning. The two of us talked about going to the church service at eleven. So that meant that we had to get up and shower and find something to wear. So we did get up about an hour later to get ourselves ready. We did not have suites and ties, but we were able to find something that we felt was nice enough to wear to church. Once we were dressed we went down stairs to get something to eat for breakfast. Then we headed to the chapel. As we walked in we found somewhere to sit, we sat side by side, and we enjoyed the service. It lasted for about an hour and a half. The two of us went back to the dome room; him and I both needed to go down stairs to do some laundry. We got our clothes together and went down to the laundry room, it took us a while to wash and dry the clothes before taking everything back up to our room.

After putting everything away we decided to go out and see what the rest of the campus was like, because so far all we had seen was our room and the building that we had classes in, and the chapel. Warren and I went down to my car and we drove around the campus stopping in the park and walked over to lake and sat down in the grass and watch the ducks and the other birds, and the people around us as we talked about things like our girl friends and family. Yes we both have girl friends, which we will not get to see for a while. We know that the net time we will be able to go home is going to be the Christmas holiday. That is months a way, so we just has to deal with it, and make phones to them. It was a little after lunchtime so we got something to eat from a place across from the park. We walked back over to the lake where we stayed for a while longer. Then we drove around a little more then went back to our dome room.

The week of classes will be starting again in the morning. Well for now we had a few more hours to relax. Both of us were caught up on all of class assignments and reading. So what we were going to do was find something on TV to watch the two of us enjoy talking with each other. After getting back into the room I got a phone call from my girl friend, she was going to see how things were going, I told that my roommate and I had made it though one week of classes, and that I like having Warren for a roommate. I asked her about the things that were going on with her. She told me that she was walking part time at a fast food place to make her own money. We didn't talk for a real long time, because she didn't have much before she had to get ready to go some where with her family, which I could understand that.

About the time I got off the phone Warren's cell started to ring it was his mother, plus his girl friend was there with her so he talked to both of them for a while. After ending his call he seemed to be a little down, so I asked him is anything was wrong? He told hearing his mother's voice kind of got to him. The two of them had always been close. He did not stay down for long. Some how we were able to cheer each other up. We found some crazy show on TV which made us laugh, and that made us start playing around with each and acting childish. We had some fun for a while. Dinnertime rolled around and we needed to go down stairs and get something to eat. After that we returned to our room, we had to put away the clothes that we had washed earlier in the day.

It was really warm in the room and I just wanted to cool off. Warren said that he felt like taking off his clothes and sitting round. He got up and started undressing when he was down to his briefs he stopped and went over to his dresser and opened a drawer pulling out a pair of those thin shorts that he sleeps in, he tossed them over to me and said try these. Then he took off his briefs and put on the shorts. That's when I got up and undressed, I did put on the shorts that Warren had told me to try. The shorts were the only things that we had on while we sat watching TV. It was now nine o'clock and it was time for us to be getting to bed so that we could get some sleep for our Monday morning class. I went into the bathroom first and took a shower once drying off I put back on the shorts then I went back into the room. Warren had to take his shower; I was sitting watching TV until he came out of the bathroom. Then I turned off the TV and we got into our beds. I have to tell you the short did feel good to sleep in just as Warren had said.

That Monday morning the alarm clock went off about six o'clock, and we got up so that we could get dressed for our class, Warren and I had a class with Mrs. Scott and we could not be late. He jumped out bed first. I don't know what he had been dreaming about, but he had a hard on. He headed for the bathroom. When he came out he only had his towel around his waist. Warren walked over to his bed and throws the shorts that he had slept in on the bed. He made up the bed then he walked over to his drawer and got out a pair of briefs so he could start getting dressed. I went into the bathroom to take my shower, after which I dried off and went back into the room so I could get ready. I took the shorts and put them on my bed. Then I changed into my clothes. We got our stuff together and went down stairs for breakfast. Then we went to class; we got there in time. The next three hours went back a little slow, but time did not stand still.

After the class was over we had the rest of the day to do anything that we needed to do. So we headed back to the dome. Once there we went into the room and put our stuff down. At lunchtime we went down and had lunch, then came back to our room so we could work our class assignment. While sitting there I started to daydream about my girl friend and the last tie we had sex. Warren asked me a question about something that we had went over in class, but I did not hear him at first so he asked me a second time, that time I heard, but I did not understand him. I asked him what did he say, he asked me again. I tried my best to answer his question.

The following days and weeks went back at a medium pace. Warren and I had been here for over two months. It was good that we had become friends, because that made it easier for us. It was a Friday night and I had just got back from my last class for the week. When I opened the door there was Warren lying on his bed watching TV. So I spoke just as I closed the door behind me. I walked over to my deck so I could put my stuff down. Then I went into the bathroom because I had to piss. After returning to the room Warren asked me how my class had gone. I told him that it had gone good.

That night the two of us found it very hard to fall asleep that night. After turning off the TV, and lights, we laid in our beds talking to each other. Some how we stared talking about how long it had been for each of us since we had sex. Both of us have girlfriends, but we both had been away from home for months. I could only think how horny I was. I cannot say what Warren was really thinking. Warren asks me something that took me by surprise, when he wanted to know if I had ever jacked off. I told him that I had when I was younger. I turned the question around on him; he told me that he had also done it when he was younger. Somewhere doing the medium of the night we fell asleep. The next morning we awoke about nine o'clock. So we got up to take our showers, Warren was the first to go into the bathroom; I sat there on the side of my bed while I was waiting for him to come back out.

Just as I heard the water in the shower turn off I got up and move closer to the bathroom door. To wait for him to come out so I could get in there to take my shower. Then he opened the door, and stepped into the room. I did not realize that why I had been sitting there I had thought about my girl and the last time we had sex. Doing that time I had gotten a hard on in my shorts. When he took a few steps out of the bathroom he made a statement that made me realize that he had seen my hard dick though the shorts that I had on. I knew that he was just joking with me. When I stood up there it was standing straight out in front of me. I walked into the bathroom, undressed and stepped into the shower. I made sure that the water was turned down so that it would be cooler. It did cross my mind to jack off, but I didn't. After showering I dried off and wrapped my towel around my waist so that I could go back into the room to get dressed.

We both dressed and headed down stairs so we could get some breakfast then we talked about going and doing something for a while. Well it Saturday morning and we just wanted to spend some time without thinking about school and school work. So we went to the local mall where we waked around and checked out some of the stores. We stayed gone until lunchtime then we went back to get something to eat. Once we had eaten we went back up stairs to our room and just watched some TV. It wasn't long before we started talking with each other. Some how the topic of sex came up again, I guest because both of us being young men, we had sex on our minds.

Warren and I were both feeling kind of horny. My cell phone started to ring; when I looked the caller ID I saw that it was my parents home number. When I answered it was my mother, she told me that she was missing talking to me, so she gave me a call to see how I was doing. I told that I was doing ok just working hard with my classes. She also asked about how things are going with my roommate. I told her that we are getting alone real good together, and that we have become real good friends. I asked her if she wanted to speak to Warren? She said yes, so I handed the phone to him, saying my mother wants to speak to him. He took the phone and said hello to her. They talked for a while, and then he gave the phone back to me. At that point mom and me did not stay on the phone much longer.

About that time both Warren and I got cell phone calls, it was very odd that both calls came from our girl friends. So we talked to them for a while, was real nice, but it seem to only make want to be with them more than ever. Now there we were to guys who wanted to be with their girl friends, to have sex, which we had not had in months. It was kind of funny how both of us were sitting there talking to our girls' friend at the same time, and both ended up having hard dicks. That's when the topic of jack off came up again between us. We said that know one would know what we did in our dome room but us. So we both removed our clothing and sat there jacking off. Well we did however get off because of what we had done. It was hard for me not to look over to see Warren sitting here working his own dick.

The two of us did end up watching each other for a while. That was the first time for me jacking off with another guy, nor had never watch any one doing that at all. Yes I had seen guys' nake before, both at home with my brothers and at school in the locker room in high school. After doing that we got ourselves cleaned up, and redressed. It took us the rest of the day to even bring up what we had done. That night when we were laying there in the dark I asked Warren how did he feel about what the two of us had done earlier. His reply was that it had relived the horniness that he had been feeling. He then turn things around on me and asked how I felt about it? I told him that it was the first time that I had ever done anything like that before.

The next few days thing between us changed. Well we started doing things like going into the bathroom together and being nake in front of each other more. It wasn't long before we ended up jacking off with each other again. As time went on we seem to be doing that more and more as the months went by. The first real break that we had which was Christmas holiday, and we both had plans to go home to see our families and our girl friends. On the day that I was on my way home, the first thing that I did was called my girl friend and asked her if she could meet me at my parents house. Because I really wanted to see so badly, it had been so long since we had seen each other.

She was waiting for me when I got there. We spent a little time talking, I was also getting turned on by being there with her, it also seem that at the same time she also was getting on. The two of us left for a while, we ended finding some where to go were we could be alone, so we can have sex. It made me feel good to be with her after being apart so long. After spending the holidays at home for a few days, it was time to go back to college. I was looking forward to seeing Warren. Will I got up on Saturday morning to get on the road to drive back to the school. After a few hours I got back to dome, when I got to the room Warren was already there.

It was go to see my friend, after spending time at home around family I still wanted to see him. We greeted each other with smiles on our faces. He asked me how things had gone with me over the holidays; I told him that it was good to be back home for a while. Then he asked me about seeing my girl friend. I told him that she and I had spent some time together while I was there. It was my turn to ask him about his time back home with his family, he told me that was good being there with them, and before I could ask he told me that yes he did spend time with his girl friend. After the two of us got everything put away, and going down stairs to get something to eat. We were back in the room where we watched some TV and talked. Yes we did talk the one thing that we both had on our minds, but did not want to be the first to bring it up, and that was the topic of if we had sex with our girl friends over the holidays. Warren and I both said that we had sex while we were gone.

The next morning we were right back going into the bathroom together and dressing in front of each other. A week or so went by then on night there we were nake and jacking off together again with each other. One thing did change however, that night we sat closer to each other with our legs touching. We took our time jacking off almost as if we were showing off for each other. I did not want to admit to myself that I was having strong toward Warren; this feeling was different from just friendship. The way that I could explain it was that I wanted to spend as much time with him as I could. We had started to make a few (school) friends, but Warren and I had a very special connection.

I kept my feelings to myself; I did not want to tell Warren how I was feeling about him. One Friday night things took a turn between the two of us. We were alone in our dome room where we sitting there watching TV, then we somehow moved real close to each other. So close that our bodies were touching, the only thing that we had on at the time were those thin shorts that we slept in at night. I was something, but I did not understand what I was feeling. Warren looked over at me, asking me you really want us to jack off again don't you? He was right I was horny, and somehow he knew that. I looked into his eyes wanting to say yes, but without saying a word we both seem to know what each other was thinking. So we removed our shorts and started to stoke our dicks.

As we sat there we stand close to each other, we watched each other jack our dicks. Then something came over me and I took my hand off of my own dick and reached over and touched his dick. I really wanted to feel apart of him in my hand. That was the first time that I had ever touched another man like that. Was I doing something wrong? Well before I could think about it he reached over and put his hand around my dick and started to stoke me. Why did I like the way it was feeling to me? He was using just the right touch. Before I knew it I was cumin all over his hand. It was only a few moments between then and when he covered my hand with his warm cum. As him and I sat there together it was like we couldn't move for a while, or should I say that we did not want to move.

After a while we both came back to reality and pulled our hands away from each other, then we got up and went into the bathroom to cleanup. There we both were standing beside each other totally nake. There were no words to be said at that time. Once we had finished what we needed to do, Warren and I walked back into the bedroom. We did not get redressed right away; it was like we wanted to be nake for each other. I was the first one to say something, when I said I hope that you are not upset with me for what I did? Warren smile and said you did not do anything wrong, we both did the same thing. So no one did anything wrong.

The months went by and before we knew it our spring break was coming up, and we would be able to leave school for a few days. I asked Warren if he would like to go with me to my parent's for spring break? He told me that he would love to meet my family. So o that Friday night we left for my hometown, we got in late that night. My parents were waiting for us to get there. That night the two of us share my old bedroom. The next morning we woke up to the smells of mom cooking breakfast. We got ready to go into the kitchen to get some breakfast.

As all of us sat at the table my parents start talking to us about school, they wanted to know how things were going for us. We both told them that things were going good for us. One thing that we could never tell them about was what we had done sexually. Because we did not want any one to know, that was something that we would have to keep to ourselves. Later that day warren met my girl friend; the three spent some time together. Then Warren and I went by to my parent's house. For dinner, also my brothers and sisters were going to be there with their families. I wanted him to meet them; I hoped that they would like him.

Before they I could tell that every body liked Warren. When we got into bed Warren and I talked about how things has been going while we are here. Then we ended up in each other's arms. For the first time we kissed, it felt good for some reason I could not explain why. Then next few days was hard in a way for me I wanted to be with my girl friend sexually, but I felt that it would be wrong for to leave Warren alone while I went off with her. So I just took him with e when I went to see her each time. It wasn't long before it was time for us to return to school. So that Saturday afternoon we started on our trip. We got back to the school later that evening, then we went up to our dome room to put our things into the room. By that time we both was ready to eat something, so we went down stairs to get something for dinner.

The two of us had spent a few days away from school together, but there was some things that we did not do the whole time we were away. I wanted to be with my girl friend sexually so bad, but didn't, was it really because of not wanting to leave Warren alone or was there something else going on? Now that we are back at school are things going to change. This was our first night back, and I know that I am feeling horny. Should I say any thing to him about what I am feeling or should I just let ride?

Once we were back into the room I didn't have to say a word. It was like when we took off our clothes that night, we knew what each other really needed, so there we were laying next to each other on his twin bed nake ready to start jacking off. That's when things took an unexpected turn; before we knew it we were kissing and holding each other close. I could feel his hands touching my skin so softly and warm. I have to say that I wanted him so badly, in away that I had not wanted him before. Holding him like this it seemed that our hearts were beating as one, what was going on between us? That night we laid there together without jacking off, we did how ever fell asleep in each other's arms. I awoke the next morning early with Warren lying in my arms, so soft and warm. I just laid there without moving a watching him sleep. Awhile later the alarm went off and he woke up, it was time for us to get ready for class. After getting dress we went down stairs to have breakfast, so we could go to class.

Later that day when we were back in our room Warren and I talked about what had happened the night before between us, we agreed that it was a very good feeling, and that we both wanted it. That night when it was time for bed there we were in bed together, lying nake and holding each other. At one point Warren was behind me with his arms around me, I could feel is dick harden against my ass, but I didn't want him to move away from me. I laid there with thoughts going though my mind of how men could allow another man to fuck them in their ass. I had never had any gay thoughts before now, what was going on with me? Am I gay?

It wasn't long before I fell asleep, the next morning I awoke with him lying next to me in his twin bed. As I turned to look at him I found that he was already woke and was watching me sleep just as I had done him before. We laid there until the alarm clock went off letting us know that it was time for to get up, and get ready for our classes. Our day went by like any other day. Once it was over we back in our room studying, and then watching some TV while we tried to relax. We also found ourselves playing around, doing little things to each other that made us laugh.

After we had taken showers and gotten ready for bed without any questions we ended up in my bed together, with our bodies touching and felling so warm against each other. What we were doing felt so right. Warren and I had gotten so close that we had a real connection with each other in a special way. When we were away from each other I thought about him, and when we were together I enjoyed being around him. The two of us like some of the same things. The week went by fast, when Saturday came around we decided to go to the mall just to be away for the school for a while. We went into this one shop were we found a pair of friendship necklaces. Which each necklace had one half of a circle that fit together, with words that read we believe in friendship, and on the back it had the year 1979. So we put some money together and brought the necklaces, once back in my car we each put one of the necklace around our neck, placing it under out tee shirts, this were be just between us.

From the mall we went to the park were we sat and watch the other people around us in the park. We walked to the other side of the lake and back before we drove back to the school. While we were sitting in our room we talked about going to Church in the morning, then it was time for us to take showers so we could get ready for bed. For some reason we ended up in the shower together, this didn't feel uncomfortable because we were use to seeing each other nake before. After our shower we got into bed, the next morning we did get up and go to Church, it was very enjoyable. Once being back in our room we both made sure that we had all of our work do for our classes on Monday.

Maybe I should take you ahead in time to what happened once we had graduated, and the two of us had move back to our own hometowns. We stand very close. We both still had our girl friends. About fourteen months later I asked my girl friend to marry me. Well she did however say yes. With in nine months all of the wedding plans had me made and it was only about three weeks before the big day. I had asked my brother and Warren to be my best men. It was going to be a Church wedding. Warren came into town two days before, so we could send some time together. I had gotten an apartment when I came back home, because I wanted to be out on my own. Well that's were Warren stayed while in was in town when ever he came to visit. I had also visited him in his hometown. We acted as if we were still college roommates, doing some of things that we had always done. The night before my wedding something happened between Warren and myself that could change everything, we agreed to keep it a secret between us. The next morning we got ready for the wedding. On our way to the Church he told me that he was happy for me, and that his wish for us was to have a very happy and long marriage. I stood there and took my vows with him right by my side.

I know many of you could never understand what I am going to confess to. I was a man in love with two people at the same time. You see one was my wife and the other one is Warren. About two years went by when I got a call from Warren asking me if I would be his best man for his wedding. I told him that I would be very happy to stand up for him. Well my wife and I went there a few days before the wedding. Warren and I spent as much time together as we could. The night before his wedding we spent the night together just has we had the night before my wedding. We stayed at his place alone, that night our secret came back up again, well I just as well tell you what went on. The two of had sex with each other. Just as we had done whenever could get together after the night before my wedding. The next day I stood next to him as his best man, just as he had done for me. I stood there and watched the man I was in love with exchange vows with his wife. As I looked across at my wife who was on of the bride's maid I knew just how he was feeling at this moment.

Well after the wedding Warren and I had a chance to be alone for a few moments, that's when he let me know that he was in love with me, I could hold back how I was feeling about him at that point, so I also confessed my love for him. From that point on we kept that to ourselves, only to talk about our feels when we were alone. Years went by and we had our affair without any one knowing. It was very hard when the four of us got together. The truth did not come to light until many years later and we were much older. It was after my tenth year of being married that everything really changed for us all. The four of us had gotten together and went away for a vacation. While there it got harder for Warren and I to keep things to ourselves any longer. The four of us had been gone for three days when Warren and I sexual needs got the best of us, as we were in one of our motel room we let go and had sex. Our wives were out shopping so we had some time alone. Once we had finished, the two of us got into the shower together just as we had done many times before, just as we stepped out of the shower our wives were right there in the room. The only thing that we could do was to come out of the bathroom, because we had left our clothes in the room. Plus we would have to explain what we were doing in the bathroom together. Well we walked out with towels wrapped and us to our waiting wives. As we walked back into the room both of them were sitting there, and they looked right at the bathroom door when it opened. As we walked though the doorway we could see the look on their faces.

The two of knew then that we had to confess the truth to them once and for all. So without even putting on our clothes we sat down and told them that we had something to confess. We started out by telling them that we never wanted to hurt them in any way. Then we went on to say that since college we had fallen in love with each other and that we had been having an affair that we keep a secret from them for years. I was bracing myself for the anger and tears, but the real surprise was yet to come. The women sit there and listen to everything that we had to say with loosing their cool.

Then after we had finished talking our wives had something to tell us. His wife start out by saying now it's your turn to sit back and listen to what we have to say. So we did. Well we had to hear the words that the two of them had form their own special relationship over years. The two them did not mean just a friendship, they meant that the two them was also having an affair. After everything was said and done the four of us made an agreement with each other that would last a lifetime.

This will have to be continued at another time. Then we well tell you what happened after that. You will have to wait to read all about it.

Beyond College (The wife's story)

You can call Dee, my husband is timothy we have been married for ten years, when the four us went away on a vacation together. While gone I found out something about my husband that would have destroyed most marriages. Maybe I should start from the top. Well my best friend was Micki; her husband was Warren, who was my husband's college roommate. The two of us left the motel that morning to go shopping leaving our husband alone to find something to do on their own for a while. Well they did however find something to do; it was something that had being wanting to do all long. We did not have any idea what was really on their minds. After shopping we came back to the motel, when we entered to room we did not know that our husbands were also there. Once we walked into the room and closed the door behind us, we hear the shower going in the bathroom. So we waited for one of them to come out. After the water stopped running Micki called by saying baby we back, because we did not know which one was in the bathroom.

After a few moments the door opened and to our surprise not one, but both of our husbands walked out with only towels wrapped around their waist. They had a look on their face that one of shock. They didn't even bother to get dressed at that point. The two men came over to where we were sitting and Warren said that they had to tell us something. That's when Timothy took over and said Warren and I have been having an affair for along time, we did our best to keep it from the two of you. Micki and I just listened to what was being said, knowing that we also had a secret that our husband did not now about. We had something to tell them about. After they had finished talking and was waiting for our reaction. I took a real deep breath and slowly spoke the words; we have something that we need to talk to you about also.

I said you don't have to feel so bad about what you have done, because you are not the only ones having an affair. I looked into Timothy's eyes and told him that I had been in love with Micki for along time now. The two of us had became close over the years, and the more that we were around each other things started to happened between us. At first I tried my very best to fight it, but after a while it became to hard to not want to feeling for her. One weekend while the two of us had gone to visit them, and the two of you had gone out together something took over and we could not hold back any longer. That's when we had our first kiss. Like the two you we had to find times to spend together. We also talked on the phone just you had done. You see we thought that the two of you were just real good friends, and I guest that you had thought the same thing about us. Without getting all crazy about the matter the four of us sat there and talked about how we were going to handle things. Micki came up with an idea, she said why don't we just keep things the way they are. No one knows about this but us, and we can keep everything between ourselves, plus we can have the things that we have now. Warren said maybe this could work.

Well that means that we would all still be in love two people. We all agreed to do just that. When we went back to our homes we did everything the same way that we had before. And this went on for months. Each of us had the best of both worlds. The people that we had married, and the people that we loved, maybe the best to explain this to you. The four of us are all bi-sexual, I made love to my husband whenever we wanted to, then I would spend time with Micki and make love to her. I knew that Timothy and Warren were having sex some of times when they got to together, but I did not allow that to make me upset, because I was happy with what was going on.

There were times when all of us would spend time together as a group, and that was very happy times. No one had to hind their feelings and when we were alone we could carry on our affairs and not feel any guilt about it. I will never forget it was on Nov. 17th, I had a doctor's appointment, before it was over she asked me if I been feeling anything unusual the past few weeks. I told her that nothing had been going on that was different. She will I have something to tell you. I was sitting on the examine table looking at her, I guest she could tell that I was bracing for the worth. So she said don't worry its good news. Then she went on to tell me that I was pregnant. I was surprised to hear the words, I was also happy at the same time. She said I can do a simple test that would show just how far along you are. The she did a sonogram. It showed that I was 12 weeks into the pregnancy.

That evening when Timothy came home from work, and we sat down to eat dinner, once we had finish-eating dinner. The two of us were sitting on the sofa in our family room looking that TV when I turned towards him, and told him that I had something tell him. I started by saying you know that I had a doctor's appointment today, he replied yes I know baby. Then I went on to say the doctor told me something that I think you will like to know. He asked me what did the doctor tell you? I said that I am 12 weeks pregnant. Before I could say anything else, he took me into his arms and held me for a while. I could tell that he was a very happy man. The next thing that ran though my mind was that I going to need to tell Micki about being pregnant.

Later that night I gave her a call. We talked for a while before I told her that I needed to tell her something. She took a few moments before she asked what do you need to tell me. Then I said I found out today that I am 12 weeks pregnant. As we talked she asked me how do Timothy feel about that? I told her that he was happy about it. I did not know that the same time her and me were on the phone Warren and Timothy were also talking with each other. I knew that he was going to tell Warren about the pregnancy. Once we all had gotten off the phone Timothy and I got ready for bed. Two weeks went by and I had gone to see Micki, while we were lying in bed together I could tell that she had something on her mind, so I asked what's going baby? She said I think that I am pregnant. After that we talked for a while, after about an hour I knew that I needed to go back home.

Before I left Micki decided to take a home pregnancy test. Later that night Warren called Timothy to talk to him. Once they had gotten off the phone he came into the family room and sat down beside me and took me by the hand, say did you know that Micki thinks that she maybe pregnant? I said yes I know she told me today while we were together. I also said I guest that we will find out soon, because she said that she was going to take a home pregnancy test. Every body found out that she was pregnant. She had not done a home test, but she had gone to the doctor to find out for sure. Once she had left the doctor's office she called me and told me the good news. But before calling me she called Warren and told him, then he called Timothy and gave him the good news.

The next few months were great the four of us shared everything about our pregnancies together. Timothy and I found out that we were having a boy, and Warren and Micki found out that their baby was going to be a girl. As our due date was coming up we had made plans to be there at the hospital for the birth of each other's baby. Well when I went into labor I called Timothy, and then I called Micki. As Timothy and I were in the hospital room waiting for our baby to be born Warren and Micki came in. The four of us were right together when our babies came into the world. Well his name is Warren Michael, because of our best friend and lovers, whom we also named as his godparents. A few weeks later timothy and I went to be with them for birth of their daughter, we were right there in the room when she was born. Deleana Timya, they named the two of us her godparents.

I know it is hard for other people to understand the feeling I have for two different people. It is said that no one can really love more than one person at a time; well I have to say they are wrong. I find myself loving the best of both worlds. I am married to a wonderful man, and in love with a very special woman. Who is also married to my husband's best friend and his lover. The outside worlds don't need to know about our relationships. As I lay here in bed with my loving husband. I can't help from thinking about my love; the reality is that she is at home with her husband. About that time the phone started ring. When I answered it Warren was on the other end, he wanted to speak to Timothy, I asked him to hold on for a moment while I handed the phone to him. He did not try to hide what they were talking about. After they finished talking Micki wanted to talk to me so Timothy gave my the phone back telling that she wanted to talk to me, so we got on the phone and talked for a while.

Once the phone call was over Timothy and I talked about our phone call. We both knew that we had shared our feelings with our lovers, and that we wanted to be with them. As we laid there together we made plans to take our baby and go to see our lovers for the weekend. Before trying to get some sleep we got up to check on our son Warren. As we stood over his crib we watched as he slept. We went back into our bedroom, which was right in the next room. Timothy held me in his arms that night. Early the next morning we were woken up to the sound of the cries of our baby. So the two of use got up out our bed. He got up to get ready for work, and I went in to get Warren. I fed him while my husband sat down to eat breakfast. Then he lend over and kissed me before going to work.

After finishing with the baby, I got into the shower; afterwards I fitted breakfast for myself. That was no different than any other day Micki and I talked on the phone. I told her that Timothy and I was planning to come and see her and Warren for the weekend. She said that would be nice, that way we could all spend some time together, and see each other's babies. Well the days went by and on Friday morning we left to drive to our friends house. The drive wasn't that long. Once we got there they were waiting on us to get there. The four of us sat around talking and enjoying the babies. Later that day we all went out shopping. We had the babies wrapped up nice warm. To any one that saw us they saw two couples out together with their babies. No knew that we were much more than that.

Later that evening Micki and I got into her kitchen and cooked dinner. While the men were in the family room watching TV. The babies were in the nursery sleep in Deleana's crib. Once the food was ready, we called our husbands in to the kitchen to eat dinner. After eating the four of use went in to the family room and sat together watching TV and talking, we were called into the nursery by the sounds of our baby's cries. Once we got them back to sleep, all of us knew that we wanted to be with our lovers sexually. Some how we started talking about who would sleep where. We agreed that Warren and Timothy would sleep in their guest room together, while Micki and I would be in their master bedroom.

While our husbands were making love to each in the other room, Micki and I were making love to each. That night it felt good to be able to hold her in my arms. The next morning our babies woke us up early. I have to say that our husbands were real good about helping out with the babies. There the four of us half nake together, while we took care of out little ones. Looking at my husband knowing what he had done tonight before, well he knew what I had also done. That weekend was a special time for all of us. Timothy and I left to drive back home on Sunday evening. Once back home we called them to let them know that we had made it home. We all talked for a while about our weekend together.

Now things were back to where they need to be. The months went by and one evening Timothy and I got a phone call from the people that we both loved. They had some great news to tell us. The company that Warren worked for was being coming apart of the company that Timothy worked for, and Warren was asked to transfer to the new office. That means that they would have to closer to us. That's when the idea came up that the four of us find away to get a house together. All of us were in an agreement. After our phone call Timothy confessed that he knew about the two companies coming together, but he did not know who was going to be coming to the new office. I could tell that he was really happy about Warren coming here. Well I have to say that I was also happy about that.

This whole thing would mean that the four of us would be together. The next two weeks the four of us looked for a house that we all liked. It was on a Friday we looked a wonderful house with a nice size yard and enough rooms for all of us. We decided to make a bide on the house, which was approved and paid the down payment. The four of us made the move the next week. We were going to live there together as two married couples in the eyes of our families and other friends, while at the same time we were going to be able to have our love affairs without any one knowing. We shared our beds and our love with each other every day. I know that some people may have said that we were crazy living together with the things going on that way. Well it really worked for us.

By the time our children were two years old, my son called Warren and Micki uncle and aunt, while at the same time their daughter called us aunt and uncle. Then one day Micki and I found that we were each pregnant again, this time I was going to 1 have a girl, while she was going to have a boy. This time it seem that our babies were going to be born maybe just days apart, not weeks. The four of use went though everything together. Micki and I went to the doctor's appointments together. We were going to us one room in the house as nursery for our babies to share.

As the months went by our due dates were getting closer. Warren and Timothy were both very happy about becoming fathers again. It was good to be living in the same house. While our husband at work micki and I shared some loving moments together. We also knew that when they had a change to be alone together that they were making love to each other as well. One night after we all had gotten into bed and fell asleep it seemed as if we had planned what happened. Both Micki and I went into labor at the same time, so we had to wake Warren and Timothy up so we could get ready to go to the hospital. One good thing our older children were not at home that night, Timothy's had them over at their house for the weekend.

About four o'clock in the morning we went to the house hospital, when we got there they put us in the same room. The four of us share the waiting time together. When the nurse did a check on us to see how much more long it might be before the babies would be born, she said that she need to get the doctor to come into the room because we were very close to giving birth. Guest what happened after that it was only a few moments later when two babies came into the world. Micki's baby boy was born first then my baby girl was born. She named him after his father Warren Evans, Jr. while my baby girl was named after me.

Two days later we carried our babies home were their older brother and sister and grand parents were waiting there for them. Our home was full of people who wanted to welcome home the two newest members of our family. The babies slept though almost everything. That night after every one left. Along with our husbands and older children we sat in the family room and watched some TV. While sitting there the babies wanted some attention. The men went in to see what was needed. They were able to take care of the problem, and then they can back into the room and joined us again. About 9:00 pm it was time for the older children to go to bed. Once we had put them to bed, Timothy and I went into our bedroom while Warren and Micki went into bed. We did get to sleep for a few hours before the babies needed to be changed and feed. The next morning we got up and had breakfast with our husbands, and then we got the older children up so that we could give them baths and breakfast. A little later the babies woke up, once we had token them from the nursery we called our older children to come in to help us with them.

After a while the children wanted to run off and play. We were able to spend some alone together, were we just sat down and talked to each other while watching our children play. Later that afternoon we had to fix dinner before our husbands came home from work. About 5:30 Warren and Timothy walked into the house. They greeted us with kisses and hugs.

After they check on the children and getting ready for dinner we sat down and had dinner. Once we clean up and put things away went into the family room and watched TV for a while. The next six weeks were going to be long because we were told by our doctor that we could not have sex until our six week checkup. So that meant that I could not have sex with my husband or my lover. At night I slept in bed with my husband, then doing the daytime

Micki and I would take moments to touch or hold each other when we could.

I know that as you read this it's hard for you to understand how any of us felt. Being in love with two people and having both of them right in reach, but having to wait. Timothy and Warren were both very good about the whole thing. I could not be upset with them if they were having sex with each other, because I know that they do have needs. One I woke up in bed alone as I got up to check on the children I walked by the guest room and found the door slightly open, as I looked in there were Warren and Timothy making love. I walked back to the bedroom and got back into bed without saying anything. The next morning I awoke to the sound of a baby crying to find myself in my husband's arms.

I got out of bed to check on the babies. Warren, Jr. was awoke but not crying, while my little girl wanted some attention, just as I had taken her out of her crib Micki walked in to check on Little Warren. We took care of our babies, while spending a little time together. As we were feeding our babies our husband came into the kitchen where we were, coming over to us putting their arms around us and giving us a kiss. It was a Saturday so they did not have to go to work; the day was going to spend with all of us together.

It was time for our six-week checkup at the doctor's. Micki and I went in for our appointments. Everything went real good for both of us, after we had gotten by home, we were alone because Timothy's mother had all four children for the day. So that gave us the chance to enjoy our time together. We made love in the same bed that I had seen Timothy and Warren making love. I never told Micki what I had seen that night.

Well I feel that I should move along with what I have to tell you. As the time passed we were able to keep our little secret just between the four of us. I know that it's very hard to keep things away from you parents, but we have been able to for all this time. We have been living in this house together for about six years now. Our children were older now and in school. That means that Micki and I have more time to be alone doing the day while our husbands and children are out of the house. We took some of this time to share our love with each other. Yes we all knew what we were doing would be seen by others as wrong, but to me it was better than right. I was in love and I had the best of both worlds at my fingertips.

One day while I was helping Micki doing some house cleaning my cell phone started to ring, when I looked at the caller Id, I saw that it was an old friend of mines from High School. I answered the call by saying hello. Her first words were hi bouncy, that was the nickname she gave me while we were cheerleader together. She went on to let me know that she was in town for a few days, and that she had talked to my mother who gave her my number. Because she wanted to see how I was doing. G.G. asked if she could come by to see me, so we could spend some time together and talk. I told her that it would be okay for her to come over. She said that she could be there by noon.

After getting off the phone I told Micki about the call. We finished up what we were doing before the call. A few moment passed there came a knock on our front door. I went to see who was at the door. When I opened it there was G.G. standing there in front of me. We gave each other a hug. Then I told her to come in. I showed her into the family room where Micki was sitting. I really wanted the two of them to meet, but there was only one thing I could not tell her what was really going on between her and me. However I did explain about the four of us living in the house together with our children. After that she told me that she was also married and had four children. The three of us talked for a while. After about an hour G.G. said that she had better get back to her parents' house. Once she had gone and Micki and I were alone again, I let her know that it was very hard for me to not tell G.G. about everything that was really going on with us. She said that she understood why I did not say anything.

We spend the rest of the day doing things around the house until it was time to go and pick up our children from school. Once we were back home it was time to work on fixing dinner for our family. About 5:30 pm our husbands got home. After coming in and giving us a kiss, they went in to change clothes. All of us sat down to eat diner together. The kids were being kids playing around with each other like they always do. The four of them were sisters and brothers.

After dinner we clean up the kitchen then we all sat in the family room and watched TV until is was bedtime. That night was a warn one I woke up in the middle of the night to find Timothy was not in bed beside me. I wasn't worried about that because I knew that he was somewhere in the house. I laid there for a while a wake. A few moments later he came back to bed. I didn't ask him where he had been, he knew that I was a woke so he told me that he needed to spend some time with Warren. My reply was I understood why he did it.

As time passed us by the days turned into months, and the months turned into years. Out lives got better as time with on. The children had gotten older and each one of them were into their own things. One day they were our babies then the next thing we knew they were teenagers. Now the four us could understand how our parents felt when we were that age. Our girls had boyfriends and the boys had girlfriends. We were now older ourselves and the love we shared had grown stronger. Over the years we had still keep our parents and other family members along with friends in the dark about our real relationship. Even though we were older our sex lives were still wonderful, having a husband and a lover in the same house was great. In away I was cheating, but in away I was not, because how can you cheat when every one in the relationship knows about each other.

The day came when our oldest children were getting ready to graduate from High School and go off to college. On the night of our children's graduation we were four very proud parents as we watched them walk across the stage. After there were going to be a party for the students, so after graduation they went to the party and we went home. The four of us took this time alone together to enjoy each other. That night I made love to my husband and also the woman that I love. As we enjoyed our lovemaking we knew that our husbands were making love to each other at the same time.

One thing we did not do that night which was sat up waiting for our children to come home. As I laid in bed in my husband's arms I thought about how wonderful my life was at that moment. How many people gets the chance to have a marriage and a love affair at the same time.

My thoughts were cut short when Timothy kissed my neck, and said I love you Deleana, replied by telling him that I loved him too. While listening to him I knew that he also loved Warren, but I was able to understand how he felt and I could handle it. The next morning when work up we checked in on the children to find them all asleep in their beds. So we let them sleep late. When they got up and came into the family room where the four of us was sitting. We were able to talk to them about their night out. The four of them were very close, and sometimes they also got on each others nerves as all brothers and sisters do from time to time. True there were two children per family, but the four of them act as if they are all in one big happy family.

The day came when both of our oldest children Warren and Deleana were leaven home to go off to college. On the ride back home I had a thought to cross my mind, I wondered if the cycle was starting all over again with our children. Even if it is we can handle it as a family. In two years our youngest children will be going off to college themselves. When we got home later that evening the four of us had some time along because our children had dates. All of us went into the master bedroom, were we undressed and got in bed together. For the first we allowed ourselves to share our sexual experience together.

I know that you could never understand the way that we did things; I hope that you could understand that we are happy together. After our lovemaking was over we got up and showered, then went to our own bedrooms. By the time our children got home they never knew anything about it. The months passed and the day came when Deleana and Warren, Jr. were going off to college, so the last of our children were leaving the house. One weekend Warren Michael came home and brought his roommate with him. The two of them reminded me of Timothy and Warren somewhat when they were roommates in college. The funny thing about that was that they almost walked in on the four of us enjoying sometime alone.

That weekend the two them spent night in the boy's room. I remembered that after the weekend was over Timothy and I talked about how we thought that the weekend had gone with the visit from our son and his roommate. He said that it brought back some memories of him and Warren when they were roommates. Now I wonder if this was a replay of the life we had years ago. Would it be so bad if one of our own children were to go down the same road that we have. As a parent I wonder if he would even tell us what was really going on with them or would they do the same thing that we had done by not telling our parents.

On their next break Warren Michael and his roommate Phillip went to visit Phillip's parents for the weekend. Each of our children were away and had lives of their own, which was a good thing for us in many ways. One thing it gave us more time to be free to love each other the way that we really want to. The four of us tried very hard not to let things get out of hand, because if it did our families might find out what was really going on. Well I know that are a lot of other things that you would like to know about how things turned out with our families.

The years went by and we are all older and our children are out in the world living their own lives. It may be best if I end this story that this point leaving you without telling about all the turns our lives took as the years went on. One day I could decide to write another story and tell you everything. Good night my friends, and sweet dreams. That's what I am going to have laying in my husband's arms, while my lover sleep in the next room with her husband.